LOVE'S FORBIDDEN FLOWER

"I did not mean to frighten you," Silver Fox whispered. "I only wanted to see your beautiful face."

Lisa could not believe her eyes. Here stood the tall, handsome man of her dreams. And when Silver Fox took her in his iron-hard arms and ravished her petal-soft lips, she knew she would surrender to him now—and each time he called.

"How is it that you have come into my life?" the powerful warrior asked softly. "You are as trusting as a newborn fawn—and as sweetly innocent."

Lisa wanted to tell her forbidden lover that nothing else but the two of them mattered, that nothing could keep them apart. But with those thoughts she saw the faces of her aunt and cousin. What would they say if they were to find out she had secretly met the enemy? But try as she might, she could not turn away. He had taught her the meaning of rapture—and his savage passion was about to become her fate. . . .

HISTORICAL ROMANCE AT ITS BEST!
by KATHLEEN DRYMON

SAVAGE DAWN (1436, $3.75)

Lisa should have been terrified of the awesome Indian who attacked her carriage and took her captive. Instead Silver Fox's touch made her melt into wild reckless rapture . . . until the SAVAGE DAWN.

TEXAS BLOSSOM (1305, $3.75)

When Sorrel's luscious curves silhouetted the firelight, Mathew felt lust and desire like he never felt before. Soon, he was enmeshed in her silvery web of love — their passion flowering like a wild TEXAS BLOSSOM!

WILD DESIRES (1103, $3.50)

The tempestuous saga of three generations of women, set in the back streets of London, glamorous New Orleans and the sultry tropics — where each finds passion in a stranger's arms!

TENDER PASSIONS (1032, $3.50)

While countless men professed their adoration for Katherine, she tossed her head in rejection. But when she's pirated away by a man whose object is lust, she finds herself willing!

by BRENNA McCARTNEY

REBEL BRIDE (1442, $3.50)

When Southern Major Brant Faulkner suggested Amber warm his bed to save her life, she was ready to hang for being a Union spy. But when his demanding lips closed over hers, the curvaceous beauty forgot dying and felt she'd gone straight to heaven!

PASSION'S BLOSSOM (1109, $3.50)

Lovely, innocent Catherine's fantasies were shattered when her aunts promised her in marriage to a rich, leering old man. When she met dashing, handsome Cameron she vowed that — married or not — only he would lead her to the garden of love.

Savage Dawn

Kathleen Drymon

ZEBRA BOOKS
KENSINGTON PUBLISHING CORP.

ZEBRA BOOKS

are published by

Kensington Publishing Corp.
475 Park Avenue South
New York, N.Y. 10016

Second printing: June 1986

Printed in the United States of America

To Evelyn, with love

Chapter One

The carriage rattled over the dirt encrusted roads. The driver, having been given orders to make haste, whipped the team of horses to an ever more hurried pace.

Inside the vehicle two women reclined against the well upholstered interior. One sat with back straight and features pinched, trying to keep her dark brown eyes from looking toward the younger woman across from her. There was no time for pity now, the die had been cast and she was not one to turn back on her first decision.

Lisa Culbreth sat across from her stepsister Sylvia, her hands clutched tightly within the folds of her black traveling dress and her china blue eyes directed out of the carriage window. Though she looked upon the passing scenery, she saw nothing.

In her thoughts were the blackest visions. She was being sent from her home, Culbreth manor and was to be foisted upon kin that she had only seen as a young child.

While growing up, her life had not been that pleasant with Sylvia being the one to tend her, but at least she had had a home to call her own and the man who stayed abed upstairs in the master bedchamber had been her father. But now all seemed lost.

Her mother had passed from this life when Lisa had been a babe, and shortly after her father had suffered a stroke, leaving her to the care of her stepsister. Then, with the passing of her father only a few weeks ago, Sylvia had come to her with the news that she would be going to America to visit her mother's sister, Adell Simmons.

Of course Lisa had been outraged and had voiced her objections strongly, but in the long run Sylvia had won out. Since Sylvia possessed papers proving that she was the sole heir to the Culbreth fortune, Lisa saw no way out except to comply.

And now, as the carriage drew them on toward London and the ship that would carry her from her home, she felt the salty dampness of tears sting her blue eyes.

Shaking her blond curls she willed herself not

to become emotional before the woman across from her. Knowing that far too often in the past she had let Sylvia see her weakness, she had determined days ago that she would be brave. How could her life with her aunt be as pain-filled as that she had known in the past? She had lived luxuriously, but she had suffered dearly.

Richard Culbreth, her father, had been her only true link with her home and life. She had never known any true love from the woman who was her sister. Sylvia had tended her only as a duty, meanwhile awaiting the day when Lisa would be dismissed from her house. And now that day had arrived.

As the carriage drove through the London streets, its destination the busy waterfront docks, passersby took second glances at the profile of the lovely girl revealed in the carriage window.

Lisa's appearance was inherited from Virginia Culbreth, her mother. She possessed blond, almost white, waist-length hair, and her eyes were of the purest blue. Her features were perfect and as delicate as the rest of her form. Her face was a heart-shaped one, set off by tiny, petal-pink lips.

Aye, she was a fair beauty. So thought all who laid eyes upon her. And this situation, though it was not of Lisa's making, was one of the main reasons that Sylvia wished to be rid of her.

Sylvia, being the elder sister, had put all her energies into running the large Culbreth estate, caring for her ailing father, and raising her stepsister. She had had little time to devote to herself. Years had passed, and when at last, she had looked about she had realized that she was no longer young. Though she had never been beautiful, she was now a tight-mouthed spinster and each time that her sister stood beside her and received admiring glances she was pained by jealousy.

The carriage finally pulled up before a long plank leading to a large ship, on which was painted the name, the *Sea Maid*. Opening the door, the driver helped the passengers from the interior. And with Tess, Lisa's maid, standing at her side they all viewed the ship for a full moment, taking in the well-tended look of her and her overall sturdiness.

"I have been told that she is a fine ship, Lisa," Sylvia stated, as she watched her sister's eyes roam freely over the length of the vessel.

"I am sure she is," was the only response forthcoming.

"Let us go and meet her captain then, if you are ready." A dark brow rose in Lisa's direction. "Henry, you can bring the bags aboard. Tess shall help you." Turning, Sylvia began to walk up the plank stretched across a few feet of water to the ship, Lisa following her long stride.

A tall, distinguished elderly man met them as they set foot on the deck of the *Sea Maid*. "Good day, ladies," his deep, commanding voice greeted the two women standing before him while his green-gray eyes appraised them.

"And a good day to you, sir." It was Sylvia who spoke up. "I am Sylvia Culbreth, and I have made the necessary arrangements for my sister and her maid to travel on your fine ship. You are the captain?" she asked as an afterthought. Nothing displeased Sylvia more than to waste her words on someone of little consequence.

"Aye, I am the captain of the *Sea Maid*. Benjamin Barlow at your service." His gray-topped head bent in the ladies' direction and his eyes once again went from the oldest to the youngest of the sisters, thereby setting Sylvia's nerves on edge.

"I have only a short time so if you will be good enough to show us the cabin you have set aside for my sister." She arched one dark, fine eyebrow at this man who, by his gray hair and hardened looks, could easily be the age of her father if he were still living, Sylvia thought with some ill humor.

Clearing his throat at this setback, the captain took Lisa's tiny hand within his own. "It shall be a pleasure to have you aboard, Miss Culbreth." And turning his back on Sylvia, he shouted for Mr. Travers, the first mate.

Lisa flushed slightly from embarrassment at the abruptness of her sister's manner toward the captain, but she held her tongue, knowing no good would come of her saying anything. Soon she would no longer have to be exposed to

Sylvia's temper, and so with some irritation, she chafed at the delay of her sister's leave-taking.

Hurried steps could be heard rushing to do the captain's bidding, and from around a corner of the ship a man of middle years approached the two women and the captain. "You called for me, Captain Barlow?" Billy Travers stood straight and tall before the man he had sailed under for the last five years, his dark eyes looking for instructions so he might do whatever his captain wished. For he knew that the captain of the *Sea Maid*, deserved all the respect due him, he being the best sea captain that he had ever known.

"Yes indeed, Mr. Travers, I did call." A soft grin came over the features of Captain Barlow. "You will take Miss Culbreth to her cabin and have one of the men help her maid with her bags."

"Yes, sir." The younger man turned toward the ladies and offered willingly, "If you will follow this way I will show you to your quarters." Then, with a hurried motion, he turned and started down the companionway, glancing back only once to make sure that the women were following.

He led the ladies in his charge down a short hallway, and at the end he opened a portal and stepped within. "This is to be your cabin, Miss Culbreth, and your maid shall have to share it with you. I am afraid that we are rather cramped for space this trip. Several other passengers are to board before tomorrow morning, and the captain is taking a full load of supplies to America."

Lisa looked about at the cabin that was to be her home for the duration of time it would take to reach her destination. The cabin was far larger than she would have imagined one to be, its flooring and walls of a dark, rich wood that shone from frequent care. In the center of the room was a large bed and on one far wall a small cot had been set up for her maid. "This shall be fine, sir," she said to the mate who stood by the door expectantly.

Being assured that all was satisfactory, he left them, saying, "I shall see that your maid has help with your baggage then if you do not need anything else."

Sylvia was impressed by the cabin but she reasoned that considering the high price she had been charged, her stepsister and the maid should have some luxury. "I see that you shall be fine here, Lisa," she said, turning about and letting her dark eyes roam over each item.

Lisa did not answer but stood near the door waiting for her to leave.

"Well I guess I shall see if Henry and that girl of yours are finished yet. I hate to be traveling at night. There are so many unsavory types out along the roads." She approached Lisa and halted before the girl. "I hope you do well for yourself, Lisa." Then, drawing open the string to the purse she had tied to her wrist, she pulled a small pouch of coins out and laid them in her sister's hand. "Perhaps this will help you somewhat."

Lisa did not answer but her violet eyes looked down with a twinge of loathing at the small pouch in her fist. Guilt must surely be pressing upon Sylvia for her foul act, she thought, remembering all of the fine new clothing Sylvia had had made up for her for this trip—and now these few coins. These acts were so unlike Sylvia. But why should she not be generous? Lisa reflected. These would be the last of her expenses for her stepsister.

Sylvia saw that she was not going to get any kind of response from Lisa, so with a turn of her skirts she was out the door and down the passage, leaving behind all the responsibility that had been thrust upon her since an early age. With each step of her slippers she felt weight being taken from her back.

Lisa threw the pouch down upon the built-in chest of drawers, and turning, she walked about, filling her vision with all the cabin offered. She felt comfortable within the richness of the cabin, though for a moment her mind went to her chambers at Culbreth manor, a picture of the large, airy room that she had slept in as long as she could remember filling her thoughts and bringing small tears of pain to her eyes for a moment. But the door was pushed open and several men bearing her trunks entered, Tess following closely behind. So Lisa pulled herself from her tormented thoughts, and needing to keep busy, she began to help her maid unpack the objects they would need for the voyage.

Tess was a bright and lively girl, and the men who had followed her into the cabin were in the same mood, their faces all wearing large grins of admiration as they set down the trunks and traveling cases.

Lisa felt some irritation build as she watched Tess's forward ways when she thanked the men and winked at each as he went through the portal.

"Oh, Miss Lisa, I think that we shall have quite an adventure. I do indeed." The girl spun about the room, her excitement intense. She had been born at Culbreth manor and had been taught by her mother, who was the mansion's cook, to be a ladies' maid. This trip was the first time she had ever been away from the manor. To her simple mind this was her first taste of freedom, and she relished the sweet, delightful feel of all about her.

Lisa, though her irritation mounted at the girl's words, thought to rebuke her for her manner and to remind her of her place, but instead she decided to let her have her way for this short time. Soon enough Tess would learn that she was still the same girl but in a different environment. So, ignoring her, she set her brush and toilet articles upon the bureau, her fingers softly caressing for a few lingering seconds the treasured articles that were all she had left of her mother.

The *Sea Maid*, though not expected to leave the London docks until dawn on the following morning, was abustle with activity, passengers arriving and luggage of every description being carried aboard her decks.

Early in the evening a young boy brought a tray of food to Lisa's room, explaining as he set it down that dinner this day would be served to all passengers in their cabins because the captain was too busy to entertain them as he would on other nights.

Lisa smiled her thanks at the lad, wondering as she did what sort of affairs these meals would be. She had not given much thought to the entertainment that would be handed out on this ship and she was somewhat surprised that the captain of such a ship would be spending each evening with his fellow passengers.

As the boy left, Tess filled two plates with the simple, but delicious-smelling fare and then handed one to her charge. "This certainly does smell good, Miss Lisa. I feel half starved. Why, do you know, it has been all day since we have eaten a thing." The girl's tone sounded incredulous as she realized that she had not eaten in so long a time.

Lisa smiled fondly at Tess, her own thoughts far from her stomach. In fact, due to the rolling motion of the ship as she lay at anchor Lisa's insides felt rather queasy. Rising, she excused herself from the plate of food before her and started to the door. "I think I shall take some fresh air. You take your time and eat, Tess."

Tess lifted her head from her plate and looked at the young woman by the door. "If that is what you wish, ma'am." She again bent to her food, not truly caring what the girl across from her did.

Going to the deck's rail, Lisa felt fresh salt air hit her full in the face and with a tilt to her head she let the full caress of the northern breeze touch her. Its coolness settled the disquiet of her stomach and made her body relax. She stood for some moments thus, her golden curls, unbound by any trimming, hanging about her waist and flowing freely as the small gust of wind captured and lightly pulled their golden mass.

From the deck where she stood, the docks and the whole of the waterfront of London lay visible to her eyes, and as those blue-violet orbs opened wide to look about her, she breathed in the fresh, salt-laced air and realized with some embarrassment that a handsomely trimmed landau had pulled up beside the *Sea Maid* and that at this very moment a gentleman stood watching her. Though he wore glasses of some kind, she could feel the warmth of the caress in his eyes even where she stood.

As though her having noticed him pulled him back to reality, the gentleman, with the aid of a dark-featured smaller man, began to make his way up the gangplank and onto the deck of the *Sea Maid*.

Lisa watched with some curiosity as the man made his way slowly up the steps with his servant.

19

She could tell that he was very wealthy for several other servants bearing luggage were following him from the landau. The smaller man at his side must be his personal servant, Lisa thought, for he seemed to flutter about him.

Lisa strained forward, trying to see, in the dimming light, the man's face. Though he wore spectacles and his hair appeared white she could not, at this distance, determine his age. Irrationally, perhaps, she felt him to be a young man despite his aged façade.

As this gentleman set foot upon the ship, the captain seemed to appear out of nowhere to stand before him, extend his hand, and call out a friendly greeting of welcome. "Mr. Rollins, it is a pleasure to see you once again. You will occupy the same cabin as on your last trip. I hope this shall be to your liking?"

"Aye, that will be fine." The gentleman's voice was soft yet seemed to be rough and grating at the same time as Lisa listened to their conversation from her position by the rail of the ship. "My man Adam sees to my comfort well no matter where I am."

The captain of the *Sea Maid* shook his head in agreement, recalling the last trip this strange man had made aboard his ship some months ago when he had come from America to England. The short, black-eyed man, who always seemed to be looking about for signs of danger, did indeed take good care of his master.

"Adam, you can direct the men with the luggage to the cabin," Mr. Rollins instructed his servant.

The smaller man looked for a moment at the man he served so faithfully, his dark eyes registering his distrust of everything about him and his reluctance to leave his employer.

"Go along, Adam, I shall talk with the captain another moment." Rollins's strained voice now contained a note of authority.

"Aye . . . but I shall be back in only a few moments." The man called Adam finally conceded and, turning, motioned to the men carrying the cases to follow him down the companionway to the cabin that would house his employer and himself.

Lisa stood to the side of the railing, her deep blue eyes studying this strange man. He seemed not as old as one would have imagined or as he would wish one to think. But for the shawl on his shoulders, draped about his large body like a dark cape of some sort, and the gray-white powdered wig he wore tied back in a small queue, he seemed ageless yet as old as eternity. His face, as he responded to something the captain was saying, struck Lisa for it seemed that the ravages of old age had passed him by. His skin appeared to be tight and free of the wrinkles of the elderly.

Her eyes dropped to his gloved hands and the cane which he clasped tightly. He was a tall man but his full height and figure were somewhat hidden by the cover of the dark shawl thrown about his shoulders. As she drew her blue eyes up once again, his cane hit the deck with a small snap, and the gentleman Lisa had been so intently looking over turned from the captain and set his full gaze upon her. His thick glasses rested low on the straight bridge of his nose and his eyes seemed to penetrate beyond her face.

Lisa felt the full warmth of her blush as his gaze, with flaming warmth, probed her body. Only a second longer she stood before turning and fleeing toward her cabin. She felt embarrassed at having been caught in her game of watching a complete stranger.

Tess had finished the last of the food on the tray and had cleaned up the remains of her meal by the time Lisa opened the door to the cabin. But her thoughts far from food, Lisa absently waved away the other's words of praise for the repast.

"I wish to retire for the evening," Lisa announced, starting to pull off her slippers and then her stockings. All she wished for now was a quiet retreat from her thoughts. She wondered for a fleeting moment if the captain had seen the small interplay between his two passengers. If he had, what on earth would he think of her? She flamed anew. Did he think she was so bold as to gaze upon any male that stood before her? Or had his thoughts been of the ill breeding she revealed by prying into others' conversations.

As she lay down upon the bed she felt the

heated stare of those black, penetrating eyes. Had this strange man boldly perused her form to teach her a lesson in manners? Or had this been a ploy to embarrass her for staring so hard at an elderly man? Lisa was mortified by her actions and buried her head deep within the softness of her covers. How could she ever face that man again? she wondered. Oh, what shame she had to bear, first being set from her home and now this—on her first day aboard ship having been caught at such an ill-mannered game.

Chapter Two

The deep, resounding call echoed across the ship—"Hoist the anchor." It pulled Lisa from the depths of sleep, and with some reluctance she forced her eyes open. As she did, once more she was reminded of her whereabouts. Her home, Culbreth manor was now lost to her. And at the gentle motion of the ship and the sound of hurried feet overhead she snuggled deeper into the comfort of her coverlet, knowing that she would make a new future—achieve some kind of happiness, for she had known none in the days behind her. Or perhaps she would find her kin in America as uncaring as her stepsister in England.

With a soft sigh for the unknown, her thick

lashes descended once again over the blue pools of her eyes. What matter, she thought fleetingly. She was but a pawn in this game called life. No matter what the cost she would survive. And as though wishing to acknowledge this thought, behind her closed lids she dreamed of herself on the back of a beautiful, sleek horse, her golden curls flying behind in the wind and upon her face a look of the sheerest pleasure as she gently urged the steed onward. She was reminded of the coast near Culbreth manor, for the horse's hoofs kicked up soft sand and beside her were foaming crests of rushing waves.

The rolling motion of the *Sea Maid* only added fuel to her imaginings. Lisa took a deep breath and the smell of the salt air made her small, pink lips break into a tiny smile. She could feel the fresh, tingling salt air hitting her full in the face, and as the horse pressed ever onward, she threw back her head and her own deep laughter filled her ears. But as her golden head was thrown back she glimpsed another rider, one on a much larger horse than her own. His male laughter mingled with hers. Try as she might, though, Lisa could not make out the features of this strange man who had entered the depths of her dreams.

He was wrapped in a large black cape that flowed behind him as his huge black stallion bore down upon her. Determinedly Lisa forced herself to study the man, his laughter now seeming to fill her whole being. Suddenly her smiling face became fearful and her race along the beach turned into a frantic flight for freedom.

The huge black beast swooped down upon her as Lisa pushed her own mount to the limits of its abilities. Lisa strained forward as she felt the hot breath of the large black stallion upon her back. With a fierce cry she struck her horse, willing him on, but with each step she felt her captor closing in upon her.

Large clawlike hands reached out from the depths of the black cape and Lisa felt a scream well up from the pit of her stomach; expressing total despair it sprang forth from her lips until all she could hear was the sound of her own voice. The darkness that had shadowed the stranger now turned to light, and throwing back his cape, she saw the form of a large man. As her screams filled her ears she saw that his face, within inches of her own, wore an evil grin. Thick glasses partially covered over his features and across his shoulders flowed white, long hair.

Feeling hands upon her shoulders, Lisa frantically pulled away. No longer did she seem to be in the depths of her dreams but in a real struggle as she tried to escape the hands that held her. Her loud screams filled the cabin.

"Miss Lisa. Miss Lisa. You are only dreaming." Tess tried shaking her mistress awake but that only made matters worse and fear crept over her features. "You must wake up, Miss Lisa," she shouted over the screams that were coming from the young woman upon the bed. Finally, after much persistence, Lisa seemed to return to reality as her large blue eyes opened.

For a second she thought she was still on the beach, that the elderly man's hands, which she had seen gloved and holding the cane, were those of a huge animal-like beast clutching out at her. But finally as Tess's soothing words crept into her brain, she focused her blue eyes upon the girl, making out the lightly freckled features and sandy-red hair before her. With a whimpering sigh of relief Lisa fell back upon the pillows as she fully realized that she was not on that beach with the strange, horrible man but on the *Sea Maid*, in her cabin where she was safe.

"Oh, Tess, it was so terrible," she finally got out as the other girl sat upon her bed, her own features expressing fright at her mistress's turmoil.

"Aye, ma'am. I am sure it must have been for you to be so upset." Tess was still not too sure that her mistress had fully recovered from her dream.

Lisa could still see in her mind's eye those terrible, beastly hands and the evil grin of the strange man she'd been viewing on deck last evening. Once again she felt the frantic beating of her heart and she began to gasp for breath. "I am quite all right now, Tess." She had detected the maid's nervousness and wished to quell her fright. "Go back to your bed. There is still some time until we should be rising."

"Are you sure, Miss Lisa? If you be wanting we could talk or do something instead of going back to sleep." She could not quite get the sounds of her mistress's screams from her mind.

With a small laugh, Lisa reached out and patted Tess's hand. "I am sure. Go back to your bed now and get your rest. I shall not be dreaming anymore." And, indeed, Lisa had no intention of dreaming again. She would only rest for a short time until it would be time to rise and get about. So, when Tess did as she was bid, Lisa rolled onto her side, and with her eyes wide open, she tried to bring some reason into her trying thoughts. She had not had such upsetting dreams since she had been young. Then she could remember Sylvia coming into her room and quieting her with harsh words. The nightmares must have been connected with her rudeness in staring at the elderly man. The only way in which she could truly punish herself for such an open display of bad manners was within her dreams and at the hands of the elderly man.

This first morning set the pattern for the days ahead. After rising and dressing Lisa and Tess broke their fast when a tray was brought to their cabin by the same boy who had come on their first evening aboard ship.

This meal, though, Lisa did not pass by. Feeling very hungry, for she had barely eaten the day before, she now finished all that had been set upon her plate by Tess. Then, sitting back with a satisfied sigh, she sipped at her tea and looked about the small cabin.

She wondered fleetingly what she was to do to keep herself busy during the days she would be on the *Sea Maid*. She had brought a small bit of sewing with her but this occupation was not truly to her liking. Though she could sew a fine stitch and had been taught at an early age, she had never enjoyed this ladylike quality. She had also brought books from the Culbreth library, but at thoughts of these she found reason to frown. Most of these books she had already read since there was little to do at the manor except to read and since Sylvia, who did not care for reading, had not purchased current books for the library. She wondered if Captain Barlow would have something that she could read. He seemed like an intelligent man and one well learned. Perhaps after a while she would be able to send Tess with a request to borrow a book or two. At this thought she felt somewhat better about her future aboard the *Sea Maid*.

Lisa spent the rest of the morning in her cabin, straightening out her wardrobe and then working on a sampler she had been given by Mrs. Meeker. With some concentration she coaxed her slender fingers to make the necessary stitches and to pull the small threads. But by the time the cabin boy brought a small tray of fruit for the noonday meal, she threw the sampler aside, and taking up a large apple, she told Tess that she was going on deck for some fresh air.

The deck of the *Sea Maid* was very active. Crew members rushed about and passengers stood along the rail, getting some fresh air and visiting a bit with the people who were to be their companions for the following weeks.

Lisa herself did not care to visit or gossip as she realized some of the other female passengers were wont to do when she glimpsed several standing to the side and looking about and whispering behind their open fans. Most of these women were much older than Lisa and the looks thrown in her direction as she stood by herself along the rail of the ship were not friendly ones. So, with a flip of her golden head, Lisa set their probing eyes from her thoughts, then leaned against the rail, and breathed deeply of the salty air which blew gently against her creamy cheeks.

She loved the sea and the feel of this ship beneath her feet. As her blue eyes skimmed over the vast blue-green expanse stretching before her, she relished not seeing any sign of land. It was as though she were all alone here on this great open sea and nothing in this world mattered except for the thriving, pulsating vastness before her.

If she were a man, she thought with a touch of envy for the opposite sex, she would sail the seas until she were old and gray, never wanting to touch upon dry land and view the enclosed structures of houses and towns. She would become a pirate, she mused as she stood holding on to the railing, her senses filled with the wanderlust of the sea. Thoughts from books she had read in the past now came to the forefront of her mind. Books about daring and boldness, about men who lusted only for the mighty ocean and for the power that coursed through their veins at the knowledge that they no longer depended upon landed men, nor upon the silly rules and laws that others had made up. They only had to answer to themselves and to the mighty sea beneath their ships.

She could almost see herself as she was now, standing upon the deck of a mighty ship but within her thoughts she was not constrained by the clothing that she now wore. Instead of her gown, corset, stays, and other undergarments, she wore only loose-fitting trousers and a flowing shirt. Her golden curls were tied back with a bright-colored scarf. Cutlass in hand, she stood, breathing in her freedom, knowing that only she held her destiny within her hands.

With some surprise Lisa was pulled from her thoughts by a heavy tapping on the deck beside her. Blinking to clear her mind of her make-believe thoughts she realized that she was no longer standing alone at the railing.

"I almost hated to disturb you, madam. I fully beg your pardon, but the look upon your features lent me to believe that perhaps you were a trifle lost to your surroundings and I did somewhat fear for your safety."

Lisa looked down and found herself indeed quite close to the rail. With a bright flush she looked at the man before her. It was the same man at whom she had been staring last evening, the one who had broken into the depths of her dreams this very morning. Now here he was, but this time he had caught her dreaming in broad daylight. Again she felt the pressure of embarrassment as she had the evening before. When his gruff-toned words came back to her mind she knew that he had been standing here for some time, watching her, and must have thought her about to throw herself over the side of the ship. "I-I was but . . ." she started to explain, not wishing anyone to think that she would wish to commit such an act.

"Do not explain to me, madam. There is no need." He sensed her embarrassment and wished to put her at ease, but at the same time he found a small delight in the pinkness of her cheeks.

As if possessing a will of their own Lisa's eyes were drawn from the man's face, which was partially obscured by glasses that rode low on his nose, to his gloved hands which grasped the gold-handled cane. A small shudder passed over her as she imagined those hands without the gloves to cover them. Could her dreams possibly be correct? As on the preceding night, he wore a shawl which covered most of his upper body. "I-I must be going." A large lump seemed to be sticking in her throat as she backed away from the man beside her. She could almost envision herself trying to flee from this man as she had in her dream this morning and her pulse raced at an unnatural pace.

"You do not look at all well." His deep, rough voice touched Lisa once again, and the black, piercing eyes that looked upon her seemed to search her every feature, intruding at will.

Lisa did not know why, but this man truly frightened her. Turning, she almost fell head over heels when she stepped into a small pile of rope that had been set next to the rail by one of the crew.

The gloved hands reached out, and for an elderly man, who to all appearances had lost the attributes of health, took hold of Lisa's forearm with a surprising amount of strength. Steadying her, he pulled her up toward his concealed frame. "You must be more careful, madam, or you shall find yourself sprawled out here upon the deck."

Lisa could only stare at the hand holding her arm, expecting at any moment that it would turn into the clawed one in her dreams. But, with some will, she shook herself and glancing about she tried to steady her frayed nerves. She would have to pull herself together, she cautioned herself severely. She could, at this very moment, feel the eyes of several ladies upon her, and with this man standing so close, she felt her breath catching from fright. "Thank you, sir. I am sorry I was so clumsy." She tried to smile as she pulled her arm free and straightened out her skirts, but the best she could manage was a slanted tilt to her petal-pink lips.

"It was indeed my pleasure, madam." His voice was low and harsh to her ears, but she was thankful, as she once again felt her face flush, that no other ears could hear his response. Though this man appeared old enough to be her father he exuded some strange kind of power that left her feeling faint and blushing. She could only pray that none of the other passengers watching this scene had noticed her apparent feelings.

Without another word Lisa turned and, grasping her skirts in her hands, hurried down the companionway toward her cabin. Reaching the safety of her room she shared with Tess she closed the portal with a loud thud and leaned her body against its wood, feeling protected now from the outside world. Aware of the trembling of her body, Lisa shut her eyes tightly for a moment and took a deep breath, relieved that here in her cabin she did not have to fear this strange man.

Tess, looking up from her own sewing, saw the look upon her mistress's face and, putting her material aside, rose to her feet. She had always thought of Lisa Culbreth as being level headed and strong willed, yet since leaving England she had been shown a different side to the girl, a side that Tess had to admit she did not care for. She was not the bravest of souls and she had always liked being Miss Lisa's maid because she had always been sure of her mistress. But now she had thrown off her normality. Her own fear growing, she went to her mistress. "What is it, miss? Has something happened to the ship?" She could only attribute Lisa's behavior to a great calamity. Perhaps they were sinking.

At the girl's words, Lisa pulled herself together, realizing that she was upsetting her maid. "No. No, Tess. Nothing is wrong. I guess I am only getting a slight headache. Perhaps the sun shining down so brightly is the cause," she lied, wishing to relieve the girl.

"Why you just come over here and lie down for a time then, Miss Lisa." Tess took Lisa by the hand and pulled her toward the bed. "Let me help you out of this gown and then you can rest much easier. I'll not be forgetting to make sure that you carry a parasol from now on. Miss Sylvia told me to be caring properly for you and I sure intend to do just that." Tess now seemed more in control, sickness she could handle. Bad dreams and other frights were not something that she wished to be around. But if a headache was the cause of her mistress's problems she could take care of that.

As Lisa lay upon the soft counterpane, Tess brought a bowl of water, laced with a touch of perfume, and dipping a cloth into the cool liquid, she placed it over her mistress's forehead. "You just close your eyes, ma'am, and rest for a time. I'll wake you in plenty of time for dinner."

Lisa did not want to sleep but she closed her eyes, wishing to avoid further upsetting her maid. She experienced a deep fear that if she were to sleep she would once again dream about the strange man. But as time passed and Tess went back to her sewing, the silence of the room quickly lulled Lisa into a dreamless sleep.

As promised Tess woke her mistress in time to dress for dinner, but at the news that all of the passengers took their evening meals with the captain and the first mate presiding, Lisa decided that she would much rather stay in her cabin and have a tray brought in.

Tess looked disappointed when her mistress said this. She herself had expected to take her meal in the galley. One of the crew members had told her that she would be more than welcome to join some of the men there. Since several of the young men aboard ship had already appealed to Tess's sense of romance, she did not relish the idea of staying cooped up all evening with her mistress.

"I am afraid that my head is still bothering me somewhat, Tess. If you would go and have someone bring me a tray I would be most grateful." Lisa had no intention of having to endure a meal with all of the passengers. She could almost feel those black, piercing eyes upon her once again and a small shudder raced over her form. "If you have made plans, Tess, feel free to do as you wish. I shall not be needing you. After I eat I think I shall lie down." In fact, Lisa hoped that the girl had something she could do to occupy herself. She already felt the lack of privacy because she was sharing her cabin. It was as though she were being forced to share all of the thoughts within her mind with someone else.

A large smile lit up Tess's face. "Yes, ma'am, I do have plans. One of the gentlemen from the crew asked me to join him for dinner." She was not about to tell her mistress that actually she would be sharing her meal with several men. "I shall tell that boy to bring you a tray, ma'am, if that will be all you shall be needing?"

"Yes, yes. Do as you have planned." Lisa waved the girl out the door, glad to have a short time for herself and her thoughts.

After finishing the meal brought to her cabin, Lisa brought out a book of sonnets and leaned back against her pillows, until finally her eyes tired and she fell to sleep, not even waking early in the morning hours as the door to her cabin was softly opened and Tess quietly made her way to her cot across the cabin.

For the next two days Lisa stayed in her cabin, not wishing to face again the strange man who so disturbed her. She ate her meals within the confines of the cabin, her only company that of her maid Tess. But on each day that passed she seemed to see less of the girl who was always hurrying about the ship.

Finally, on the third evening Lisa announced that she would be having dinner with the rest of the passengers aboard the *Sea Maid*, her boredom finally getting the better of her.

Tess did not care whether her mistress stayed in her room or dined with the others. She was having the time of her life. This evening, after her own dinner, she would be going for a walk about the ship with Timmy Welks. She had already been out with the good-natured, fun-loving Timmy twice, and she could already feel the strength of his strong arms wrapped about her frame.

With hurried movements Tess helped her mistress to dress in a black satin gown, its bodice trimmed delicately with the sheerest of white lace that barely concealed the swelling fullness of her breasts.

It was easy for Lisa to sense that her maid's heart was not in her work this evening. With some irritation she endured Tess's hands which pulled and tugged the material about her hips and waist. But when the girl began to arrange Lisa's coiffure after a few seconds she swung about with a small yelp of pain. Her golden hair had been pulled. "Begone from me!" Lisa had borne all she could from this clumsy girl. She would rather face the evening ahead with her hair arranged by her own hands than to be pulled baldheaded.

Tess looked with some astonishment at her

mistress. She knew that she had been rushing and not taking the time that she usually did with her mistress's toilet, but there certainly was no reason for the girl to snap at her in this manner. "I am sorry, Miss Lisa. I certainly did not mean to pull your hair." She stood, guiltily looking down at the golden head and holding the hairbrush.

For a moment as Lisa looked into Tess's freckled face she regretted her waspishness, but quickly she recalled the girl's actions of the past few days, her frequent absences from the cabin. She felt this was a good time for her to mention them to her maid and to remind her that she was not simply on this ship for a pleasure cruise. "Tess, I am sorry I was harsh but lately you have not been behaving as you should. I am afraid that your performance of your duties has been quite lacking. This evening you were in such a hurry to help me on with my gown that when you pulled my hair I am afraid I could bear no more."

"That is quite all right, Miss Lisa. I did not take offense." The girl smiled toward her mistress.

Lisa stared incredulously at the girl, not believing the words she had just uttered. Tess had acted as though her mistress were in the wrong and as if she were, in fact, accepting an apology. "Tess, perhaps you do not understand. What I am trying to say is that you must start acting the part of ladies' maid or else I shall be forced to dismiss you."

Quick tears came to the girl's light green eyes,

as comprehension dawned. "I am sorry, miss," she apologized, dashing the wetness from her cheeks with the backs of her fists.

The girl's mournful look softened Lisa's heart and quickly she regretted her harsh words. Rising from the chair before the dressing-table mirror, she faced the young maid. "Oh, Tess, I am sorry." She took hold of the girl's shoulders and gently squeezed.

With a sniff Tess shook her head from side to side. "Oh no, ma'am, you had the right to rebuke me. I guess it's this sea air that's got my head up in the clouds nowadays." She omitted the effect that Timmy Welks and the other young crew members had had on her since she'd boarded the *Sea Maid*.

"Well let us think no more about this then." Lisa patted the shoulders under her hands. "You go on to dinner. I can finish my hair myself."

"Are you sure, miss?" Tess's green eyes dried instantly and a bright sparkling light quickly came into their depths.

Not missing this quick response to her words, Lisa sighed deeply before sitting once again before the mirror as Tess hurried from the room without another word. With some exasperation she began twisting her hair into tiny ringlets and binding them securely atop her head with pearl hairpins as Tess had started to do. She truly could not fathom what had gotten into the girl. In the past she had never acted in this manner. She had always been such a good and helpful maid, never seeming to be slack in her duties until now, aboard the *Sea Maid*.

Well, mayhap the girl was right and it was the sea air, she thought as she patted the last curl into place and stood. For a moment she lingered before the mirror and looked over her reflection. The gown, though designed for evening wear, was also in the color of her mourning. Now as she, at the last moment, fastened a strand of pearls about her neck, she smiled with some small satisfaction. She had to admit she was well able to tend to herself. She had never looked finer than she did this evening. The tiny hairpins winked lustrously from within each curl, matching the pearls about her neck which hung above the depths of her lace bodice. The black satin seemed to shimmer elegantly with each movement of her petite form, adding an extra depth to her creamy complexion and her dark, violet-blue eyes.

Aye, she thought to herself, none could find fault with Lisa Culbreth this evening. This confidence in her appearance gave her the added strength she would be needing for the hours ahead. Again, as she had for the past few days, she pictured the piercing black eyes of the strange man she had met on deck. She dreaded meeting him again this evening at dinner, but she had cautioned herself that she would not be able to keep to her cabin during the whole of this voyage. If she were to get this night behind her, the meeting she most dreaded would be in the past.

Strengthening her backbone she took up her black cape and small, beaded purse and left the cabin. She realized that with each passing day she was having to depend more upon her own wits. She was truly alone here on the *Sea Maid*, and though she had to admit that she missed her home and familiar surroundings at Culbreth manor, there was a challenge to her life now that she had not known before and she realized that her spirit was intrigued by this new aspect of being her own person.

She soon reached the dining area, and entering the portal, she was surprised to see so many passengers seated and already beginning their meals. Quickly her blue eyes checked the room, discovering with some relief that the man she had dreaded facing was not present in the lively group.

"Why, Miss Culbreth, I am so glad that you are feeling well enough to join our friendly group." Captain Benjamin Barlow hurried from his place at the end of one of the long tables and rushed to Lisa's side, taking her arm and directing her to a place at his right hand.

"Thank you, Captain. I do feel much better." Lisa went willingly with him and politely replied to his questions concerning her health. She had told Tess to tell any who asked that she was feeling a bit under the weather during the past few days, but now she had to admit that she was only harming herself by staying away from these dining affairs. She glanced at the colorful gathering, smiling softly at those who looked in her direction. Some of the passengers who had not seen her since she'd boarded the *Sea Maid* wondered about the beautiful woman who was finally making an appearance in their midst and who seemed to captivate their captain.

"I must admit that I have been most anxiously awaiting your recovery. I would have come to your cabin to see to your health but I am afraid that my ship and crew keep me quite busy." The captain spoke as he filled a plate with the tempting food set in bowls down the center of the table.

Lisa smiled at the captain, finding his manner quite gracious. He was, in fact, much older than she, but he had a very distinguished manner which any woman would find attractive and for some reason Lisa knew that he also was aware of this simple fact.

As he set her plate before her, his gray-green eyes gazed into her own for a fraction of a moment longer than necessary before he once again spoke. "Your sister mentioned that you were going to visit your aunt?"

"Yes, that is so," Lisa replied, taking a bit of the food on her plate and hoping that he would not dwell upon this subject for long. She found no pleasure in being reminded of the circumstances which had placed her on this ship.

Captain Barlow must have noticed her mood, for he quickly changed the subject by introducing her to a gentleman sitting on the other side of him. "May I present to you, Miss Culbreth, Mr. Dwayne Simon."

Lisa nodded her head at the portly gentleman as his dark eyes rose from his plate and settled upon her for a full moment before once again going back to the repast set out before him.

Captain Barlow smiled toward Lisa as though sharing some great joke he saw in the actions of the other gentlemen. "Some men have no taste for the truly finer things in this life." His comment was spoken softly so only Lisa could catch the words.

Two bright red spots colored Lisa's cheeks at the captain's words and she also quickly went back to her meal.

The talk at the tables was loud and lively as the passengers conversed and became friends. Lisa's attention was distracted when the door to the dining room opened and a rather short, squat dark-skinned man entered. He went to a side table, took up a tray laden with food, covered it with a small cloth, and started from the room.

The captain also had noticed the man, and seeing where Lisa was staring, he supplied the information she wished to know. She had seen this man before, she knew. He was the one who had come aboard the *Sea Maid* with the strange, elderly man that first evening she had been aboard ship. His master had called him Adam.

"He takes a tray to his master each evening. For

a time I was beginning to think that you also would be of the same nature as Mr. Rollins."

Lisa looked to the captain, not quite understanding his words. How was she in any way like the elderly man who so frightened her?

Rich, deep laughter filled her ears as Benjamin Barlow saw her look of incredulity. "I see that you have seen the man I speak of. I am sorry I did not mean to offend you, Miss Culbreth, or to slur the good man who stays to his cabin. I meant only that your maid also came each evening and reported that you were in need of a tray to be sent to your cabin."

Lisa smiled as she realized his meaning. "I see what you mean, Captain. Though I was confused at first, for you see I have indeed met Mr. Rollins. Is that his name?" When the captain nodded his head, she continued. "I am afraid that the gentleman does rather unnerve me." She felt her face flame at this confession, and she hoped that this kind man would not think ill of her for feeling this way toward an elderly man.

"I can see how he would do that Miss Culbreth. Indeed I can see how any young woman would feel some small discomfort about the gentleman." Captain Barlow pushed his plate away from him and relaxed in his chair. "He is a strange one, this Mr. Craig Rollins. He has been a passenger aboard my ship before and that time also I saw little of the gentleman. He only ventures from his cabin during the morning hours, when he will stroll slowly about the ship, and at these times he is usually seen with his man, the one who just left. The man's name is Adam and he caters to Mr. Rollins with some faithfulness."

"What line of business does this Mr. Rollins pursue?" Lisa could again feel those black eyes upon her and see those gloved hands reaching out for her.

"He does not as far as I know have any special interest. I have heard it rumored that he has an estate in England and also property in America. But any more I do not know. He does not venture any information. Stays pretty much to himself I'm afraid."

"Humph . . . more people should do the same I say." These were the first words that Mr. Simon had ventured during the repast. "Aye, there are far too many busybodies about nowadays to my way of thinking."

At first Lisa thought the fat, little man was speaking about her and the captain, but he quickly dispelled this thought as his dark, brown eyes went to the far end of the table where a small group of ladies had gathered to whisper in low tones.

"Aye, I take your meaning well, sir, but what would you have when even your own wife partakes in such lively amusement?" Captain Barlow smiled at the man.

"I am the first to admit the truth of your words, sir. Why think you that I am so set about keeping to myself? For twenty years I have lived with that woman down there and for twenty years I have heard of nothing except what other women wear and the ways in which they tend their hair."

Lisa smiled at the man, feeling some compassion for his plight. No wonder he keeps his head over his plate and does not concern himself with the happenings about him. She looked toward the end of the table, at a large, sharp-featured woman wearing a red dress. By the glances she threw in Mr. Simon's direction and the constant barrage of twittering behind her fan, Lisa surmised that this indeed must be Mrs. Simon.

"I think it about time for me to collect my wife and retire for the evening." Mr. Simon rose to his feet and nodded his round head in Lisa's direction. "It has been a pleasure, madam. Good evening, Captain." After turning toward the captain for the briefest of seconds he went to the end of the long table, stood next to his wife, and said a few words in her ear, whereupon she also rose and followed her husband from the room.

Lisa's look was contemplative as her eyes followed the pair from the room.

For a moment Captain Barlow looked at the beautiful features before him, feeling a peace grow within himself from just watching this young woman. She seemed at ease in this gathering, he noticed, and then as his eyes went over her small heart-shaped face and lingered for a second on her soft, petal-pink lips he realized that throughout all of his travels he had never met a more desirable and lovely woman. He had remained a bachelor, avoiding the many traps set for him by women he had known, but this young innocent who, as far as he could put together from the information that he had gleaned from her sister, was being sent from her home and pushed upon her kin, was different from any woman he had ever met.

There was a bit of an age difference, he cautioned himself sternly, but then another portion of his brain told him that this woman was really different. She seemed to be the woman of his dreams, the woman he had all these years been awaiting.

As her blue orbs fringed with dark lashes again turned toward the captain of the *Sea Maid*, Lisa noticed something in the depths of his eyes that caught her off guard. There was tenderness deep within his gray-green orbs, but even deeper within their depths there was something stronger, something she had not seen before. It frightened her to see the raw intensity of his desire. She felt a blush overwhelm her features and began to excuse herself from the table, thinking that perhaps it would be best if she were to gain the safety of her own cabin.

But as she stood the captain also gained his feet. "Allow me to escort you to your cabin, Miss Culbreth." He did not await her answer but took her elbow and gently steered her toward the door, smiling and greeting his passengers as he did so.

Not being well versed in the arts of flirtation and deception, Lisa was at a loss regarding how to act when the handsome, elderly captain of the *Sea Maid* steered her out toward the deck in order to accompany her to her cabin door.

The evening was warm, but a slight northerly breeze stirred the small waves, slapping them against the hull of the silent ship. A full, bright, orange moon rode high over the ocean, dispensing light as if it were a huge lantern set above the ship and leaving only the farthest corners to the blackness of the night.

Lisa took a deep breath of the sweet, salt-tanged air, again rejoicing at the feeling that came over her when she stood on this ship and looked out across the endless display of water.

"'Tis beautiful is it not, Miss Culbreth?" Captain Barlow heard the soft sigh that escaped Lisa's lips, and though he did not look at her, he knew her feelings well. There was a kinship here as the couple stood on the deck, next to the railing, and looked over the green-blue depths. Without being told he knew that her feelings were similar to those that he had felt for years each time he stood alone at sea, with all quiet about him, as though only he, this mighty ship beneath his feet, and the ocean were real.

"Aye, quite beautiful indeed," Lisa breathed, hating even to say these few words to disrupt the quiet spell of the moment. But this slight distraction reminded her that she was here alone with this gentleman. She had best make her way to her cabin before she suffered some injury to her reputation, she thought as she looked from the sea to the face of the man at her side. "Captain, I am afraid that I should be getting back to my cabin. My maid shall be waiting up for me, and I would not have her unduly distressed with my delay."

"Aye, you are right. I am sorry that I have kept you so long." He turned and once again took hold of her elbow. "It has truly been a pleasure to be able to share your pleasant company this eve. I hope tomorrow evening you will allow me to escort you to dinner?"

They had reached Lisa's cabin door and were standing without as his words came to her. "I also have enjoyed this night. Of course, I shall be honored to dine with you tomorrow evening." Lisa thought him quite pleasant for a ship's captain, and though she knew that he was going out of his way a touch more than necessary for one of his passengers she did not truly think of him as more than a friendly gentleman trying to be of assistance to a lady with no family or friends.

As her hand started to turn the doorknob, down the hallway another door opened and the small dark man called Adam stepped out. His dark eyes took in the scene—the young woman and the captain—and without preamble he strode purposefully in their direction. "Good evening, ma'am. Captain." He nodded his head in their direction. "I would have a few words with you Captain Barlow if you have the time to spare?" He stood awaiting the captain, not in any way conscious of the ill manners he'd displayed by interrupting the couple.

Captain Barlow was annoyed with this intrusion, but as a gentleman he said nothing to the smaller man. "If you will excuse me, Miss Culbreth?"

Lisa was of the opposite disposition. She had felt somewhat trapped as she stood out here alone in the hallway with this captain. She had not known what to do for he had seemed to wish to delay her, whereas she wanted only to attain the safety of her cabin. So she responded to the smaller man's intrusion by experiencing a sense of relief.

"Good evening, Captain Barlow. Thank you for your company and for escorting me to my cabin." Upon saying this she entered her quarters, shutting the portal behind her.

To Lisa's relief Tess had not as yet returned from her own dinner, and relishing the freedom of being alone in the cabin, Lisa began to pull the gown from her body. She dwelt on Captain Barlow and on the strange man, Craig Rollins, and his manservant. It was lucky that the dark, small man had appeared. Lisa thought the captain of the *Sea Maid* most gracious, but she knew that she could never harbor stronger feelings than those of a friend for the elderly man. It was not his age that put the restraint upon her feelings or even his appearance, for she had to admit that he was a most handsome man. With this thought, she stood before her mirror, pulled the pins from her hair, and brushed out those long golden tresses. It was something else. Somehow her heart seemed to be waiting for the right man to come into her life. She had always envisioned this faceless man of her dreams as being strong—dashing—and had seen herself drawn by inner responses toward him. She knew that Captain Barlow was not this man of her dreams, and she was not the type of young woman to throw her favors carelessly about. No. She would guard her heart well for the one who would one day claim her.

As she slipped the light blue satin nightgown over her head her thoughts went to Craig Rollins. Why she could not put this man from her thoughts was a mystery to her. There was nothing appealing about the man whatsoever. In fact, he was just the opposite, quite displeasing to her young eyes. So what was it that kept her mind busy with thoughts of this strange man? She shook her head, knowing that her answer was far from her at this moment.

Perhaps, she reasoned, it was the sense of mystery that he seemed to exude. His manner, his dress, and even the small man who worked for him were mysterious. Perhaps this was what drew her thoughts ever to him.

Trying to clear her mind of thoughts of the captain and of Mr. Rollins Lisa prayed as she had for the past few nights that she would not dream, that her sleep would be devoid of anything except the slumber she sought. And so finished with this prayer, she pulled the coverlet up under her chin and shut her blue eyes, forcing all thoughts from her mind. But for a moment she thought back to the great cliffs along the back side of Culbreth manor. She could feel the soft wind gently stroking her face and sense the calm of the mighty ocean below. These fancies soothed her feelings and brought her the slumber she desired.

Chapter Three

The days aboard the *Sea Maid* passed slowly; yet their pace was pleasant. The weather held fair and warm, only a few occasional showers dimming the late afternoons with slight sprinklings which chased the passengers from the deck of the ship to the safety of their cabins.

Lisa spent her mornings on deck, sitting leisurely upon one of the chairs placed about for the passengers' use. In the warmth of the sun, she passed the time reading, losing herself, the future, and the past in the lines written upon the pages before her. At these times she forgot that she had been sent from her home and was being forced upon kin she did not know. Indeed she did not even know if they truly wished her to come to them. She completely lost herself to all but the words before her, delighting in the romances of other young women who had found true love or feeling her heart beat rapidly at the soft, gentle love words written upon the pages of the book of poetry that she had brought with her from home.

Her pleasure in these morning intervals was interrupted only when she happened to look up from the pages before her and glance into the face of Craig Rollins. This strange man always seemed to be watching her whenever he was on deck at the same time as she. And Lisa felt some annoyance when her blue eyes clashed with those of piercing black.

Always, though, this strange, mysterious man would turn away from her a moment after their eyes had made contact. And with slow movements, usually with his servant at his arm, Craig Rollins would leave the deck and go toward his cabin.

Each of these encounters left Lisa with shaking limbs. Indeed her whole body quaked with unreasoning, spiraling fear—fear of what she had no idea. How could she be so afraid of an elderly man? she asked herself time and again. But always the answer eluded her and she only knew that whatever the reason it was there and she could not shake it.

It was after one of these morning encounters, when Lisa had left the deck of the ship to seek out the privacy of her cabin, wishing to put as much distance between herself and Mr. Rollins as possible, that Tess entered their small quarters, her arms laden with books of all descriptions.

Lisa herself had only been in the cabin a few moments and was in the process of wiping her brow with cool water in an attempt to ease the disquiet that had settled over her after, on deck, she had felt the distinct presence of eyes upon her and had looked up to be greeted by a dark intense stare. She had wondered for a moment what this man could wish of her. But quickly she'd dismissed this thought, and gathering her book and her skirts, she had hurried from the deck and sought out her room.

"Why, Tess, you finally did what I asked of you." Lisa dried her hands upon the soft towel and quickly went to the girl's side, believing her maid had asked the captain for books for her to read while on board the *Sea Maid* as she had requested her to do some days ago.

Tess looked at the young woman she served with some irritation. It seemed her mistress was forever saying something to offend her. With a loud sniff she straightened her back and looked Lisa directly in the eye. "Aye, Miss Lisa, I asked the captain days ago and he told me then that he did not have anything to read. I took it that he had better things to do than to spend his time reading some old books."

"But if you asked him days ago why did you not

tell me of his answer and wherever did you get these?" Lisa had already started pulling the treasure of books from the maid's hands.

"I guess that I forgot to tell you what the captain said." When Lisa directed a look of irritation at her, she continued. "These here belong to that strange man who wears that black shawl draped about himself. His manservant told me that I was to take these to you and that you could return them at your leisure." Tess did not think seriously about this man letting her mistress read his books. To her way of thinking this whole incident was a bunch of nonsense. She had better things to do with her time than sit about and read pages from books that could not possibly have anything to do with her life at this moment.

Lisa dropped the books upon the bed as though she had been burned. "Mr. Rollins gave you these books?" She could not believe her ears. Why would this man lend her books?

"His manservant, that dark foreign-looking man be the one give them to me," Tess rejoined with some displeasure. She had tried the power of her womanly charms on this small man called Adam. Something about his dark, strangeness attracted her. But he had looked at her as though she had been of no concern to him and had left her where she'd been standing as he had went about his master's business. She had only been insulted for a short time, for on board the *Sea Maid* she had found too many men starving for the attention she could give. Within a short time she had attracted Timmy Welks. To Tess he was a man who could show a woman that she was wanted. That exchange with Adam had taken place several days before. Then today, as she had been walking toward the cabin, Adam had stopped her before she could pass through the door. She had thought that at last he had come about. Instead he had only wished her to carry a bunch of no-account books to her mistress.

For a moment Lisa was tempted, as she looked down upon the small pile of books, to make Tess gather them into her arms and take them back to the man from whom she had gotten them, but as her blue eyes lingered on the expensive leather bindings boasting of fine authors she had read in the past, she stayed this temptation. Sitting down slowly upon the coverlet she let her hands slowly reach out and take one book and then another. As she opened each to the front page she saw in a bold neat script the name Craig Rollings. For a moment Lisa was reminded of the gloved hands that could bring such a shudder to her body. These same hands had written this name? she wondered.

Meanwhile Tess had stood, waiting for her mistress to make some other remark. But seeing Lisa's absorption with the books she started toward the door, her mind already going to her next rendezvous with Timmy Welks.

Without even glancing in her maid's direction,

Lisa became involved in the first page of a book of poetry. Thinking the words lovely, she sighed and soon was lost to all about her.

The next morning while Lisa sat on deck, enjoying one of the books she had been loaned, she slowly looked up as she felt eyes upon her. Craig Rollins stood only a few feet away, his piercing black orbs seeming to sear her to her very depths.

"Forgive me for staring," his voice sounded hoarse to Lisa's ears.

She did not answer but could not pull her own blue eyes from his penetrating gaze.

"I hope you did not mind my boldness in sending you those books. My man Adam mentioned one evening that he had overheard your maid asking our good captain if he had any books that he could let you read while on ship. I am afraid that when my man reported to me that our captain did not have any of the desired articles I took it upon myself to see that you were not deprived of your pleasure."

Lisa clasped the book tightly in her hands. She had never imagined this strange man would approach her and talk in such a companionable way. She felt her body tremble as she started to offer her thanks to him for his generous loan. "Thank you, sir, for your kindness." She lowered her eyes, no longer able to gaze into the ebony depths before her.

Grating, rasping laughter touched her ears. "I myself find no greater pastime than to sit and lose myself in the pages of a good book. Your thanks are not necessary, madam." His shawl-draped frame bowed in a courtly manner before her.

Lisa sat, awaiting his departure, but as he stood, not moving on about his business, she felt some discomfort in his presence.

"I imagine that my passion for reading is my main reason for these spectacles." His grating voice held a touch of humor that was lost upon Lisa at this moment.

Not knowing the reason for his amusement she found herself nevertheless tentatively smiling, a small tilt overtaking her delicate petal-shaped lips.

Craig Rollins instantly picked up on her little smile and deep within his chest he felt a small throbbing pain. He wished to view her laughing gaily. What was there about this young woman, he wondered fleetingly as he stood over her, that pulled him and sought him out? Never before had he felt this strongly drawn toward any woman. "So I have finally pierced that hard shell?" He laughed as he looked toward her.

"Sir?" Lisa questioned, finding that as she looked up at this man she no longer feared him. It must have been that terrible dream that had made her react to him as she had throughout this first portion of the voyage. But now as he stood before her, his features smiling down upon her, she could not help but feel a bit foolish. Why had she feared him? In fact, now that she looked into his face, she noticed a kindness that rarely showed upon his features.

"May I sit down?" The rasping voice touched her, but this time she did not experience the shiver it had always touched off before. Lisa looked from him to the empty chair next to her own and, with a small smile, nodded her head.

"Thank you." He slowly sighed and gingerly sat down, pulling the dark shawl tighter about him as he stretched out his long legs and held the gold-handled cane with a loose grip. "At times standing plagues me dearly." He grinned toward Lisa, his white teeth gleaming.

Lisa did not answer, not knowing the real reason for the cane's use or if this man had problems with his health.

"You seem to be a mystery to me, Miss Culbreth."

Lisa's reaction was one of surprise: first at the idea that she was any kind of mystery, and second that he knew her name. But then she quickly realized that he had probably heard one of the passengers or even the captain of the ship mention it. "However could I pose as a mystery to you, sir?" she questioned, truly wishing to know the meaning of his words.

"From all sources I have heard that you are going to your aunt's for an extended amount of time and that this aunt lives in Missouri. I must admit that perhaps the word mystery does not suit you well for perhaps it is just my own curiosity that has been piqued." At the raising of her shapely brow, he continued with a deep-throated laugh. "I also live in Missouri and I wonder if perhaps you could be going to visit Adell Simmons?"

Lisa's mouth opened at his question. "Why how on earth did you know my aunt's name?" She could not remember mentioning that name to anyone aboard the *Sea Maid*.

Again the laughter touched upon her with a grating rasp. "I was not that sure that I was right until this very moment. But I gather by your surprise that your kin is mistress Simmons."

"But who told you?" Lisa was still amazed that he would know the name of her aunt.

"No one told me your aunt's name, Miss Culbreth. I but put together all of the pieces of information that I have heard about you since the beginning of this voyage. And knowing that you are to go to Missouri and that your only kin is an aunt who owns an inn and a few other things that were mentioned, I thought to venture a guess. I can see now that I was right in my assumptions."

"But do you know my aunt or have you heard of her?" Lisa continued her line of questioning in the hope that this gentleman could give her some information about her kin, information that might ease her mind about the outcome of this trip. But to her regret the man sitting next to her did not react as she wished.

With some thoughtfulness he looked her full in the face before speaking again. "Your aunt runs an inn not far from my own property and upon occasion I have eaten a meal at her establishment."

"But what of Aunt Adell? Have you perhaps met and spoken with her? You see it has been years since last I saw my aunt and I am somewhat curious." As Lisa tried to explain her line of questioning, she felt his black eyes watching her closely.

"I am afraid that I am not the one to tell you about the woman. Of course, I have met her but I hold no opinion of her or her affairs."

Lisa would have felt some embarrassment at his words if not for his patient smile that lightened their effect. "Thank you," she said softly and then added, "I am sure that I shall find her most pleasant."

No response followed, but Craig Rollins did smile as though he had some understanding of her plight.

"Perhaps you would care to dine with me this evening, Miss Culbreth?"

His words took Lisa totally by surprise and for a moment she did not respond. "That would be pleasant, sir. I will meet you in the dining area and perhaps you would care to join the captain at his table. I usually dine there."

Craig Rollins directed an intense look at her features, his piercing black orbs taking in each movement of her face as she spoke. "I do not take my meals in the dining area but have a tray brought to my cabin."

His words were left hanging in the air for a full moment before Lisa began. "I-I do not think that I could possibly—"

He did not let her finish before he interjected, "All shall be proper. Adam shall serve us and if you would like you can bring your maid along with you."

"I have no doubt that all would be quite proper." Lisa's face became warm because of his penetrating gaze. She felt obligated to provide a reason for not being able to dine with him this evening. "It is only that I usually dine with the other passengers and the captain."

"I shall have Adam inform the good captain that your plans shall be changed for this evening." Craig Rollins started to rise from the chair. "Leave all to me, Miss Culbreth. Adam shall call for you at your cabin at the dinner hour." And without awaiting an answer he turned and started from the deck area, leaving an open-mouthed Lisa staring after him.

Lisa sat dumbfounded for a full moment before she truly realized what had just taken place. She was going to dine with this Mr. Rollins, in his cabin, this very evening when only yesterday she had been so frightened of this man she had avoided the merest glance in his direction if he were about. How could he have so easily and so quickly arranged for her to be his dinner guest?

Gathering up her books and the light robe she had laid across her lap, she started slowly toward her cabin. She would have to send Tess, of course, with a message to this Mr. Rollins that she wouldn't be able to dine alone with him. But as this thought came, another one, more daring, followed. What harm would there be in sharing a meal with an elderly gentleman? His manservant would be in the room the whole time—and he had even told her to bring Tess. This, of course, she knew would not set well with the girl, but after all, she was the one who gave the maid her orders.

It might just be a splendid evening, she thought as she reached her door and started through it. Mr. Rollins was by all appearances a well-learned gentleman, and perhaps she would be able to learn more about this place called Missouri where she was going. Mayhap he would be able to remember some small thing about her kin that he had not thought of earlier.

With her mind now set on going through with her plans for dinner, Lisa went to the dressing-table mirror and brushed out her long, golden hair. She would have to choose the right dress and hairstyle for the evening ahead. After all she would not wish to appear without breeding. But in a distant part of her brain, the portion that seemed always to be daring and full of life, she again experienced that dark gaze upon her as she had such a short time ago. She marveled at her reaction to it, knowing that Mr. Rollins was much older than she. Nonetheless she had to admit that some mysterious quality in the man seemed to pull her toward him.

Tess, as Lisa had expected, had become sullen and rather upset at the news that she was to attend her mistress this evening by accompanying her to Mr. Rollins's cabin for dinner.

"You should have told me before I made my own plans, Miss Lisa," the girl said to her mistress on first hearing this news.

Lisa was irritated by the girl's words. Here they were on a ship heading for her aunt's home, and this girl, her maid, was standing before her and telling her that she had other plans. Well, it was time she set the girl straight, she thought as she viewed Tess's freckled features. "You are not free to make your own plans, Tess, and you know this. You have worked long enough at Culbreth manor as a ladies' maid to know your duties prohibit your running about at your own whim. You are needed tonight and I shall hear no argument about it." Lisa hated to be so firm with the girl, but since they had boarded this ship, she had taken all that she could bear from her.

Tess did not answer her mistress but went to the wardrobe to get the dress Lisa would wear this evening.

When she placed it upon the bed Lisa looked at it with some dismay. The gown had the lowest bustline of those in Lisa's collection, its bodice plunging to a daring degree and displaying much to any eye.

When the dress had been made for her Lisa had turned a rather dubious eye upon its style, but she had been told this low cut was, indeed, the rage now and she could not possibly have a complete wardrobe without such a gown.

Still, Lisa thought, this evening was not the time to wear such a daring creation. Then, looking up from the dress into the face of Tess, Lisa knew that, indeed, this would be the evening she would wear the dress. She had pushed her maid as far as possible, and she could easily see that it was her turn to give in.

The gown was made of the richest French lace. Slipping it on, Lisa again looked toward the bodice as she stood back from the mirror and viewed herself. So low was the gown cut, Lisa worried that her breasts might fall out of their small confinement. So, taking up a black lace handkerchief, she carefully placed it over her breasts and tucked it into the gown, thereby adding some measure of comfort to her outraged modesty.

The rest of the gown, Lisa had to admit, was truly lovely. It was a rather simple gown, with sleeves tightly tapered to the wrists at which small gatherings of black lace delicately fell over her small hands. The black material of the gown gracefully molded Lisa's body.

Feeling more at ease now with the handkerchief safely tucked within the bodice, Lisa carefully put on her diamond earrings and necklace, and after Tess had finished with her coiffure, she looked at her reflection with some pleasure.

"I think that we are about ready, Tess. As soon as Mr. Rollins's man comes we shall be on our way."

Lisa felt some excitement as she anticipated the evening ahead, and this she attributed to the fact that she was doing something out of the ordinary. Since being on the *Sea Maid* she had either taken her meal in her cabin or in the dining area with the captain. She liked the excitement of the unknown, and going to Mr. Rollins's cabin for dinner would be an experience she had never before in her life had. Even though her maid and his servant would be in the room, still she would be dining alone with a gentleman. Here she reminded herself that this gentleman was not one about whom she would have desired to hold any thoughts of romance. He was elderly and rather strange, in fact, he was quite the opposite of what she would have wished for in the man of her dreams.

A knock at the portal aroused Lisa from her thoughts, and Tess went to the door.

"Mr. Rollins has sent me to escort you ladies to his cabin for dinner." Adam stood at the door and in a stoic manner addressed Tess.

"I know what you are here for." The maid replied and Lisa felt her face flame as she hurriedly made her way to the door.

"Thank you," she told the small dark man who awaited them, acting as though Tess had never spoken.

"If you will follow me, ma'am." He turned and started down the hallway, then stopped outside the cabin that belonged to the man he served so faithfully.

Lisa followed closely behind, her anger at her maid having reached a new peak. Perhaps she had been wrong in deciding that Tess should accompany her this evening, but she would not have been able to dine with Mr. Rollins without some companion.

"So you did decide to come after all?" Craig Rollins met Lisa at the door and with a smile took her hand within his own gloved one.

As Lisa looked down at the hand holding her own, for a moment she was reminded of the dream she had had, but quickly this thought flew. Dreams were not reality, she reminded herself, and this man had shown her this afternoon that he was not the person she had imagined him to be. So, with a smile, she responded, "You held doubts that I would come?"

"Truth to tell I did, indeed, Miss Culbreth." Craig Rollins held her hand a bit tighter in his grip and led her into his cabin, saying, "Make yourself comfortable." He himself selected a comfortable-looking chair next to a small sofa.

Lisa felt at ease in the surroundings of the cabin and with the gentleman at her side, so without a second thought she took the seat across from him on the sofa. "I did in fact think strongly of sending Tess with a message that I would not be able to attend dinner with you, but upon reflection I thought better of it." Lisa knew her truthful statements to this man were occasioned by her need and her desire for a friend, something she never had.

Craig Rollins smiled, displaying a small measure of amusement at the young woman across from him, and at the same time his dark eyes perused her form from head to slipper. She is magnificent, he thought, as his eyes swept over her and for an added second lingered upon the small touch of lace handkerchief tucked away in her bodice. "I am certainly glad that you did not decide to send your maid with that message."

"So am I." Lisa spoke softly, not able to regard him directly any longer, she looked about and let her blue eyes sweep the room.

His cabin was quite different from her own, her's consisting of only one stateroom, whereas the cabin they were now in was a front parlor of sorts and an open door off to the side indicated that there was at least one other stateroom adjoining.

As soon as they had escorted Lisa to the cabin,

Tess and Adam had both left in order to bring back the trays that would contain dinner. So Lisa, feeling the bite of discomfort at being alone with Craig Rollins, held her hands clutched tightly on her lap and searched her mind for some bit of conversation.

Craig Rollins sat back in his chair, gazing intently at the light blush provoked on Lisa's cheeks by his words that he was glad she had come. Then his eyes lingered on her as he watched her look about his cabin. There was something about this woman that seemed to create a tight restraint within his chest. Never had he met another who had this effect upon him.

Clearing his throat he straightened in his chair and turned toward Lisa. "Have you found the voyage pleasant thus far?"

The question led Lisa toward mutual ground and she answered with truthful words. Though the *Sea Maid* would not be many more days at sea but would soon be arriving at her destination, Lisa knew that she would miss the fresh salt air and the slight rolling motion of the ship beneath her feet. "This has been my first trip upon a ship, but I find that it has been most enjoyable." She left out the only dim spot in her days, her maid Tess and the problems the girl seemed constantly to be arousing.

Their companionable talk went on for a short while longer until Adam entered the cabin bearing two large trays laden with their evening repast.

"The captain extends his wishes for an enjoyable evening, Miss Culbreth," Adam said as he set the trays upon a table near at hand and began to set the bowls and plates in order.

Lisa smiled at the small man but did not respond. Instead her blue eyes watched the door, awaiting Tess's entry.

Looking at the girl, Adam sensed her thoughts, and clearing his throat with a small sound, he began. "I am afraid that your maid shall not be joining you but has asked me to inform you that she has made dinner plans of her own."

Lisa could not believe her ears. Tess was not coming back to Mr. Rollins's cabin? How could the girl do such a thing? Did she think that she could do whatever she wished? Lisa tried not to let her face reveal her anger at her maid. But her fury was beginning to mount.

"Perhaps the girl has found herself a friend aboard ship," Craig Rollins said kindly, trying to put Lisa's mind at ease.

Lisa looked toward him and some of her anger did seem to disappear due to his kindness. But what should she do now? she wondered to herself. Should she make her excuses and go to her own cabin? What would be thought or said of her if it were to be known aboard the *Sea Maid* that she had been entertained by and had dined alone with a gentleman in his cabin?

These thoughts, though, seemed to desert her as Adam pulled the table up near the sofa and began to serve the food upon the plates. There seemed to be no polite way that she could leave, she told herself. She would eat quickly, she thought, and then she would make her excuses and leave for her cabin.

After putting down the plates before the couple, Adam left the room silently, going through the adjoining door toward the back of the cabin.

"Everything looks delicious, Miss Culbreth. As usual, the captain serves the best for his passengers."

Lisa smiled toward the man across from her as she picked up her fork and sampled the fare before her. His mention of the captain brought the image of that man sharply to her mind. Each evening in the past she had supped with Captain Barlow, though after that one evening when he had escorted her to her cabin he had not again offered to do so, nor had he acted as eager. He seemed preoccupied with his ship and men, and was often rushing from the dining table to check upon something aboard the *Sea Maid*. Lisa wondered fleetingly what the captain had thought when he'd been told that she was to dine with this strange, mysterious gentleman who stayed so much to himself.

Quickly her thoughts turned to other subjects,

however, as Craig Rollins asked her about her home in England and then questioned her further about her trip to America.

During the course of the dinner he told her of the countryside surrounding her aunt's inn and described some of the people she would be meeting. Lisa listened avidly, eager to hear all about the place that would figure so prominently in her immediate future.

Craig Rollins described Missouri, bringing to Lisa's mind a vision of delight that she could barely wait to see.

"You truly love your home there?" she asked, already knowing his answer.

"Aye, I love Missouri. My grandfather built my home, and he also loved the land and the people." This strange man looked deep into the liquid, blue orbs before him as though searching out her very depths. "Here, have some more of this cobbler," he said huskily, pulling himself back to reality.

Lisa sat back on the sofa, a satisfied grin on her face. "I am afraid that I could not dare any more, sir." And with a small laugh she added, "If I keep on I shall not be able to fit into any of my gowns."

Craig Rollins also grinned, but his black eyes belied the truth of her words as they traveled over her petite form. "Nay, madam, much would have to be consumed to harm the vision before me in any manner."

Again Lisa felt a sting pinking her cheeks. It seemed that at each compliment offered by this man she was embarrassed.

At that moment, the quiet was shattered as Adam entered the cabin and, seeing that the couple was finished, started clearing the trays before them. "Would you wish coffee now?" He looked to the man he served and awaited an answer.

"Would you care for coffee, Miss Culbreth?" Craig Rollins questioned before answering the smaller man. But at Lisa's negative nod and her answer that she would have to be going back to her cabin, he shook his white wigged head and sat back upon his chair to watch the woman across from him with some admiration as the dark small man cleaned up the dishes and then started from the room.

Neither Lisa nor the man across from her spoke for a moment after Adam left, both seemed pulled by some mysterious force just to keep their eyes on each other.

Lisa was the first to pull herself together. Rising from the sofa, she stood and gathered up her small purse. Then looking at the man across from her, she stated, "I truly must be getting back to my own cabin. I am sure that Tess will be there by now."

Craig Rollins also rose, and with a gentleness that amazed Lisa, he reached out his gloved hand and took her arm. "You cannot leave without an escort. Adam will be gone only a moment longer. Wait this short time."

Lisa seemed capable only of nodding her golden head in assent.

Noting this movement, the man next to her seemed to draw ever nearer, making Lisa's breath catch in her throat.

With no words spoken he seemed to be upon her, consuming her with his heated look. The touch of his gloved hand upon her arm seemed like a fiery brand through the lace of her gown.

Lisa knew the moment that his head lowered and his lips touched her own that she had lost her control. His lips were feather light, a butterfly's touch, but beneath his gentle caress she sensed a touch so molten that a warning was elicited from her brain. She was aware that this simple spark could set off a consuming fiery explosion.

She drew away from the man who held her and by this slight movement she won her release. But as his dark eyes looked deep into her own she was not so sure of what she had won.

It was a full moment before either spoke. Lisa felt her limbs shake and knew that there would be little for her to say.

Craig Rollins's dark eyes never left the lovely features of the woman before him, noting the flush on her cheeks and the torment of passion written deep within her blue eyes.

The rasping huskiness of his voice broke the quiet spell of the cabin. "Please forgive me, Miss Culbreth. I am afraid I was totally unprepared for what occurred, as I am sure you were." He tried to put her at ease and to voice what was on his mind. It was true he had had no intention of taking this woman in his arms. He had only wished to dine with her and to talk to her. None of what had just happened had been planned.

The sound of his voice pulled Lisa back to reality. His tone reminded her that he was an older man, wrapped within the folds of his dark shawl, and that he wore a wig to cover some oddity of his hair. What had happened moments ago had been nothing. But deep in her mind she could again feel those lips and taste the strength and tenderness of his caress. Shaking herself she stood more firmly. She was being silly. Her thoughts were only those of any young woman who had never before been held in a lover's arms. She had never tasted the lips of a young man of her choosing, so naturally she would be a bit spellbound by this gentleman's warm kiss. But she would have to put it all into the right order, she warned herself sternly. He was much older and quite mysterious, nothing at all like the man that she would one day choose for herself. This man was only a friend, and she would have to put from her mind that one flaming kiss.

With some will she tried to smile. "I think I should go to my cabin now, Mr. Rollins."

"Adam should be here in a moment. Please await him." Craig Rollins stepped back a few feet to allow her to feel safe in doing as he bid. "You must believe me, Miss Culbreth, I did not plan what happened." He tried once more to assure her that he had not asked her to his cabin for any purpose other than dinner and conversation.

"I know," she whispered, trying to block from her mind what had occurred as she was forced to wait for Adam. And finally when the cabin door did open, before the smaller man could enter, Lisa swept out of the room and started down the hallway.

With a knowing look at his employer, Adam quickly turned and followed the lovely girl, keeping his quick steps some space behind her but making sure that she arrived at and safely entered her own cabin.

The days passed swiftly aboard the sleek ship, the *Sea Maid*, and to Lisa's delight she found that she could easily shrug off any thoughts of that night in Craig Rollins's cabin or of the touch and feel of his arms about her and of the pressure of that searing kiss.

The day following their dinner together found the couple on deck, reading and talking as if they were old friends, neither mentioning the night before. And for the remainder of the voyage this was how the two conducted themselves, as though they were old and valued friends.

And Lisa thought of Craig Rollins in this light. She was in dire need of a friend, someone to whom she could talk, someone who knew of her plight but who did not pressure her or question her about her reasons for leaving England and going to her kin.

On his part, Craig Rollins was intrigued by this young girl, and whenever he could he would seek her out when she was on deck, enjoying her company and sharing her joy when she laughed at some amusing anecdote he told her.

Between the two a comfortable friendship began to grow, but all too soon the day drew near when the *Sea Maid* would dock. Lisa was experiencing trepidation over what lay ahead and she tried unsuccessfully to extend these last moments.

On the morning the *Sea Maid* docked Tess entered the cabin and, with a large grin, went directly to Lisa who was packing her gowns.

Looking up with some irritation, Lisa did not straighten but kept on with her work, knowing she could not depend upon the girl to do this task that was truly her job. In the preceding days Tess had done less and less.

"Miss Lisa, I must talk with you for a moment." Tess stood, grinning and looking down at the young girl she had served as ladies' maid for some time.

With a weary look at the girl, Lisa slowly rose. "What is it, Tess? You can see that I am almost finished with my packing. I have but a few more things to put into the trunk and the captain has said that a man will be in here shortly to take my things on deck."

There seemed to be a sparkling gleam in the girl's eyes as she took a deep breath and in one gush of breath responded, "I'll not be going along with you to your aunt's home. Timmy and me are going to get married up when we dock and before he has to put out to sea again."

Lisa stood for a moment and stared at the girl, but then using simple logic she put the girl's actions over the past weeks into focus. Indeed, this had to be the cause of her behavior. She had found herself someone to love, someone, it would appear, who felt the same about her.

"Are you sure, Tess? Is this what you want?" Her heart warmed at the glowing face before her and all of the anger she had harbored against the girl seemed to vanish.

"I know that you were counting upon me, Miss Lisa, to go along with you but your sister Sylvia did tell me that once I arrived here in America I was free to do whatever I wished."

Lisa had no idea that Sylvia had told the girl this, but she realized that she had no idea of the circumstances of her family here in America and that, perhaps, Sylvia, who knew more of matters, did not think that Tess would be able to be kept on as her personal maid.

"Oh, Tess." Quickly, she went to the girl and wrapped her arms about her. "I am thrilled for you. I only hope that you are not rushing into anything."

The two girls hugged and kissed each other, and Tess, tears now rolling down her cheeks as she realized she would miss this young beauty she had cared for, spoke up, "No, ma'am, I'm not making a mistake. Timmy is a hard worker and he has plans to, one day, be a captain of his own ship."

Lisa knew that Tess's head was in the clouds but she held her peace, hoping only that all would come right and wishing the girl before her all the luck in the world. "I have something for you." Quickly, she went to the trunk she was packing and, pushing her hand between the neatly packed gowns to the bottom she pulled out a small pouch. "Perhaps this will help you and Timmy with your life ahead." She smiled at the girl and once more hugged her tightly.

Tess was dumbfounded as she stared at the coins in the pouch. "Oh, Miss Lisa, I couldn't be taking all of this."

"I wish to give it to you, Tess. Do not worry about me. I have the necessary coins for my stage and the trip to my aunt's. Once there I doubt that I shall be in need."

Then with one more tight squeeze to her mistress's waist Tess ran out the door in search of Timmy.

"Well." Lisa sighed aloud as she went back to her packing, she was truly alone now. But hardening her spirit, she knew that she would survive no matter what.

Standing at the railing along the deck, Craig Rollins slowly approached Lisa. He smiled, and taking her hand in his own and bringing it to his lips, he began to bid her good luck on the trip ahead. With rasping words he promised that he would visit her aunt's establishment soon and that, perhaps, the two of them could share a meal and talk about old times.

Lisa smiled her thankfulness at this kind man and, nodding her head, agreed that anytime he could visit her he would be more than welcome. He had grown into the best friend she had ever had and she did not want him to step completely out of her life.

She had thought that he might be taking the same stage as she, but he told her that he had business in town and his own vehicle awaited his pleasure. So again Lisa must trust to herself and hope that all would turn out for the best.

Chapter Four

With each turn and clatter of the great wheels of the stage Lisa felt the shattering force of the hard, thinly cushioned seat make contact with her body and send piercing pains up through her backbone.

Today was the second day of enduring the bumpy roads and the dust that cruelly struck her nostrils, at times threatening to strangle her. Once more she wiped at her forehead with her scented handkerchief, wishing as she did that Tess had not deserted her but had come along on this miserable trip.

This part of her trip was by far the hardest thing she had ever experienced in her life. It was a seemingly endless ride in the confinement of this carriage with only a thin, angular woman, who rarely made a sound, not even to complain about the hard trip, sitting next to her. The only other passenger in the vehicle was an obese man who nearly filled up a whole opposite seat and whose small black eyes, set deep within the folds of his face, kept a steady gaze upon Lisa throughout the long day.

Yesterday Lisa had felt her cheeks flame each time she looked across at the man but after hours of travel she had grown used to his impolite stare. He had spoken only a few words throughout the ride but Lisa nonetheless had received the impression that she was indeed lucky to be sitting next to Mrs. Abigail Beilier. Something plainly visible in the fat man's gaze spoke of his evil intent if given the opportunity.

Lisa spent most of the time in the vehicle looking out of the window or wiping at the continual dust upon her black gown. The only break in the long ride had occurred the previous evening when the driver had pulled up before an inn and announced that all passengers could alight and procure lodgings for the night.

Lisa shared a room with Mrs. Beilier. But it seemed to her that she had barely touched her head to the pillow when their door was being rudely knocked upon and a shout from the hall announced that it was almost time for the stage to be on its way. Hurriedly, the passengers ate breakfast, and then, once again, the small group climbed back into the waiting vehicle.

As the threesome settled back against the seats and the driver pulled back his long whip and cracked it over the heads of the team of horses, the monstrous man across from the ladies settled his black orbs once more upon the sight he had missed while in his own room in the inn. To this fat man the night had, indeed, been long. He had never set eyes upon a lovelier creature than the woman sitting across from him and if that skinny old biddy were not sitting beside her, he would have tried to draw her out with conversation. Who knew where their talk might lead. The driver and his helper atop the carriage would have no idea of what was happening inside the vehicle until they pulled to a halt, and that would not be done, he was sure, until dark was fast approaching.

"There was talk among the men at the inn about that accursed Indian, Silver Fox." Seeing that both women's eyes were drawn toward him, he pulled out his dingy handkerchief to wipe at the dribble on his chin and, holding his audience with his sly gaze, went on. "You ladies have undoubtedly not heard about this fierce Indian. It is said that he is chief of his tribe now and that he hates all white men with a ruthless passion which bodes ill for all who get in his way."

Before he could say any more, Mrs. Beilier spoke up haughtily, "Gossip is the devil's tool,

Mr. Moore." Stonily, she stared him into silence for a moment.

Truly upset by this rude setback, Mr. Moore wiped agitatedly at the water coming down his chin from his lower lip. "You'll be wishing you had listened to this gossip if that redskin stops this carriage as he's done in this area."

Lisa had not heard much about the Indians of this area. She had presumed that most of them had made peace with the white man and that all was going well here in the wilderness. But now, with this man's words filling her mind, she thought back to all the stories she had ever heard about Indians. There truly were not many, for she had led a sheltered life until her stepsister had forced her out of her home. But some stories of tortures and killings did come to her mind and as her hand clutched at her white throat she paled.

Leroy Moore quickly spotted Lisa's response to his talk of Indians, so ignoring Mrs. Beilier completely, he focused his beady eyes upon the young lady sitting across from him and continued. "Why, the stories that have circulated in this area about this Silver Fox keep even the bravest souls watchful lest he come upon them unaware. They say that a white man was found hunting near his village and that he, that is this Silver Fox, came upon him. The man had only been trapping a few animals, but Silver Fox had some of his red friends hold the poor bloke while he used his knife to slowly take the man's life.

Then, when the man drew his last breath, the savages took the poor bugger and hung him at the beginning of the path leading into the forest, as a warning to others who might dare to approach Silver Fox's domain."

Lisa could not believe that this form of raw savageness could exist. She had only known the civilized world of England, where there were no red men, no savages. "Why surely this cannot happen in Missouri, sir. Why my own aunt owns an inn there and lives among other people. Surely there is some form of order and protection?"

"I know well where your aunt lives, miss," the portly man responded, surprising Lisa by knowing such a thing about her. "I heard you speaking to the driver about your destination yesterday," he explained. "But if you think that all shall be roses because Adell Simmons owns an inn and lives among others you will find that you can be quite wrong. You see the Simmons' inn is not all that far from the forest and mountains that these Blackfoot savages claim as their own."

Lisa paled. Had she endured so much to find that now she was to be thrust into the wilderness where she would have to worry about losing her life to savages? Had she left her sweet home for this manner of torture? A terrific fright came over her, and clasping her hands tightly within the folds of her black gown, she had to will herself not to tremble.

Leroy Moore saw that his words were hitting

their intended target. He had gotten where he was by using his slyness. He loved wealth, and what he wished for he tried hard to obtain. "I cannot imagine what a lovely little blossom such as yourself is doing in this hard land? One would think that your family would have more of a care for where you are bound?"

Lisa lifted her chin a notch at his inquiries. It was none of this fat man's business what she was doing in America or why she was on her way to her aunt's inn. "As you yourself said, sir, I have an aunt in this country."

"Indeed you do, miss, indeed you do. I just cannot figure out why you are traveling alone through this heathen wilderness."

"I can hardly see how this should affect you, sir, in any way." Lisa had heard enough from this man. He was becoming too friendly to her thinking.

Mrs. Beilier turned from the window and gave the fat man a shriveling look, as though daring him to say another word.

Seeing the glance directed toward him, Mr. Moore decided that the best thing for him to do at this moment was to be quiet. Perhaps he would get another chance to find out more about this intriguing girl-woman across from him.

Satisfied for the moment that this vile man was to remain quiet, the older woman looked at Lisa, as if she were rebuking her for talking to such a low creature as the one across from them. Finally, satisfied that no more would be said, she expelled a soft, "Hauff," through her nostrils and turned toward the window.

Lisa had the rest of the morning to sit and reflect on the fat man's talk about the Indian, Silver Fox, and the images it conjured up in her mind. What would it be like to come face to face with a fierce and dangerous Indian? What had this Mr. Moore called him? A redskin savage. She could not imagine what it would be like to face such a one.

The day finally drew to a close, and with the lowering of the sun, the vehicle halted before an inn. After Mrs. Beilier, Lisa was helped down by the driver. Mr. Moore was the last to alight and both the driver and his companion helped the huge man to step from the carriage and gain his footing.

Lisa stretched her cramped muscles, feeling the full weight of the past two days' ride in the stage. For a fleeting moment she thought of the day still ahead of her. How was she to endure another day such as this? During the last hour of this afternoon she had wished several times to scream with pain as the stage jostled about on the road, bouncing over ruts and holes.

"Come along, Miss Culbreth." Mrs. Beileir took Lisa in hand as she started toward the inn. "We had better seek our room and a meal. The morning shall be here quickly enough."

With no will of her own Lisa followed the thin

woman, her blue eyes resting upon the blackness of the woman's skirt. But once inside the large wooden door, she sat down upon the first bench that caught her eye.

"I shall procure us a room together, Miss Culbreth, and then order our dinner. I hope you do not mind my taking over in this manner, my dear?" Not waiting for an answer she went on. "I can see how tired you are. You just relax while you are able."

Lisa did not argue. She was glad to have someone take control of her life, even for a few minutes. She felt as though she had been thrown into a world full of confusion. Placing her arms on the table and laying her head upon them, she shut her dark blue eyes and for a moment fell asleep. Feeling something tapping her on the shoulder she jerked upright, only to find a grinning Mr. Moore sitting across from her.

"Your dinner is on the way." He nodded his head toward Mrs. Beilier as he wiped his lower lip, a sly grin upon his features. He had sat for a time across from the young girl until he'd seen Mrs. Beilier—he cursed her silently—coming from the inn's kitchen area. Then he'd reached out one of his fat hands and touched the girl's soft, golden curls. When he saw that Mrs. Beilier was talking to the proprietor about some detail concerning their stay, he let his hand caress the silkiness of the strands beneath his fat fingers. But as soon as Mrs. Beilier approached, he lightly tapped Lisa on the shoulder.

Lisa felt distinctly uncomfortable as she looked into the beady eyes before her. When her dark blue eyes went from his face to his hands now folded across the table from her, she felt her body tremble as though those same hands were upon her flesh.

As though reading the thoughts which were going through Lisa's mind, Leroy Moore chuckled softly to himself. He had decided earlier in the day that he would make a bid for this young lady. He would appeal to her aunt. From what he knew or had heard about Adell Simmons he did not think it too forward of him to consider the possibility of a future with this lovely young thing at his side. He put from his mind thoughts of his wife who was waiting for news of the deal he had come to Missouri to make. He would start a new life here in Missouri and he would also have a new wife. He would approach Adell Simmons with an offer of money and perhaps she would relinquish this treasure that sat before him. Excitement filled his soul at the prospect of this young thing sharing his life. He could envision her creamy white skin lying soft and pliant beneath his touch. Then those silky threads of gold would be his to caress and run his fingers through at will. Saliva drooled even more swiftly down his chin at this greedy thought, leaving a trail of spittle which he left unattended.

Lisa was relieved when Mrs. Beilier sat down

next to her on the bench and directed a hard look toward Leroy Moore. Having noticed the liquid rolling down his chin and the look of pure lust written in his dark eyes, Mrs. Beilier turned toward the girl. "Our dinner will be here shortly. I myself had to go to the kitchen to tell the girl there how we would wish our meal cooked. The proprietor was too busy. We shall also have to share a room with one of the girls who work here. I only hope she does not snore and stays to herself."

"Thank you, Mrs. Beilier. I do not know what I would do without you." Lisa appreciated the woman's generous concern for her welfare.

"Think nothing of it, my dear. I have a daughter myself. That is who I am going to visit. And I know how I would hate for her to be left to the fates and to have to defend herself from all manner of rude attentions." She looked directly opposite her into Mr. Moore's eyes. "There are some who would not think twice about forcing their attentions upon a lady."

Mr. Moore scowled darkly at the thin woman, but then, with a fatherly smile, he looked to Lisa. "You must listen to the good Mrs. Beilier, Miss Culbreth. There are, indeed, all manner of vile-mannered men about these days. I must say that your family should have thought ahead and sent someone to accompany you on this long trip." He ignored the dark looks given him by Mrs. Beilier and turned his attention toward the young lovely before him, hoping to establish some form of friendship with the girl.

"My maid was to travel with me to my aunt's, sir. But I am afraid that she quit her duties the day our ship docked. That left me quite alone." Lisa spoke softly, hating to tell this nosey man any of her affairs but seeing no way out.

Before Leroy Moore could say any more the meal was brought to the table and spread out before the threesome. With his usual gusto for food Leroy attacked all that was before him, leaving no room for talk or even a sideways look.

As soon as the women had finished their repast, Mrs. Beilier hurried Lisa from the common room and up the stairs to the chamber they had been given. "Let us rest while we have the time. All too soon we shall have to board that dreadful vehicle again." She opened the door and, lighting a small wick candle, made ready for the night.

Lisa was of the same mind and hurriedly pulled her nightgown from her small bag. "I wish to thank you for your friendship, Mrs. Beilier," she said as she lay upon the lumpy mattress, next to the thin woman. Then she closed her blue eyes.

"There is no need, child. I can see that you are in need of someone to give you a hand. There are certain men that young ladies have to be wary of because of their bad intentions. Mr. Moore, I am afraid, if I am reading the man correctly, is just such a man."

As Mrs. Beilier's snapping eyes looked toward

Lisa's face to see if the girl were taking her meaning, she found the young girl already fast asleep and oblivious to her warning. With a thin smile the older woman also closed her eyes. She would have to watch out for her. She would think of her as her own dear Beth, her own sweet daughter. It had been nearly three years now since last she had seen her only child, and enjoying these thoughts of her Beth, she fell into a deep sleep.

The next morning Lisa was pulled from the depths of a sound slumber by someone shaking her shoulder. "What? What is it?" she drowsily rose on an elbow, forcing her eyes to open.

"The old lady said to let you sleep for a few moments before telling you to go down to breakfast." A heavyset young girl with dingy, stringy brown hair spoke. Then turning her back upon the bed and going to the single bureau in the room, she took up the lone comb there and started pulling it through her mass of brown hair.

Lisa rubbed her eyes, realizing that this must be the girl with whom she and Mrs. Beilier had shared the room. "Thank you." She brought her hand up and stifled a yawn as she tried to pull herself from the confines of the bed.

"The old lady said that she would have some rolls and tea for you so you had best hurry," the girl threw over her shoulder as she started from the room.

This time Lisa did not respond to the girl's

words. She had found her rather rude. Perhaps the girl had resented having to share her room with strangers, Lisa thought. She herself would not take kindly to having to share her bed with two women she had never met.

Pushing the girl from her thoughts, she pulled the nightgown over her head and began to dress in a black traveling gown. Its neckline was trimmed with a touch of soft creamy lace, some of which also adorned the cuffs. Going to the small, cracked mirror over the bureau she glimpsed her reflection, and with a sour look at what she saw before her, she went to her bag and took up her brush. She was glad that this would be the last day that she would have to endure such discomfort. By this very afternoon she would, according to the stage driver, arrive at her aunt's inn.

Keeping in mind that she would be meeting her kin and that this would be her last day aboard the rolling, bumpy vehicle she brushed out her long, golden tresses and carefully pinned her curls atop her head, after which she placed a small black hat, trimmed with the same creamy lace, at a jaunty angle upon her curls.

With a last glance in the mirror Lisa took up her bag, left the room, and started down the hall. Seeing Mrs. Beilier sitting at a table, she also sat down and began to eat the breakfast that the good woman had ordered for the two of them.

They were only alotted a small amount of time before the stage driver called them to board the stage.

As Mrs. Beilier and Lisa both started from the common room, Lisa noticed that Mr. Moore was nowhere in sight. For a fleeting moment she thought that perhaps he had decided not to pursue his journey any farther. And at this thought she experienced a feeling of relief. The man made her quite uncomfortable. His dark eyes always seemed to be upon her. For a moment she was reminded of Craig Rollins, the man she had met upon the *Sea Maid*, but as she thought of the mysterious older man, she wished wholeheartedly that it was he sitting across from her in the carriage instead of this Mr. Moore. She truly missed the kind man she had found to be a true friend aboard ship.

"Now, Mike, I be seeing you in a few days if'n you don't get your scalp lifted by that red devil, Silver Fox." A large man sitting near the vast open hearth shouted out to one of the drivers of the vehicle in which Lisa had been riding.

Before stepping through the portal, Lisa turned and looked at the man who had just spoken. As she did so, she noticed the concerned look that crossed the driver's features.

"Aye, Ben, me and Tod are watching every bush for that redskin and if'n he crosses our path the country won't be having to worry no more." He patted the long rifle that he held casually in his right hand.

"That's brave talk but I be hearing that the Fox

was sighted near here only yesterday evening," the man called Ben rejoined.

These words seemed to bring a different response than the first. "I be watching then. Thanks for the warning." With this the drivers started toward the door and Lisa hurriedly accompanied Mrs. Beilier to the carriage, her thoughts again dwelling upon Indians. All the talk she had heard so far about Indians had concerned one Indian in particular, Silver Fox. Indeed, he must be fierce and terrible, she thought as the driver handed first her and then Mrs. Beilier up into the vehicle.

Lisa soon realized she would not be free of Leroy Moore's probing eyes for the rest of her trip. As she entered the carriage she at once noticed the fat man.

With a large grin of greeting Mr. Moore looked at Lisa and then Mrs. Beilier. "I took my meal early this morning and then visited with some of the men staying at the inn," he said as though addressing one in particular, but having no response from either of the ladies he went on. "I trust that both of you had a good evening's rest?" He cocked his head toward the two opposite him to discourage them from neglecting his question.

"Is our sleep of any importance to you, Mr. Moore?" Mrs. Beilier had also thought that this fat, intrusive man had left their company. So with some disappointment she now looked full into his face and answered his question with one of her own, expressed with some haughtiness.

Leroy Moore did not let this woman put him off. Last night his dreams had been of the lovely Lisa, and this morning nothing could upset him in the least. "I did not mean to intrude. I but hoped that you had rested well for the day ahead of us. I expect it to be as arduous as the past two."

"Neither Miss Culbreth nor myself expect this day to be different from those we have endured already, sir. But Miss Culbreth can be comforted by the fact that for her this shall be the last day in this carriage."

"Aye, she can be comforted there. As for myself, I have been thinking of staying at her aunt's inn for a few days. I have been there on past occasions and have met the dear lady who is her kin. I find her inn most pleasant so I think I shall also take my leave of this dreadful coach."

Mrs. Beilier sighed with irritation. Mr. Moore seemed to be intent upon bothering this young woman seated next to her, but there was nothing further she could do about the matter. The girl's kin would have to set this odious man straight. She was sure the girl's aunt would, at once, put Mr. Moore in his place concerning this young woman. She could not imagine anyone's kinfolk allowing this man to be around.

Lisa could not believe her ears. Why on earth would this fat, unpleasant man wish to stay on at her aunt's inn? The thought of having to endure for several more days this man's eyes upon her sent cold chills coursing over her form. Her blue eyes swiftly went over his form, taking in the bountiful proportions bulging out of his food-stained suit and vest. She raised her eyes from his body to the folds of soft white skin on his neck and then farther to his slack, drooling lips before her eyes were drawn to his small, dark brown predatory eyes. A dark flush graced her cheeks as she fully realized how repulsive this man across from her was, and at the same time she noticed his small eyes were looking her up and down. With a hurried motion she pulled her head from the sight before her and swiftly looked out the window, watching as the drivers got the team of horses started down the dirt road.

Mrs. Beilier noticed the interplay going on between the couple in the carriage but she held her peace, knowing that the girl found this man not to her liking and hoping that she would find kin to defend her from such men as he.

Mr. Moore, though, was in the mood for conversation. He had talked with the men at the inn and this had seemed to stimulate him with the desire for companionship. "There was more talk of that Indian from the men at the inn. They say he's been stirring up more trouble."

"Mr. Moore, if you do not mind I would take it very kindly if you would let this talk of Indians drop." Mrs. Beilier pulled her knitting from the bag that rested at her feet and began to work on the shawl she was making for her daughter.

"Just trying to make conversation, Mrs. Beilier."

"I think you men try deliberately to frighten us women with this talk of Indians and the like."

"There is no need for you or Miss Culbreth to be afraid." His small dark eyes caressed Lisa, watching her profile as she, oblivious to the conversation going on about her, looked out the window. "I would deem it an honor to protect both of you ladies from any form of harm." With these words he puffed out his already too large chest.

Mrs. Beilier did not respond. Her eyes, as they went over Leroy Moore, told all that needed to be said. Her doubt of the veracity of his boastful words was plainly visible. Leroy, sensing her mockery, wiped his lower lip and then he also stared out the window, his mind seething at her insult. He did not have to take her ridicule, especially in front of the woman he desired to claim as his own. Keeping his mouth shut, he sat and stewed with anger.

After the noon hour had passed, Lisa became impatient, her desire to reach her journey's end building as each moment passed. Again and again she fidgeted on her seat, her hands occasionally going to her hair to make sure that her coiffure had not begun to droop and that her curls were still in place. She wished to make a good impression at this first meeting with her aunt. A deep-gnawing fear had begun to grow in her, a fear that if her aunt was displeased by her and did not offer her a home, she truly had no place to go. She was alone in this vast wilderness full of fierce Indians and men such as this Mr. Moore whose eyes told only too well of the fate she would meet if she were left on her own and somehow fell prey to those greedy fat hands. And she truly did not know the ways of the world. If the need to defend herself arose, she doubted that she would know what to do. With a soft sigh, she brushed at the black material of her gown, wishing that the dust were her thoughts and could as easily be removed.

Mrs. Beilier looked up from her knitting and, seeing the sad, worried look upon Lisa's features, patted the hand that lay white and soft upon the black gown, wishing to relay some strength to this young girl.

Lisa smiled at the elderly lady, knowing her kindness came from a gentle heart. And as she smiled she felt some of her courage return. Of course her kin would wish her to come. Hadn't her aunt invited her? Had she not herself read the letter written to her stepsister?

A sudden lurch and sway of the coach almost slung Lisa into Mr. Moore's lap, and she was pulled sharply out of her thoughts. Jerking herself away from the fat man's pudgy hands which reached out to steady her, Lisa grasped hold of her cushioned seat and tried to reposition herself next to Mrs. Beilier.

That good woman herself was almost in the same fix but she had reached out at the first odd motion of the stage and taken hold of support. "What on earth?" she exclaimed as she reached out a hand to prevent Lisa from falling again.

The coach was now being pulled by the horses at a harrowing pace, its drivers shouting and the whip cracking loudly overhead. Lisa regained her seat and sat white-faced with fear. She clutched the upholstery desperately as her small hat flew to the floor and her golden curls began to fall about her face.

Leroy Moore pulled his huge weight to the window and peered out. What he shouted back into the vehicle resounded like the hammer of doom. "Injuns. They're chasing close behind. Must be at least a dozen of the red savages!"

No! Lisa thought, this cannot be happening. She clutched at her throat, afraid that she was going to be sick as she heard a rifle shot sound. With the will of one who was truly lost to the world of fear she shut her eyes tightly together and began silently to pray.

Mrs. Beilier was of the same mind, and she sat as though numb, mumbling prayers to the Lord for rescue and the strength to endure what was to happen.

No more shots ensued after the first one but within minutes the coach was being pulled to a fierce halt.

Lisa held her breath as she heard the sound of horses' hooves surrounding the vehicle.

Mrs. Beilier took Lisa's hand and tightly clasped it within her own. She had said only the night before that she would consider this young girl as her own, and now, in the face of danger, she knew that the child needed all the courage that she could gather.

Lisa directed a small, trembling smile toward the older woman, knowing that Mrs. Beilier would stand at her side and be her support.

Mr. Moore, after looking out the coach window, had sat back against the seat not saying another word. His features were pale and his breathing was shallow. And when the carriage door was pulled ajar and an Indian with a painted face stuck his head within, Leroy Moore all but collapsed upon the seat.

"Tell your passengers to step out." These words were spoken to the driver who had been pulled down from the top of the carriage and who was now standing and looking up into the face of the Indian leader.

To those inside, the words spoken to the driver had sounded as loud and hard as a clap of thunder, and all braced themselves for the ordeal ahead.

Mrs. Beilier was the first to respond to the driver's command that all within should alight. "Come along, child. It is best to have done with what shall happen. Remember that you are an innocent. The Lord above shall look after you." She took hold of Lisa's trembling hand and started out the coach door.

The women got to the ground with the help of the drivers. Then Mr. Moore clambered down, panting from exertion and fear.

As the three passengers and two drivers stood next to the coach, Lisa looked up for the first time. Her blue eyes were twin slivers of fear as they rose to take in the horses that surrounded them, also noting the leather leggings worn by most of the Indians, the dark tanned thighs of those in breechcloths, the naked chests, and finally the fierce faces, painted with varying designs.

Lisa's eyes went over first one and then another Indian until they finally rested upon the man astride a huge, magnificent black stallion. He stood out from his cohorts. He seemed a size larger than the others, Lisa thought. Or perhaps it was the way he sat his mount. He seemed to exude power and strength. He was clothed as those about him, but his frame seemed larger. His face was painted with only two streaks of yellow under his right eye and a small half moon on the same cheek. She was certain that this man was the leader of the group and that their fate depended upon his words.

As her blue eyes studied the man upon the black horse they were drawn to his own black orbs which bore down upon her. Lisa felt her limbs begin to weaken, and in that instant her blood felt as though it had turned to warm jell. Mrs. Beilier tightened her grip upon her as she felt Lisa's frame begin to sag.

Pulling his mesmerizing gaze from Lisa, the Indian looked over Mrs. Beilier and then glanced at the fat man standing next to the women. An angry scowl came across his features as his black eyes took in all of Mr. Moore. He was the symbolic white man. His gluttonous appetite consuming all that stood in his way. No matter the results, he would devour all until there was nothing left, no land or food. With one last look at the fat man's face, the Indian's eyes returned to the girl. His expression changed as he regarded Lisa, his black eyes again going over her form and resting upon her golden hair which had tumbled loose from its confinement before gazing into her gentle heart-shaped face which displayed fear and panic.

For a second courage came to Leroy Moore, and before he could think he blurted, "If it's money you want take what we have but leave us be." He had seen the way the leader had looked at Lisa Culbreth and something within him rebelled. He desired the girl and a surge of jealousy came over him at this Indian's bold perusal of her.

The others from the group gasped at the fat man's words. But finally the Indian settled his coal black eyes upon the man and spoke. When he did Leroy Moore felt the full bite of his mistake in speaking.

"You have nothing with which to tempt me. Not even your scalp could be called a worthy prize." The Indian's black eyes rose for a second to the stringy, greasy brown hair atop Moore's head and then with a thin irritated smile he looked back to the man's face. "But if you are wishing to breathe your last, one of my brothers will be happy to help you."

Lisa gasped at the Indian's harsh words, and as fear gripped her, she looked with frightened blue eyes into his face.

The Indian, his attention drawn by the small sound coming from her lips, noticed her white look of fright and scowled darkly upon the fat man once again. "You shall be allowed to pass this day," he said. Then he looked at the driver. "But remember the words of Silver Fox well. The whites are trying to strangle my people and my land with their presence. Each day they foul our women and our hunting grounds. You came talking truce and friendship, but we have seen the taste of this thing called friendship by the whites and it sours bitterly in our bellies. The time has come when we will not see our people abused and treated as dirt. I, Silver Fox, have said this and I will see that my tribe is dealt with fairly no matter the price."

The driver did not speak but merely nodded his head, afraid that any words he might say would only evoke a denial of this Indian's earlier words. By some miracle this fierce Indian chief Silver Fox, had said they could go free. The driver had no idea why, but he was not one to argue with an Indian who held the power, by merely raising his hand, to have the lot of them killed.

For a moment the Indian's black eyes went back to Lisa, and studying her features carefully, he gently nudged his stallion's sides, commanding him to slowly go forward.

At this movement the relief that Lisa had felt briefly when he'd said he would let them pass safely swiftly disappeared. He was coming closer with each passing second, and not knowing his intent, she backed up until she was tightly pressed against the coach.

What happened next seemed to occur within a flash. At one moment Lisa was standing next to Mrs. Beilier and looking up with frightened blue eyes toward the towering Indian, while in the next she was held tightly in a viselike grasp, her form having been pulled up securely into Silver Fox's arms, her black skirts draped about his horse.

It was a full moment before she understood what was taking place. As realization came to her she opened her mouth to scream, but swiftly her words were muffled by a large, tanned hand. And allowing Lisa only a glimpse at the horror-struck features of the kind lady who had watched over her so lovingly and those of a white-faced Mr. Moore, the Indian swung his horse about and started off down the dirt road.

Panic consumed Lisa as she heard the whoops and screams of the other riders about her. An arm held her tightly about the waist and a hand remained over her mouth. With fierce determination she began to struggle, flaying her arms about and trying with all of her might to win her release from this horrible man, but swiftly her mouth was released and her arms were pinned to her body. The Indian had encircled her form with his own arms, pulling her ever tighter into his embrace.

All that was left to Lisa now were her tears, and these she let flow as she realized that she was lost. God only knew where these men would take her, and she feared that they would perform the most evil of tortures upon her. She had heard stories of women being taken by bands of Indians and never being heard from again.

So now after all she had endured this was to be her fate, to be taken and tortured and killed by a pack of savages. Wrenching, pitiful sobs broke from her chest.

When they had ridden some distance down the road, the Indian who held Lisa brought his stallion to a halt. Those about him looked to him for direction and he signaled them to go ahead.

Looking down, his black eyes softened as they viewed Lisa's tortured face, and as her sobs of fear touched his ears a tight band squeezed about his heart. Bringing one of his hands up he gently reached out with a long dark finger and followed the line of the crystal tear that ran down her soft, creamy cheeks.

At the feel of his tender touch Lisa looked up into the face of her captor, and what was plainly visible to her was even more frightening than thoughts of torture. There was something within his dark eyes that she had never in her young life seen before—lust, passion, desire were the thoughts that swept over her. Again she tried to get free, struggling in his tight hold upon her, but still the face before her remained set and its black eyes bore down compellingly and left her powerless.

"Do not fight me for it shall profit you nothing."

His voice was as tender as the touch he had used to wipe the tear from her cheek. Lisa became still at the sound of it and against her will her liquid-filled blue eyes looked up at the dark, handsome face before her. His features were tan, but unlike the coloring of the Indians who had ridden off, his seemed to come from exposure to the sun. His hair was midnight blue-black and a thin headband held the shoulder-length straight mass from his face. That face was the most compelling feature about him. His eyes were as black as the night but there was an intelligence and an understanding within them that belied referring to him as a savage. His nose was straight and suited his other features. As Lisa looked lower on his face, a slight blush touched her own when the thought came to her that this sensual slanted mouth could easily hold promises that she had never touched upon. Gleaming white teeth were visible and the mouth that she had been admiring turned up into a grin as the Indian noticed the direction of her thoughts and also viewed the soft blush that graced her features.

Lisa was afire with shame as he sat grinning at her, but she was powerless to do aught but shut her blue eyes tightly and will her thoughts from the direction in which they had turned.

"Your beauty surpasses any my eyes have ever viewed before." His words were like a velvet whisper as they came to Lisa's ears and they brought an even darker hue to her cheeks.

"Rarely has fortune looked so favorably on me as to allow me to glimpse such perfection, let alone to hold it within my arms."

Lisa could not believe her ears. Little did she know of Indians, this was true, but she would never have suspected that a man who rode about the countryside with little more upon his frame than a breechcloth, and whose antics were generally described as savage and barbaric, could possibly talk in such a manner as this. His tone was that of a well-educated man, one well learned and quite intelligent. But despite these thoughts her mind rebelled against what he was saying. He was her captor and she had to gain her release before it was too late.

"Please let me go." She begged and began to weep.

His dark eyes looked deep into her own and with a soft, gentle smile he nodded his dark head. "Perhaps. If the payment is agreeable."

Her tears came to a slow halt and Lisa began to feel the pounding of her heart. He had said payment. There was some chance then to attain her freedom. "What sort of payment? I myself have few coins left to me, but my aunt, I am sure, would be willing to pay you whatever you would require." She watched the smile upon his features grow deeper and her hope grew at the thought that he only cared for wealth and would hold her for ransom.

"Ah . . . let me see." For a moment he thoughtfully rubbed his naked chin as though in deep thought. "You say you have a few coins and would have to get them from your aunt?" At a nod of her head he went on. "I am afraid that I never do business in this manner. My people receive payment for a service when the deed is done. You would be willing to stay with me until I receive the required amount of coins from your kin?"

Lisa's form began to tremble in response to his question. It meant that she would be his captive until he received the money from her aunt. And what if her kin refused? What then would happen to her? She had no idea whether her aunt would care to rescue a niece she had not seen in years.

Once again her tears began to flow and shaking her golden head Lisa wept. "Please let me go."

It was only a moment before the Indian reached out and took hold of her small chin, bringing her blue eyes up to look directly into his own. "I do not wish for coins as payment."

"What then?" Lisa wondered aloud but before she could say another word she had her answer.

The lips that had only a moment ago been turned up into a grin now descended with a soft, gentle caress, demanding and deliberate, seeking and sensual, not allowing release or escape.

Lisa struggled in his arms as she first realized what he was about but firmly, yet gently, the Indian took hold of the back of her head with one hand, while he wrapped his other arm about her, drawing her closer to his naked chest and preventing any movement on her part.

As his dark head lowered and his lips claimed her own, Lisa realized the payment that was expected of her and with the little self-control that remained to her she tried to push at his chest, wanting only her freedom and release from the consuming lips that were pressing her down.

But her release was not to be, and as though she were a wild mare needing to be gently broken in, Silver Fox placed his hands on either side of her golden head and made his suit more intense.

Lisa had only known one other pair of lips and they had been those of Mr. Rollins, the older man aboard the *Sea Maid*. So though her mind fought for release from Silver Fox's grip upon her, from somewhere in her inner depths she began to respond to his sweet persistence. An inner desire seemed to claim her, her mind telling her what was happening was wrong but her body beginning to respond. Her arms reached up and entwined about his strong shoulders, and, with a sigh, she threw caution into the farthest corners of her mind. The sphere of desire that was forming about her was too powerful. There was something here that she could not resist.

With a searing joy Silver Fox felt her change. And the pressure of his lips increased, banishing thought for the moment.

Expelling a large sigh, he finally released her, his head going back for a fraction of a second so that his black eyes could read the expression on her face. What he saw brought gladness to his heart. With slow, tender movements, not wishing to scare her or to destroy the beauty of the moment, Silver Fox took Lisa in his arms and climbed from the back of his horse, his lips now tenderly speaking soothing love words to her as he carried her from the road and toward a group of trees.

There was no longer any resistance on Lisa's part. All that her senses could feel were the arms about her and she was lost as he gently laid her down under a large oak tree in a soft bed of moss.

Silver Fox stood back to view the woman lying upon the ground, his thoughts on her beauty and his vision soaking up her delicate features. Never had he dreamed that he would have a creature such as she, and bending a knee upon the soft moss, he reached out a large browned hand and with easy movements caressed her creamy cheek.

Lisa lay with her eyes tightly shut, her breathing shallow and low as her body waited expectantly for what was about to happen. The physical desire that was overwhelming her was new to her, but she knew that this moment in time, this place, and what would soon happen were destined to be.

With infinite care Silver Fox slipped his arms about her. His handsome, dark face brushed against her golden hair, arousing the sweet fragrance that was only hers and thereby sending his senses reeling. Silver Fox was mindful of the need for slowness and gentleness lest he spoil the moment, for he knew that, although at this moment, she was willing, her passion could easily turn to fear for hers was an innocence he had rarely seen.

Slowly, Lisa was swept into a world of burning passion as her body made contact with his lean frame. She felt the hard, manly boldness of him, and she closed her blue eyes as his searing lips slowly traced her throat and shoulder. His hands caressed her and, with little effort, freed her of her traveling gown and undergarments.

Still, his actions did not frighten Lisa, so swept up was she in the moment that only what was to come and the wonder of it were real to her. His hands caressed her, leisurely arousing her, stroking her breasts, and moving downward over her belly. A warm tide of tingling, expectant excitement flooded her being. Her mind seemed to be whirling giddily, and she forgot completely that she did not really know this man and that she should not just give herself to any man, let alone to one her people called a heathen and a savage. A whisper of a sigh escaped from her soft, petal-pink lips as his mouth ceased to caress her and he looked into her face, trying to read her thoughts. But soon enough Silver Fox discerned what he wished to know. Again his mouth claimed hers and he held her body tightly against his own. As the pair came together in the forging of two beings, their kisses became more compelling, seeking and drawing—devouring—when their tongues met with hungry anticipation.

As Silver Fox rose above her all time seemed to stop for Lisa. There was a magic here, upon the soft moss bed, that was shattering. It flowed and expanded into a voracious rapture that made her body arch against his, driven by a compelling ardor that matched his own. A wild, soaring ecstasy burst within them, clasping them together in a scorching caldron of passion. Pulled tightly to him as though almost a part of him, Lisa felt the heavy beating of the Indian's heart and his deep ragged breathing touched her ear.

Her innocent woman's body reacted instinctively to the pulsating, blooming, indescribable feeling that seemed to be budding deep within her body and she let herself be led by him, delighting in the pleasures this man was revealing to her.

It was as though all eternity stood silent for a moment, as a showering, brilliant, sparkling burst of passion descended upon the couple, and Lisa caught her breath as the fires within her raged. Silver Fox, his body spent, clasped her tightly in his arms, his heart bursting with more than the pleasure that he had just received.

Neither moved for a few moments, their soft moss bed surrounding them and sheltering them from the outside world, but when their eyes opened their sated bodies came back to the earth about them.

"I am afraid the payment was far beyond any I had expected." Silver Fox leaned over her and looked deep into her face.

Lisa felt her features pinking at his words and now that her craving for him had been satisfied, she realized what she had done. She had given herself as ransom for her own release, or so this Indian thought. But deep within she knew there was more. This Indian had only taken a part of her that she had freely given, and her thoughts kept asking why. She could have done the same in the past with any number of men, but with none of them had she felt what she had this day. He had drawn from her secrets she had never known existed. "And are you satisfied then?" she softly ventured, keeping her eyes tightly shut, so as not to see his smiling features when he answered her.

"Aye, indeed I am." His tone was soft to her ears and she was compelled to open her blue eyes. His black ones were not mocking her folly in giving herself to him but they were tender and caring. Stinging tears came to her own as she saw this.

With a gentle caress Silver Fox reached up and lightly brushed the crystal tear that slowly rolled down her cheek. "Do you weep for a mistake, my golden flower?"

Lisa knew that she would never consider the time here in this glade a mistake. No. Her tears were for the concern that she read in his features. In the past she had never known love, had never had anyone care for her. "I do not weep for what has happened," she said truthfully.

"I am glad this is the way of it." Boldly he let his lips touch down upon hers once again. And when he raised his head, he gave a large sigh. "We had best hurry and dress, your carriage should be coming soon."

Lisa did not respond, but as he rose to his feet and she to hers and they began to dress, she felt a deep sadness. He had taken her from the carriage only to use her, and now he would leave her as though he had never known her. Could she ever do the same? she asked herself as she watched him out of the corner of her eye. He stood, relaxed, against the oak as he waited for her to finish dressing.

When she finished he came to her side, and with

easy movements, he swung her up into his arms, saying, "It is easier if I carry you to the horse." And with a grin he kissed her pink lips.

Lisa felt confused as he released her. He seemed to truly like her, but still he was going to send her back to the carriage.

For a few lingering moments he stood beside his horse with her in his arms, as though he could not bear to set her down. But when a noise could be heard from the dirt road he took her lips once more with a burning kiss.

"I shall see you again, golden flower." With these words he set her down and jumping to the back of his horse he kicked his sides and started off in the opposite direction, turning only once to look back at her.

Lisa stood alongside the road, her thoughts in disarray as she wondered if what had taken place had actually occurred. Had she given herself to this Indian? Had she allowed herself to become so lost to reason that she did that? And he had left her. Swift tears stung her eyes at the thought. He had taken her and then left her standing beside the road waiting for the carriage.

Drawing on a reserve of self-control, Lisa braced her back and dashed her tears away. She would put this Indian from her thoughts. She would wipe from her mind what had occurred this day.

As she came to this decision she caught sight of the carriage. Taking a last deep breath she braced herself for what she would tell its occupants and driver.

Now that she had decided how to deal with this situation, it was a relief to see the carriage pull to a halt at the side of the road.

Mrs. Beilier was the first to react when the vehicle came to a complete stop. Without any assistance she flew from its interior and within seconds she was holding Lisa tightly in her arms. Her tears of delight and relief covered Lisa's face as the woman turned her this way and that to make sure that she was sound and was unharmed.

Lisa hugged the woman tightly to her, realizing the full extent of the thin woman's concern. "I am fine, Mrs. Beilier. The Indian but wished to frighten us, and for no reason that I can think of, he let me down from his horse right here and then went on his own way." Lisa was not sure why, but she knew she could not tell anyone about what had actually taken place while she was the Indian's captive.

"Thank the Lord above for his goodness and mercy, child." The woman wept anew and dabbed swiftly at her tears with a delicately embroidered handkerchief.

"Let us hurry and be on our way." The stage driver motioned the ladies aboard as soon as he had made sure that all was well with the young girl who'd been taken by the Indian. It had certainly been a surprise to him to see her standing on the side of the road, but now was not the time to try to figure out the workings of a heathen mind. He wished to hurry and get to some form of safety before dark. There was no guarantee that this band of Indians was not still lurking about.

After the two women were handed up into the vehicle they clung together again until Mrs. Beilier pulled herself upright and, taking one more satisfied look in Lisa's direction, blew her nose, then sat back against the cushion, her hand still holding Lisa's as though she thought the girl would vanish at any moment.

Leroy Moore was the first to break the quiet in the carriage. "You are safe I hope, Miss Culbreth?" His small eyes went over her form with a question of their own. At first when he had seen the young woman standing off by the side of the road he had thought that he was imagining things, but here she was. And though he was quite thankful he still wondered why any man would easily give up such a prize once he had it within his grasp. Why had the Indian let her go and what had he done to her during the short time that she had been with him? Moore wondered and looking over her form, he tried to determine just what had taken place. After all, he told himself, he wanted this young woman for his own. He had the right to know just what had occurred.

Lisa blushed brightly at his look, and sensing his dark thoughts, she merely nodded her head in response to his question.

Mrs. Beilier now took her post against this man

as she had on the preceding day. "Of course she is all right, Mr. Moore. She is simply frightened and weary. Have you not eyes that can see?" Mrs. Beilier knew that he had eyes and she also had seen the way the fat man looked at the girl. "We should just be thankful to the good Lord above that we have her back with us."

"Yes, we should be thankful, Miss Culbreth. Women taken by those savages usually are not heard from again and the few who do return to civilization are looked at in rather a dim light."

Lisa knew all too well what this man was implying. He was telling her that she was lucky she had been released for if she had remained longer with the Indian her own people would regard her accusingly. It was, indeed, well for her that the Indian had released her, she thought. But then a part of her mind reminded her of their kisses and she wondered what it would have been like to have been kept a captive by the handsome Silver Fox.

Leroy Moore, as though reading her mind, sat back against the cushion, breathed deeply, and settled his arms over his large chest. Without saying another word, he let his dark eyes rest upon the woman across from him.

Mrs. Beilier seemed satisfied with just this small reprieve from the fat man's prying, and though she was aware of the discomfort his gaze occasioned in the young girl next to her, at least he was being quiet and not expressing his black thoughts for the time being. Giving one last pat to the hand lying next to hers, Mrs. Beilier looked out the window and became lost in her own thoughts.

She was certainly glad no harm had come to this young lady. She had seen the look the Indian had directed toward the girl when they had been standing before him outside the carriage, and she was truly amazed that he had let her go. She had been sure that she would never see Lisa again. The girl was bringing something to this wilderness that men of all races wanted. She possessed a beauty of which she seemed unaware and which would rule her destiny. Mrs. Beilier could only hope, for in the past few days she had begun to care for this young girl, that her kin would watch over her and realize what a treasure she was. Her own child, Beth, she had to admit had not been as lovely as this Lisa. In fact Beth had been rather plain in her youth, but she had loved her with a mother's love and she had watched over her, wishing her only the best. And Beth had been given the best when she had met the man she'd married. Nathan Lane had been a hard-working, Christian man who had loved her daughter from the first moment he had seen her. After courting her for several months he had married her, and then the couple had moved to this wilderness in order to build a future for themselves, which was exactly what they were doing. Mrs. Beilier only wished that Lisa Culbreth could have the same chance for a happy life.

Lisa's thoughts were quite different from Mrs. Beilier's. Hers were on the Indian that had spared their lives and let them go free. She released a sigh, simultaneously experiencing a small pain in her chest. His bold masculinity seemed to have made an impression upon her that she could not sweep from her mind. She again went over his features in her mind's eye, and as she remembered his lips lowering to her own, she strongly cautioned herself that she should try to forget what had taken place this afternoon and to suppress the feelings this Indian had evoked in her.

It was late in the day, almost dark, when the team of horses pulled to a halt before a large stone building with a sign that read Pheasant's Inn hanging over its front eaves.

Lisa craned her neck this way and that but was only able to see a small portion of the building, although off to the side she could glimpse the stables and a few outbuildings. She took a deep breath and forced a small smile for Mrs. Beilier. "I wish to thank you for all of your kindness."

"It is always a pleasure to make a new friend, my dear. And that is exactly how I shall always think of you—a dear, sweet friend." Mrs. Beilier patted Lisa's hand affectionately, knowing how nervous the young girl must be after traveling so many miles, having experienced what had just happened to her, and now having to face kin she barely knew.

"We shall stay the night here at The Pheasant's Inn," the driver called as he opened the coach door. "Wouldn't wish to run into that injun again this day so I think we shall seek some shelter while we are still able."

Mrs. Beilier herself still had two more days of travel before reaching her daughter's home, but seeing the relieved look on Lisa's face, she was glad that the driver had wished to stay the night. At least she would have a little more time with the girl. "Now I shall be able to go along with you when you meet your aunt, my dear." She smiled good-naturedly.

"Thank you so much," Lisa said softly.

Mr. Moore smirked at the women across from him. "There is nothing for you to fear, Miss Culbreth. I have met the good Mrs. Simmons before and she is a most pleasant woman to be around. Still, it is a good thing that the Indian did not hold you captive for a long time for most people about these parts will have little to do with a white woman after she has been taken by one of those heathens." He added the latter remark to remind her of the near mishap she'd had earlier.

Lisa experienced no relief on hearing his words about her aunt. She could well imagine what type of woman he found pleasant. And as for the Indian she had determined during the long ride this afternoon that she must drive their love-making from her thoughts, and though she knew there would be questions asked and looks directed toward her, she would hold her head upright and not flinch from cruel words. She had done nothing wrong, she told herself.

As the group left the carriage and entered the front door of the Pheasant's Inn Lisa's eyes took in all about her. From the outside she had realized how large her aunt's property was, and as the horses tied in front implied, she found the inn to be busy.

They stepped into a large common room, much bigger than any they had seen during their trip. On one side of it was a long bar, behind which stood a portly man who was filling glasses with ale and cider. The opposite wall contained an open hearth, but since the weather was still warm no fire had been lit. There were several comfortable chairs placed near the hearth for the customers' use, and the rest of the room was filled with small tables and chairs at which several men were sitting and eating delicious-smelling meals.

Lisa took all this in with a glance, and then, as her eyes went about the room, she noticed a plump woman sitting at a table near the bar and talking with an elderly, gray-haired man. As the woman looked up, some form of recognition sparked in her eyes, and Lisa immediately knew that this was her aunt Adell Simmons.

With slow steps she started toward the couple sitting at the table, her hand pulling Mrs. Beilier along with her.

Adell Simmons knew at a glance that this was her dead sister's daughter. The girl looked just like Virginia. "So you have finally arrived?" she asked as the girl stood before her table. "I had thought that perhaps that stepsister of yours would not tell you of my invitation." Adell spoke loudly, not caring who heard their conversation. She was a rough woman.

"Yes, Aunt Adell. I have come for the visit that you requested. Sylvia gave me your letter." Lisa swallowed hard as she looked down at the heavy woman before her.

"She did, did she? Well I truly did not expect it of her. She always was a snooty thing. Except that you are my sister's child, I would have long ago stopped writing to Culbreth manor."

Lisa did not respond when she heard this woman she did not know talking about her stepsister. "I hope I have not come at an inopportune time, Aunt Adell?" She could think of nothing else to say.

"The time matters not. Who is this with you?" Adell questioned, arching an eyebrow at Mrs. Beilier. Had the girl brought a maid with her? The idea brought a tight smile over her hard features.

"Oh, this is Mrs. Beilier. She has been traveling on the coach with me and has become a dear friend. She will be staying the night here at your inn because our coach was stopped by Indians and the driver fears that this Silver Fox might try to stop them again if they go on." Lisa wanted to

128

tell her aunt about the Indians and about what had taken place this afternoon so she would not have to be questioned about the matter later.

This topic seemed to spark some attention in Adell Simmons. "You say you were stopped by Silver Fox and his men and that they let you pass unharmed?" She pulled her bountiful bulk from the chair and directed her gaze at the two women before her.

"Yes, Aunt Adell," Lisa responded rather softly, aware now of her aunt's huge form standing over her. Then, with a tight swallow, she added, "There is also more. This Indian, Silver Fox, did not quite let us pass as easily as that."

"Well spit it out, girl, what did the dirty savage do?"

Lisa found it difficult to respond to this direct line of questioning, and as she tried to form her reply, she was saved from making the effort by Mrs. Beilier who placed a gentle hand upon her arm.

"What your niece is trying to tell you, Mrs. Simmons is that this Indian leader did attack our vehicle, and though he did not harm any of us, he did give Lisa quite a fright by taking her upon his horse and riding off with her. But I assure you that it was only a short matter of time before we found her standing alongside the road. She was well suited and not harmed in the least."

Adell Simmons stood, horrified, and glared at her niece. "This Indian had you upon his horse?

Am I hearing correctly? And then for no reason he let you loose?"

Lisa felt her body start to tremble, but she nodded her head in agreement at her aunt's words. "Yes, Aunt Adell. He did not harm me. He but took me down the road a pace, set me down, and rode away."

Adell Simmons could not believe her ears. Why would the Indian do such a thing? This girl standing before her was a beauty as her mother had been. Any Indian would be more than glad to get his red hands upon a piece such as she, for if nothing else she would bring a good price from another tribe. She did not speak again, though, about the girl's near abduction. She would ask the stage driver how long the Indian had the girl. "I can hardly believe that this Silver Fox did not do some harm to the lot of you. Why, there is a large reward posted for him and every man hereabout is this very day out looking for the savage. Even my own dear son, Willie, is with the others scouring the countryside," she added gruffly, her words directed more toward Mrs. Beilier.

Lisa listened, and when the woman mentioned that she had a son called Willie, her eyes brightened. Why then, she would have a cousin.

"Come along and I shall show the pair of you to a table and have some food sent to you. I must talk to your drivers and find out all that I can for the men shall wish to hear about Silver Fox."

Lisa and Mrs. Beilier were pulled along behind

the tall, heavyset woman and then shown to a table at a corner of the room near the kitchen door. "I shall have Milly bring out food and drink shortly." Having said this, she turned and, with a walk that looked more like a march, she went to the bar and approached the two drivers.

Lisa's first impression of her aunt left her at a loss. The woman seemed hard and businesslike about everything, the only exception had been when she had mentioned her son's name. Then she had shown a spark of warmth beneath her hard shell.

Mrs. Beilier did not know what she thought of the big woman either. She thought her hard, but she realized that in this country a woman without a man had to be hard. And the woman, with only a son, had built up this busy establishment, so in a way she could well understand her. There was little warmth to Adell Simmons but perhaps she would mellow toward her niece with the passing of time. At least she had not been outright nasty in any way.

Lisa and Mrs. Beilier watched the activity about them until their meals were brought out upon a large tray. Lisa sat and watched her aunt talking to Mike and Tod, the coach drivers. As she observed the hard, unmoving woman sitting nearby, she remembered her childhood. She had disliked the woman who was her mother's sister when she was a child, but now she was not sure what her feelings were. Perhaps she was too weary to make any judgement at this time, she told herself.

After eating her meal with some gusto, Lisa felt the full pressure of her tiredness. It would be good to be able to sleep and not be awakened before dawn simply to get back into the coach. With her hand, she stifled a small yawn just as her aunt once again approached their table.

"I see that you have both finished, so if you would like you can go to your rooms. I know that it is still early in the evening but I expect that the carriage ride has been a strain and that you are both quite tired."

"Thank you, Aunt Adell." Lisa smiled, thinking that she had indeed misread the woman. "I am quite tired and I am sure Mrs. Beilier is too."

"That girl Milly, from the kitchen, shall show you up the stairs then, if you are ready. Get yourself a good night's sleep for we rise fairly early to begin our day."

Lisa sighed as she rose from the table. At least she would be able to get to bed early—that would make up some for her lack of sleep.

Adell Simmons left the women without another word or glance, went to the bar, and began talking to a group of men who had just entered through the front portal.

"Well, dear, if I do not see you again let me tell you that I have been very pleased to have met you on this trip and that I shall be praying for your future." Mrs. Beilier hugged Lisa tightly after

Milly showed her to her room and then started down the hallway to show Lisa to hers.

"Thank you again for all of your help, Mrs. Beilier." Lisa kissed the elderly woman upon the cheek and then hurried behind Milly.

Lisa was shown to a room at the end of the hallway which Milly told her was next to her own. "Your bags have already been brought up by some of the boys that work here," the girl said as she opened the door and handed Lisa a small key.

"Thank you, Milly," Lisa said as she went through the door, but when she turned toward the girl she found Milly already going, at a hurried pace, back down the hallway.

There must be some mistake, Lisa thought, as she walked about the tiny room. It was not much larger than a closet. Her aunt could not have meant her to be placed here. Why there was barely enough room for her bags and the cases containing her clothes. Where was she to hang her gowns and to place all the fine things Sylvia had purchased for her?

Climbing over her bags, Lisa sat down upon the bed. She would talk to her aunt in the morning and tell her of the mistake that had been made. Rising, she pulled her gown from her body, and leaving only her chemise on, she lay down upon the small, single mattress.

Because of the strangeness of her surroundings, though Lisa was extremely tired, she could not sleep. All the events that had occurred on this day ran through her mind.

At long last she was here at her aunt's home. After many miles of travel and uncertainty she was finally here. But was this the place where she would find happiness? she wondered. Would her cousin Willie be the friend she needed? Would her aunt treat her kindly or harshly?

Then, as though these matters were of no real concern, her mind went along a different path. She saw the handsome face of Silver Fox. His features seemed only a few inches from her own. How strong and invincible he had been this afternoon when she was in his arms. What was it her aunt had said downstairs that now came to mind? There was a large bounty for this Indian. All the men about were out looking for him. And what if they were to find him? Of course, they would kill him. Her heart began to pound at a rapid tempo when she thought of that strong virile man who had held her close and shown her that his nature was not that of a hard savage. In those moments she had shared with him he had displayed a tenderness and warmth she had not known at the hands of any other. She could not envision him dead. There was an aura about him that proclaimed life.

The whites had come to this land, bringing killing and greed in their wake. Would they not delight in killing such a brave and fierce defender of his people? But as these thoughts of the Indians' struggle came to her mind so did the knowledge that all would be well with this man who had so suddenly come into her life.

Never had she met a man with the strength and will she had seen in Silver Fox. He would never be taken lightly by any man. As sleep finally crept slowly into her senses, she felt a soft gentle wave of surrender sweep over her and she imagined that bronzed, tanned body pulled up tightly to her own. A soft sigh escaped her lips as Lisa found sleep and the embrace of a gentle dream.

Chapter Five

As the sun dawned the next morning and the cock's crow came through the open window, Lisa awoke to a gentle tapping on her chamber door. "Just a moment," she called, rising and opening the door slightly.

Milly smiled at her. "Mistress Simmons asks that you come downstairs as soon as you dress."

"Why thank you, Milly," Lisa said to the girl hoping that the two of them might be on friendly terms.

"You had best hurry. She can be very hard if kept waiting long," the girl added before turning and hurrying back down the hall.

Lisa donned a soft, black, day dress which

boasted a silver sash at the waist. Running a brush through her long hair she pulled her locks back and tied them securely with a matching silver ribbon. She had no one to help her with her appearance so she did the best she could considering the need to make haste.

When she went down the stairs and into the large common room, she found all quiet and only Milly standing about.

"You are to go into the mistress's room. It is this way." The girl directed Lisa to a door near the stairwell.

"Thank you, Milly." Lisa murmured once again. She felt nervous as she knocked upon the large oak door. She would soon find out what her fate here with her kin was to be.

"Come." The booming voice of her Aunt Adell penetrated the thick door.

Without delay Lisa entered and shut the portal softly behind her. "You wished to speak with me this morning, Aunt Adell?" Lisa asked as she approached the huge woman sitting up in bed, propped by numerous pillows.

"Yes, yes. Take a seat." She pointed to a chair next to the bed, and as Lisa settled herself her aunt studied her with curious eyes. "You have worn nothing but black since I have set eyes upon you. Is there a reason for this?"

Her question quite took Lisa by surprise, and remembering the reason for the color of her clothing, quick tears came to her blue eyes. "I am in mourning for my father, Aunt Adell. He passed on before I left England."

"So he finally gave up what little life he had, did Richard? I am surprised that he did not leave this world sooner, but I guess that each of us have a strong will to survive, no matter the circumstances."

To Lisa's tender ears this woman seemed hard and uncaring. But keeping a tight clamp upon her jaw, she withheld the rebuke that easily came to her lips in defense of her father.

"You wonder why I have called you here?" Her gray eyebrows cocked as Adell Simmons waited for a reply. Lisa nodded. "I thought it would be best if we were to come to a mutual agreement on your circumstances." Now, at Lisa's look of wonder, she added. "Your stepsister Sylvia wrote to me sometime before I wrote to her. I am afraid that it was completely her idea that you make this trip and come here to my home. It would seem that your sister was sorely pressed to be rid of you."

A livid blush caressed Lisa's face at her aunt's words. How could Sylvia have been so cruel?

"I can well imagine your thoughts about your stepsister and I cannot say that I do not agree with you. She has always been a hateful minx. Even as a child I could not stand the girl," Adell Simmons added and then went on. "But this is neither here nor there. The point is what are we to do with you, Lisa?"

Lisa could feel her face warm. She tried to answer. "I-I . . ."

"I have given the matter some thought since I wrote the letter of invitation. You are my sister's child and I was fond of Virginia in my own fashion so I have decided that I shall take hold of your future. You shall stay here under my care. Of course," she continued before Lisa could say anything, "you shall be obliged to work for your food and bed. We cannot afford to have any petted and lazy girls about when there is plenty of work to be done here at the inn."

"But of course, Aunt Adell, I shall work for my keep. I am not lazy, nor do I wish to be petted. I am more than willing to do my share." Lisa had never shied from work and she would not now.

"Well, fine then. You shall start the day by helping Milly in the kitchen and then perhaps we shall have you help serve dinner to our customers. I'm sure they would appreciate a fresh, pretty face." A sly grin crossed the woman's large features. "Yes, you do look quite a bit like your mother. She, too, had a rare beauty."

Lisa found that she was quite uncomfortable at her aunt's words. The woman seemed to be calculating her worth with a critical eye. "Whatever you would have me do, Aunt Adell, I shall attempt."

"Yes, yes. I think you shall be a great asset to my establishment." Adell Simmons was quiet for a moment as she looked Lisa up and down.

"There is this matter of what took place yesterday with the Indian, Silver Fox."

At the mention of his name, Lisa's complete attention was directed toward the woman upon the bed.

Adell smiled thinly seeing the reaction to her words. "There shall not in the future be any talk about this Indian having taken you from the stage. I spoke to the drivers and they both assured me that he only kept you for a small amount of time. But some people might get the wrong idea even though you were only held a short time by this savage, Silver Fox."

Lisa could only nod her head. She herself did not wish to have to repeat her story of yesterday's happenings to anyone so she was more relieved by her aunt's words than upset.

"You may go then, if you have nothing to add to the conversation." Adell waved her hand in Lisa's direction as though excusing her from the room and dismissing her from her thoughts. "Oh, yes," she added as her niece rose to her feet. "Your choice of dress shall be quite suitable for your work. Tell Milly to find you an apron and then tell her to show you where to start."

"Yes, ma'am." Lisa turned, her mind numb as a result of the conversation she had just had with her aunt. She was to work for her keep. Her place in her aunt's house was no more than that of a maid's. She was a servant of sorts, the only difference being that there would be no remuneration for toil.

As she reached the kitchen she realized that she had forgotten to ask her aunt about her cousin and to express her thought of the preceding night that a mistake had been made in the room she had been shown. She now knew there would be no reason to question her sleeping arrangements. Her aunt had put her in the right quarters—at the end of the hallway where the rest of the inn's servants were allowed to sleep. To think she had traveled so far only to become a maid for her own aunt.

Milly looked up from stirring a pot over the hearth and quickly put down the spoon in her hand and went to Lisa's side. "Miss, come and sit over here at this table." She pointed to a small wood table sitting near the back door of the kitchen. "The cook's still sleeping and won't be up for a time yet. She's the only one allowed to sleep after the sun rises for she usually doesn't get to sleep till the early hours of the morn and the mistress would be lost without Hanna's cooking. Most of the folks that come here to Pheasant's Inn wish to have a meal cooked by Hanna. They come from miles away just to taste one of her pies."

Lisa did as she was told, pulling out a chair and sitting down. "Milly, Aunt Adell told me to ask you for an apron and to tell you to show me my duties here in the kitchen."

Milly shook her head as though she'd known all

along that this was going to happen. "I told Hanna only a week ago that if'n Mrs. Simmons's niece comes here to the Pheasant's Inn she'd have to work for her keep. Yes sir, you can ask her yourself, I sure did say it and now here you are and anyone can see that you ain't used to no hard work but already the mistress is setting you to work."

Lisa felt some embarrassment at the young girl's words and her face began to flame.

"Oh, miss, I didn't mean to upset you none." Milly hurried to the table and patted Lisa lightly upon the shoulder. "Here now. I'll be getting you a cup of hot tea and a sweet roll." She looked with some concern toward Lisa as she hurried about the kitchen. She had no wish to hurt such a tender, young girl as the one before her. She had only meant to let the girl know what kind of kin she had here. Placing a small saucer with a roll upon it and a cup containing tea before Lisa, Milly smiled pertly into her wounded face.

"Here now, love. Don't you be worrying over what I just said. I talk too much at times and everyone about these parts be knowing it."

Lisa could not keep from smiling at the red-haired girl. "Thank you, Milly. I do not take your words unkindly. I know that you did not mean to hurt me." She took a small sip of the tea before her. "It is true, though, that I have never had to do much labor. I do not mean that I will not try, for I am not averse to hard work. It is only that I may need direction. You see I have never before cooked or cleaned. At home at times our head groom would allow me to help him with his chores as long as my sister did not find out."

Milly grinned as she sat opposite Lisa at the small table. "Don't you be worrying none about learning the ways at this here inn. The learning comes quick enough. I only hope that you be strong enough. You be a mite small built to be lifting heavy trays and the like."

"I shall try though," Lisa put in quickly. "You see I have nowhere else to go but here with Aunt Adell. I do not know what I would do if she were to turn me out."

"There ain't a likely chance of that." Milly smirked. "As long as that old sea horse has herself a free hand to order about the likes of yourself she ain't going to be sending you far."

Lisa smiled at the reference the girl had made concerning her aunt, but she refrained from making any comments of her own regarding her aunt's appearance.

"As soon as you finish with your breakfast, I'll show you about the kitchen and the common room. You'll find Hanna will help you all she can, the same as I. There are only three other girls working here, but they don't be working out here in the kitchen. Mostly they tend to the upstairs rooms and help out with serving the meals in the common room. You shall probably get along well enough with them. The only one who might give you a time is that big girl Brandy. If'n she be thinking you'd be taking any of her regular customers or that the men might favor you with a bit more of a tip of the coin than they usually leave her she might give you some trouble. But I be thinking you can handle yourself pretty well. If you be needing me though, just you call. I'll not let any harm befall you."

Lisa's smile was genuine as she looked at the freckled girl. "I shall consider you the first friend I have made since arriving at my aunt's inn. I surely do need a friend, so I shall try and stay out of trouble and do as you say."

Milly grinned once again. This pretty little girl before her was more like a little child than a grown woman despite her alluring petite figure and stunning face. "I be right glad to be your friend, Lisa." She patted the other girl's hand with genuine warmth.

An hour before the dinner hour Lisa was exhausted. Never in her life had she worked so hard as she had on this day. Milly had sent her to her room to change her gown for she had almost ruined the beautiful dress that she liked so well.

That morning, when the cook, Hanna, had come into the kitchen, she and Milly had whispered softly together for several minutes off to the side while Lisa had stood stirring the pots upon the hearth as Milly had told her to do. When the two ceased talking, Milly had introduced the tall, thin woman to Lisa, and the two of them had, with some kindness in their voices, given Lisa her instructions for the rest of the day.

First she had been allotted the chore of bringing in buckets of water from the well outside the kitchen door. This done, she was given the job of peeling vegetables for the evening dinner hour. Lisa knew from the friendly smile that the middle-aged woman, Hanna, directed toward her each time she looked in her direction that Milly had explained the circumstances of her arrival. She sensed that both of these women were willing to help her in any way they could and to be her friends. She was thankful for them because she'd realized that morning what it would be like to find herself entirely alone. Yet now through some small miracle she knew two women who were willing to be her friends.

She went about the rest of the morning happy that she had been able to accomplish whatever she'd been told to do. But by midafternoon her muscles, which found this tedious work so alien, were weary. So, after she had swept the large brick kitchen floor for the second time that day, she felt relieved when Milly told her that she could go to her room and rest for an hour, then change her gown. The girl also added with a smile that perhaps Lisa had something more suitable to wear. Milly had noticed the long tear near the hem of Lisa's gown, and though an apron partially covered the dress, still dust and dirt clung to the black material.

Lisa had smiled her thanks, but as she hurried up the stairs and into her room she doubted that any of her gowns would be suitable to her present position.

Her bags were still scattered about the small room when she entered, but not having the strength at this moment to put them into some form of order, she went to the bed and sat down. She felt as if she had been here at her aunt's inn all of her life, working and grubbing for her sustenance. It was hard for her to imagine that she had only just arrived the day before. Still, she knew it was true. Only the evening before she had bidden Mrs. Beilier goodbye, and only the evening before she had had such peaceful, wonderful dreams about the forbidden Indian, Silver Fox. She felt worn and much older from only a single day of such living. What would she be like a year from now? she wondered fleetingly.

Rising she went to the bowl and pitcher resting upon the night stand, but finding no fresh water there, she again sat back upon the small mattress.

Reminding herself that she had only an hour in which to freshen herself, she looked down at her torn and tattered gown. Brushing at the dirt and grime, she sighed wearily. She would never have come to America if she had known the plans her aunt had for her. Somehow she would have made Sylvia see reason and let her stay on at the manor.

Even if she had been forced into the same situation at Culbreth manor at least she would have been in her own home surrounded by the familiar things she loved. But here she had nothing—only this small, cramped room—and at each turn she must face the unknown.

She dashed back a few tears with her hands and began to pull the now-ruined gown off her body. She would not let herself be so easily dragged down by the forces about her. She could work— and work hard. Never mind that each muscle in her body cried out with pain whenever she moved. She could endure more than this. She was a Culbreth and she would not sink into weariness but would force it from her mind, endure, and survive. She would take whatever came her way.

Determinedly she began to go through her luggage until she found a sturdier gown of heavier material than the one lying at her feet. Pulling this over her head she then set about arranging her hair. Knowing that this evening she was to help serve the meal, she neatly pulled her long golden curls to the nape of her neck and, finding a black, diamond-shaped snood, she encased the mass, arranging a few tiny curls about her face to enhance the coiffure.

There was only a small mirror over the night stand, but Lisa took her time. Then she looked over her reflection, noticing the high cut of the collar of her gown and making sure that no fault would be found with her appearance by her aunt or anyone else.

The minutes quickly passed while she was finishing her toilet and soon a small knock at her door announced Milly who stood without, a small smile upon her features.

"You look lovely," she said as she took in the girl before her. "But do you not have a gown of a simpler cut?" she asked. Although Lisa's gown had a high collar and long sleeves, and was unadorned, Milly could not quite put her finger upon it but there was something about it that attracted the eye and held it.

"Is this not all right?" Lisa asked with some concern. "I am afraid that I have nothing else that is as plain and serviceable. Should I perhaps look again?" Lisa had thought this gown would do quite nicely for the job ahead of her, but now seeing the other girl's looks, she had some doubts.

"Nay. We haven't the time and I guess that anything you would be wearing would still seem wrong here at this inn. You had best, though, take this word of caution and stay clear of Brandy this eve. I heard tell this afternoon that she had herself a fine rage with one of the other girls. They say that her and the mistress's son Willie had themselves a fight last night and she's still got a sting in her hide over the matter."

Lisa had all but forgotten that she had a cousin until Milly mentioned him. "What is Willie like?" she asked as she started to follow the girl down the hallway.

"He be a mean one, that Willie Simmons. Thinks that he can have his way with all about here at the Pheasant's Inn, he does. He has a look that can chill you through if'n you let it. The way he eyes you as though he be seeing right through your clothing." Milly stopped and turned about to look at the young girl behind her. "You had best stay clear of him, Miss Lisa. He ain't the type of man for a girl like yourself to be around. Besides Brandy thinks she has a claim on him, and you don't want to be having it out with her."

"Oh, but Willie is my cousin. Though I have not met him I am most anxious to. You see I have no other kin but Aunt Adell and this Willie."

Milly chuckled for a second at Lisa's innocence. "You be listening to me, Lisa, and stay away from Willie Simmons. He's a mean one who won't be caring that you and he be kin. He takes what he be wanting without a thought to any."

Lisa gave a light shudder at the crude picture this girl was painting of her relative. But seeing the seriousness in the green eyes before her, she nodded her head in agreement. If her cousin was so unpleasant, she certainly would have nothing to do with him.

"That's the girl. You just keep in mind what I been telling you and you will make out all right here at the inn. You ain't got nobody to fend for you so you have to be ever on your toes. You be something special that these men hereabouts ain't seen before." Milly hoped her words of caution were understood. This girl was so young and untouched by the world. She reminded her of her own dear sister who had died at the young age of twelve from the fever that had also claimed the lives of her mother and father. She had always loved her sister best and had spent much time with her so now she felt a similar bond with this young girl and wished to protect her from harm.

Downstairs, the large common room was already loud and boisterous as overnight customers of the inn and neighbors who had come to share a meal or a glass of ale with a friend talked companionably to each other.

Lisa's hands shook at the knowledge that in a few moments she would be down there serving that throng, many men and a few women, their meals.

"Come along to the kitchen, Lisa, and let's see what Hanna has to tell us. If there is not too much business this eve perhaps the regular girls can serve and you can rest. I know how tired you must be after your work today, you being not used to such."

Lisa hurried along now, hoping that perhaps she would be able to wait another day before she would be forced to carry the large trays laden with food.

It was with little humor that Hanna, wiping the sweat from her brow called the two girls to her at the hearth. "Fetch me those bowls there on the table. One of you can take these out to mistress

Simmons. Her and her boy are eating and if this don't find it's way to them soon she'll be in here yelling her head off."

Milly quickly brought the bowls to Hanna. Then, looking at Lisa, she told the girl that this would be an easy job for her and also an opportunity for her to meet her cousin.

Though Lisa was nervous, she nodded her head in agreement. And after Hanna placed the bowls, now filled with vegetables upon a tray, she started to the door, her arms feeling the weight of the tray at each step she took.

Looking about the crowded room she sighted her aunt's large form at the same table she had been occupying when Lisa had first seen her the day before. With some regret she also noticed that Mr. Moore from the coach was sitting with her aunt and a lean dark-haired young man was seated at her other side. Making her way through the throng of people, she stood next to the table.

Adell Simmons was the first to look up from her plateful of food. "Why here is the rest of our dinner." She smiled toward Lisa, a small crook of her mouth. When the two gentlemen looked up from their plates, upon Mr. Moore's features Lisa could plainly read recognition and delight. But as she glanced at the younger man, whom she surmised to be her cousin, her thoughts wavered. At first she thought she read surprise but that was quickly replaced by something in his light eyes which told her to be wary. She had seen this same look on other men's faces and always it was the same, revealing hunger, greed, and cruelty. Mr. Moore's eyes had looked upon her with this same expression.

"Well, set the bowls down upon the table, girl," her aunt cruelly ordered as Lisa hesitated. She did as bid, and as she started to turn away, she heard the younger man's voice. He was rebuking his mother.

"Mother, must you be so hard on the new help? Why didn't you tell me you had hired a new girl?" He grinned at his mother and then at Lisa.

Lisa had frozen in her tracks at the sound of his voice, not knowing whether she did so because of her fear of this man or if she wished to hear her aunt explain to her cousin that she was forcing her own sister's daughter to do the most menial labor.

"I told you weeks ago that Virginia's daughter was coming to stay with us, Willie. You got back from hunting down that Indian so late last night there wasn't much time to inform you that Lisa Culbreth had arrived." As Adell Simmons spoke she looked at her only child almost adoringly. Then she turned back to her meal as though Lisa were of no consequence.

"Ah, yes. Lisa Culbreth." The man seemed to savor the sound in his mouth before going on. "Then you must be my cousin?" He looked at Lisa, a new light now within the depths of his silver-colored eyes.

Clearing her throat to dispel her nervousness,

Lisa replied, "Yes, I am your cousin."

"Well, fine." Again those eyes went over her form and Lisa knew what Milly had been talking about when she had stated that this Willie Simmons seemed to undress a woman with his very eyes. "You and I shall have to get together and talk about whatever it is that cousins talk about when they have just met." He winked at Lisa sending a vibrant blush to her cheeks.

Leroy Moore cleared his throat, and his large belly shook as he abruptly put down his fork. "It is a pleasure to see you once again, Miss Culbreth. I trust that you are settling in well?" He looked at the apron about her waist and knew that she was no more than a hired servant to this kin of hers, but this fact, he thought, would perhaps further his suit. Yet looking at the younger Simmons, he knew he would have to make his bid quickly in order not to be gaining damaged goods. For given the time and opportunity, he knew that Willie Simmons, cousin or not, would go after the girl.

Lisa shook her head and stared down at Leroy Moore as if she had just remembered his presence. "Good evening to you, Mr. Moore." Having said this, she turned and hurried back toward the kitchen, but when she was about through the door she noticed a dark form sitting alone near the front door of the large common room.

Why it's Mr. Rollins, she thought, and changing her direction, she walked toward his table.

Craig Rollins had been watching the girl from the first moment she had come through the kitchen door. Now with his head lowered, his dark eyes watched each step she made toward his table. With a studied glance, he also took in all of the other male eyes that were watching her shapely movements and the swing of her skirts.

"Why, Mr. Rollins!" She smiled down at the man she had met aboard the *Sea Maid* and who had become such a welcome friend. And remembering her first impression of him, she felt a small twinge of shame hit her chest. "It is so good to see you and to know that you made the trip back home safely."

"It is also good to see you, Miss Culbreth. Though I had not expected to find you in quite these circumstances." His black, piercing eyes went to the tray in her hand and then to her white apron. He said no more on the matter, though, to Lisa's relief. "Why did you mention my trip home, Miss Culbreth? Did you have any trouble on the way to your aunt's inn?" He looked with concern at her features, noticing as he did so the tiredness in her blue eyes.

Lisa smiled at his concern. How truly kind this man was. Suddenly she wondered where his man Adam was, and before answering, she turned to let her eyes search the room.

Mr. Rollins, knowing her thoughts, answered her questioning eyes. "Adam is tending the horses in the stable. He will be here soon enough. Now answer me. Was there any trouble with your coach?"

"Well, not exactly. I mean there was an incident of sorts. But it turned out all right."

"Go on," he prodded her.

"Indians stopped our vehicle but no one was hurt." Here Lisa felt her face begin to flame as she remembered the tight embrace of the Indian leader.

"Indians you say?" Mr. Rollins's brow rose at her words. "I do hope that you were not unduly frightened?"

For some reason Lisa wanted to tell this kind man what had taken place. Oh, she knew that she could tell no one exactly what had happened while she had been alone with Silver Fox, but she wanted to tell Mr. Rollins that she had been taken and released. However, her aunt's words came to mind and her promise not to talk about having been taken from the coach by Silver Fox.

"At first I guess I was a bit frightened, never having seen such men before, but I have had time to consider, and although I should not say this, I think that somehow you can understand. Actually I feel rather sorry for this Indian called Silver Fox," she blurted out.

"Sorry you say?" A spark ignited in the black orbs that looked up through the thin rimmed spectacles. "How so can you feel sorry for an Indian?"

The words Silver Fox had spoken to the coach

driver came back to her mind and she said softly, "He spoke of how his people were being treated and there was something about this Indian. Oh, perhaps you do not understand." Lisa felt her face flush. "I only meant that I feel sorry for any man who tries to protect what he considers to belong to him, especially when all that he gains is a bounty upon his head and to be hunted as though he were an animal."

Craig Rollins did not speak but sat and watched the beautiful woman standing next to his table. He probed her features as though seeking out some hidden information.

Lisa felt that her words had seemed stupid. Of course, this elderly gentleman did not understand how she felt. No one could, for she herself did not know what power this Silver Fox held over her. Why did her thoughts become so jumbled when she was thinking of him? "I am sorry, Mr. Rollins. I guess I should not have talked so much. I do hope you will forgive me." Catching herself she asked, "May I bring you something to eat?"

Craig Rollins was not quick to answer. Instead he sat studying the girl. "No, Lisa. That is all right. Some other girl has already taken my order."

"Well, I had best get back to the kitchen and see what they would have me to do." She turned to go but was halted once more by his grating voice. "Perhaps tomorrow eve you could join me for dinner?"

Turning slowly, Lisa shook her blond head. "I

doubt that my aunt would allow that during working hours, sir. But perhaps tomorrow eve I can wait upon your table, and we shall have a chance to talk a bit more. It surely has been nice seeing you once again." She sighed and then headed toward the kitchen, leaving Mr. Rollins with a frown upon his features.

In the kitchen, feeling depressed at having left her home in England only to become a serving maid, she almost bumped into a tall, buxom girl. "Oh, excuse me," she said and set her tray upon the table.

The girl watched Lisa with eyes as shifty as a cat's; she also watched Hanna the cook. She was awaiting the tray for the gentleman that the new girl had just left and she was furious because she had seen the girl approach him and then stand by him and flirt and talk. Though the man was elderly and not to her liking by any means, he was a regular customer, at least he had been until he had gone away for a few months. But now that he was back she was not about to lose such a good tipper to the likes of this simpering little blond bit of fluff. Going over to where the girl was standing Brandy sneered. "You had best watch who ye be flirting with ye little doxie."

Shocked, Lisa looked at the other girl. Who was this blond woman who seemed ready to pop out of her bodice with each breath she took and what was she talking about? Flirting, she had been flirting with no one. Surely the woman could not be talking about Mr. Rollins. She shook her head trying to make some sense out of the girl's accusation. Then she realized that this must be Brandy, the girl Milly had told her about, the one she said was in love with her cousin. "I am afraid you are mistaken. I was only talking to my cousin Willie. I was not flirting."

Brandy looked hard at the beautiful young creature in front of her. What was she talking about? She had not meant her Willie. She had not even seen the girl talking with Willie Simmons. Now, with an angry flush, she became even sterner as she reproached the girl before her. "You be leaving me Willie be. Cousin indeed. If ye be thinking to stay on here and work ye best not let me catch ye near Willie again." Forgotten now were Brandy's earlier thoughts of Craig Rollins.

That was fine with Lisa for she had instantly disliked her cousin. So with a small shake of her head, she lowered her frame wearily into the chair at the table. This day had been too much. First the exhausting work, and then the insults of her kin and the humiliation of having even Mr. Rollins know that she was a servant, and now this overblown woman accusing her of flirting with her own cousin.

"Come and take this tray while the food is still hot," Hanna called as she looked over to the table and saw Brandy's angry stance. "Be leaving the young girl alone, Brandy, she be kin to the mistress and she won't be taking it kindly if any harm should befall her."

"Kin or no she had best be staying away from my Willie. It be bad enough that he watches every skirt that passes by without having this little bit of nothing right under me own nose trying to steal me love away." Huffily, Brandy went to Hanna and took the tray, forgetting for the moment that the original cause of her anger was that Lisa had been talking with one of her customers.

"Don't be stupid, girl. That young thing"— Hanna nodded her head toward Lisa—"could not give a fig about the mistress's son. The lad is her cousin. Now get yourself out of my kitchen until you can act better." Hanna had rebuked the larger woman freely, knowing that she would not dare to argue back. With just a word to the mistress, Hanna could have any of the girls who worked at the inn fired, so they all knew that they had better respect Hanna and heed her orders in her kitchen.

As she went through the door Brandy threw one last look in Lisa's direction. That girl had best beware, she thought as she went about her duties.

Hanna approached Lisa, carrying a plate of steaming delicious-looking food. "Here, love, you eat this and then make your way up to your room. You've done enough for this first night. There be plenty of time for you to do more tomorrow." Turning, she went back to her cooking.

Lisa ate some of the repast, even though her appetite had been diminished by the happenings of the evening. Pushing the chair from the table, she started through the door.

"You be locking your room now, honey," Hanna called over her shoulder as Lisa left, bringing a small smile over Lisa's features. At least Hanna and Milly would give her support.

Before climbing into bed, Lisa forced herself to unpack and arrange her clothes as best she could in that small chamber and to straighten out her room. Finally, after the last bags had been cleared away and she had taken a sponge bath, Lisa donned a fresh nightgown and sought the comfort of her small bed. No sooner did her golden curls touch the pillow than her blue eyes shut and she was dreaming. Once again Silver Fox occupied her mind, however, asleep she enjoyed a peace and freedom with him that she could know nowhere else. She was able to talk with and to touch this forbidden fruit that everyone about her wished to harm. In the folds of her slumber she desired Silver Fox and her desire was returned.

The next day was much like the one before except that Lisa was now used to awakening early and was dressed before Milly knocked upon her door. She found her work was again restricted to the kitchen area and this knowledge gave her a sense of relief. She would dread having to work with Brandy. But out here in the kitchen she was free to be herself and to enjoy the friendliness of both Milly and Hanna.

Grimacing because of her sore muscles, she went about her duties. But she was only given light tasks, both the other women having noted her discomfort. However, at the dinner hour she was told to wait on the tables and serve with the other girls.

Knowing that she must be efficient, Lisa did as she was bid. Most of the customers were genuinely kind to the young girl, delighting in her beauty when she reached over and set their plates in front of them or just watching her gentle movements with a degree of longing. Others though, who were a bit farther into their cups, were more wont to pinch and pat her bottom as she passed their tables or served them.

Lisa found to her horror that her own cousin was one of the worst of the latter type. Each time she went by his table he would reach out and lay hold of her, and though she knew by his laugh and loud voice that Willie was drunk, she felt her face flame at his advances. To make matters worse, whenever she looked about to see if any of the customers were witnessing her embarrassment she always found the eyes of Brandy following her about.

It was now well into the dinner hour, and wearily, Lisa awaited a tray of food in the kitchen when her Aunt Adell approached her.

"You may take the rest of the evening off, Lisa."

With surprise written upon her features, Lisa looked to the elder woman. "I still have this tray Aunt Adell to take to a table." This was the only response she was able to make to the woman's unexpected kindness.

"Do not worry about that. Just tell Brandy what table it goes to and then go upstairs and freshen yourself up. A gentleman wishes you to dine with him this evening and I have kindly given my permission for you to do so."

With some panic Lisa saw, for the first time, the small pouch clutched in her aunt's large fist. No doubt coins for a bribe, she thought. But who, she wondered, would wish for her to dine with him. Then, like a clap of lightning, it struck her. Mr. Moore, of course. That was why he had stayed on here at the inn, and now he was giving her aunt money to court her. "I would rather go to my room and rest, Aunt Adell." She attempted to reason with the woman. Her aunt must realize that she could not sell her favors.

"Pooh, you shall do as you're told. Mr. Rollins is an important man and he wishes you to dine with him this evening. I know that he may not be too pleasing to look upon but that is of little concern." She lightly hefted the coins in the small bag. "His family was the first in this area and he is quite wealthy. By some odd chance he has taken an interest in you. Do not disappoint me, girl, do as you are told." This last was spoken as a command.

Retaining a semblance of her composure, Lisa nodded her head. She would agree. Though she did not wish to be sold to any man for an hour of time, she would relent to dine with Mr. Rollins. She had come to like the elder man, and her relief at hearing it was not Mr. Moore with whom she was to dine, made her more readily agreeable.

"Do not stand here dallying then. Hurry to your room and tend to yourself." Her aunt's hard voice hurried her out the door. Adell Simmons watched the slim back of her dead sister's child. Perhaps the girl would become a valuable piece to have about, she thought, reflecting on the previous evening when that fat, obnoxious man Mr. Moore had spoken to her privately about the girl. He had offered her quite a handsome sum if she would somehow convince the girl to decide to wed him. At the time she had thought the idea quite ridiculous, and reluctantly, because she thought of the wealth he had offered her, she had told the man that she would have to think over the matter. But now, with this Mr. Rollins also interested in the girl, she would think the matter over with more consideration.

She sensed Craig Rollins was interested in the girl, though for the life of her she could not understand his interest. He barely went anywhere without his body servant, so what on earth would he wish of a young beautiful girl? Perhaps decoration. Lots of men who were too old wished to have women about them. She knew Craig

Rollins was not that old in years, though she did not know how old he was. She had seen little of him in the past, and only knew that he came from England and that as a boy he used to visit Charles Rollins.

Lisa descended the stairs and entered the common room, her blue eyes searching out the tables as she looked for the man with whom she was to dine. And there at a comfortable-looking table near the hearth was Craig Rollins talking in lowered tones to Adam his manservant.

With cautious steps and avoiding the drunken hands reaching out for her, Lisa made her way to the older man's table.

Smiling with appreciation, Craig Rollins greeted Lisa and nodded to Adam in dismissal. "See that all has been prepared as I ordered," he reminded his servant.

Lisa waited for an invitation to sit before spreading her skirts out and taking the chair across from Craig Rollins. "I deem it a pleasure that you have consented to dine with me, Miss Culbreth." His rough, shallow voice crossed the small space between them, filling her ears.

Lisa smiled at this kindly man, glad to be with a friend, even though he had had to bribe her aunt so that she would be allowed to share a meal with him.

Craig Rollins's breath caught when she graced

him with a smile. She looked exactly as he'd pictured her each time he'd thought of her—dressed in a beautiful gown, her hair coiled and fashioned into curls about her face, and her soft, golden features smiling her pleasure. The picture of her serving all of these rough men passed swiftly through his brain leaving a red fiery pain, but pushing that image aside, he spoke as gently as possible. "My man has gone to see to our meal."

"You needn't have sent him. I am sure that Brandy will be over in a moment," Lisa answered, seeing Brandy at one of the tables being fondled and petted by one of the men who had earlier reached out for Lisa's trim form.

Craig Rollins also looked in that direction, his mind imagining how hard it must be for this sweet innocent to have to work with a woman of Brandy's sort. "Adam doesn't mind doing my bidding. In fact, he likes to stay busy," the older man reassured Lisa.

Leaning back against the rim of her chair, for the first time in days Lisa felt at ease. She had learned on board the *Sea Maid* that she could relax and be herself around this strange man.

"Would you care for something to drink, Miss Culbreth?" Mr. Rollins questioned.

"No thank you, Mr. Rollins, I do not drink any strong spirits. My sister Sylvia used to tell me that as a lady I should acquire a taste for wine. But I am afraid that it disagrees with me."

"I dare say that is a favorable trait, madam. I am afraid that I have seen some so-called ladies who should have learned to practice abstinence long ago."

Sometimes the gentleman across from Lisa truly perplexed her. It would seem that they were in agreement about so many things. She looked him over now with a critical eye, not having done so since the first time she had laid eyes upon him. With a soft smile she wondered idly why on earth he wore those wire-rimmed glasses. He seemed to peer over them to look at her while they rested low on the bridge of his straight nose. His white-powdered wig also puzzled her. Was there no hair under the man-made material? Had he had a disease which had left him bald or was there some other reason for the wig? Lisa herself could think of none, except that it made him appear older than his features proclaimed.

"Is there something the matter?" He looked deep into her violet-blue orbs, his ebony ones seeming to bore into her very depths, and his grating, low voice seemed to be urgently seeking an answer.

Shaking her blond hair, Lisa sipped at the glass of water at her elbow. "I was but wondering what type of man you truly are," Lisa answered truthfully. "You have been so kind to me, but my lack of worldly experience has made me untrusting. I apologize for my rudeness in staring."

Before Craig Rollins could respond to her

answer, Adam came to the table, bearing a large tray of food.

"I am afraid that the large blond-haired she-cat over there is a bit angry with me, sir," the small dark man said as he placed the plates before his master and the lady at his table. "She thinks that I am stealing her fine tip of the evening." There seemed to be some humor in the little man's voice.

"You had best have a care for yourself then. I would hate to have to drive the carriage back to the estate in the dark. I do think that Brandy may be able to give you a go for your money." Craig laughed aloud to his servant.

"Aye, sir. I be watching myself."

Lisa looked at the pair and then over at the girl who was now directing angry brown eyes toward their table. "Oh dear. I do think she is upset. Perhaps we should have let her wait upon our table. It is such a little thing to do, but she seems to take it so seriously." Lisa was worried for she did not wish to be in the middle of another conflict with the large girl.

"The problem is the coins she is missing," Craig Rollins said as his glance followed Lisa's. "Do not worry about her, Lisa. Let us enjoy our meal before it cools."

Lisa pulled her eyes from Brandy and looked at the man across from her. This was the first time he had used her given name and though she did not mind, for she considered him a good friend, hearing her name from his lips struck her.

"I hope you do not mind my calling you Lisa instead of Miss Culbreth?" He seemed to have read her thoughts, and taking a bit of the beef upon his plate, he looked at her with dark, unreadable eyes.

Shaking her head Lisa mumbled, "No indeed not." But there was something about his use of her name that drew her to him. The way that raspy voice pronounced the simple word touched some deep chord in her spirit.

"Do not worry about Brandy, Lisa, I shall take care of her with a few coins and she will think no more about the matter." With a sigh, he looked intently at her before continuing with his meal. "Tell me how you are adjusting to your new home."

Lisa was caught off guard, and as she swallowed the food in her mouth, her blue eyes filled with tears. It would be so easy to tell this kind man all of her hopes for kind kin and a pleasant place to live had been a mistake. He would understand her feelings, she was sure, but bracing her spine, she willed the tears away. She would endure her misery by herself. She need not share it with another. "I am doing fine, Mr. Rollins. This is not quite what I expected but I am able to make my way."

He made no response to her statement, but looking up from her plate, Lisa could see that her words had caused him some displeasure for the tensing muscle in his jaw showed that he was angry.

And, indeed, Craig Rollins was angry. How could any woman, even Adell Simmons, treat this girl in such a fashion? He had seen her quick tears and had understood that she had tried to keep herself from stating the truth of the matter about her life here at the Pheasant's Inn. How could people treat their own kin in such a manner? What would become of this innocent petal of trust and beauty if she was left much longer under this roof? he idly wondered as he toyed with his food. He had noticed last evening when Lisa had gone to Adell's table, how the woman's inept son Willie had looked at her. That repulsive, fat man had had an expression on his face that had revealed all of his rude thoughts too. There was something about this girl that touched him and the feelings would not leave. "What day do you have off, Lisa?" he asked her softly as he pushed his plate from him, having now lost all appetite.

Lisa had not even thought of a day off. She had been so concerned with her work and doing as she was bid. "I have not asked my aunt," she answered honestly.

"I was thinking that perhaps you would care to come to my estate on that afternoon." With her questioning eyes upon him, he continued. "I have a fine stable and thought that perhaps you would care to spend some time riding. I am afraid that I am not quite able to join you, but if you do care for horses . . . ?" He left the question unfinished.

"Oh, I love to ride, Mr. Rollins. I rode as much

as possible in England and I would love to again."
She could not resist this invitation to enjoy an
afternoon away from this inn. "I would have to
tell Aunt Adell, though, and I am not so sure that
she would approve." Her features, which only
seconds ago had been alight at the thought of
riding and enjoying an afternoon of carefree
abandon, quickly slipped into an expression of
abject misery. She was sure that her aunt had no
intention of letting her have a day off, nor would
she allow Lisa to enjoy an innocent afternoon
with Mr. Rollins.

"Leave your aunt to me, Lisa. I shall talk with
the good lady," Craig Rollins spoke softly.

"Oh, but you mustn't give her any more coins
for me," Lisa blurted out, imagining what he
would do to get her aunt to give in to his wishes.

So she knew that he had had to bribe her aunt
for this evening's appointment for dinner. A thin
smile slanted across his dark face. He would pay
any amount in order to have her free from that
loving aunt for a day. "Do not worry yourself on
the matter. If a few coins are all it takes for you to
have a moment's happiness the money is well
spent."

"But . . ."

He did not let her finish but held up a gloved
hand. "The matter is settled. I shall find out the
day which shall meet with your aunt's approval
and Adam shall bring the carriage to pick you
up."

There was nothing left for Lisa to say. Here was

a man used to giving orders. He was not used to having them disobeyed, and Lisa wanted to do as bid anyway, to be able to enjoy herself and to share a carefree moment. So she said no more about his spending money upon her.

The evening progressed and by the end of the meal Lisa's small hand was stifling yawns of tiredness.

Craig Rollins smiled fondly at her, knowing that she had more than likely had a hard day and that she was now forcing herself to stay seated in her chair. "I must be leaving now, Lisa, but do not forget our appointment." He rose slowly to his feet, picking up the cane hooked upon the back of the chair.

Lisa also rose, glad the evening was over and she could make her way to her room.

"It truly has been a pleasure." He reached over before she could leave the table and took her small hand in his gloved one. "Until I see you once again, have a pleasant evening."

"Indeed, it has been wonderful Mr. Rollins and thank you again." She turned and started across the room.

Craig Rollins stood, watching her as she went up the stairs. Then looking toward the long bar, he spied Adam eying him intently, as though knowing his every thought. Nodding his head slowly in his servant's direction, he slowly made his way toward the door.

But once outside with his manservant he pulled

out his wallet and handed the smaller man a handful of bills. "Take this to the good lady Simmons and tell her that your employer wishes that her niece has the day off from work tomorrow and that my carriage shall be by just before the noon hour to pick the girl up."

Adam looked directly at this man that he served and then hurried off to do his bidding. Within a few moments Adam had returned to the carriage where his employer was awaiting him. "She shall be ready tomorrow as you wish," he told his master before closing the carriage door tightly and climbing upon the outside seat and calling for the pair of matching horses to be on their way.

Inside the carriage a smile came to the dark face of Mr. Rollins, and pulling off his gloves and rubbing his knuckles in the palm of his hand he sat back against the cushioned seat. Thoughts of Lisa Culbreth flitted through his mind, her gentle beauty leaving him somewhat at a loss. There had been other women in his life in England but never one of her caliber. She was a rare find and tomorrow he would start to woo her. He could not let her slip away. "Nay, Lisa, no harm shall find it's way to your door as long as I am about." His words rang clear and crisp in the empty carriage.

Chapter Six

As the carriage driven by Adam carried Lisa toward Rollins's home, she breathed deeply of the fragrant taste of freedom and gazed at the land glistening in the bright sunlight.

The morning had flown by on the swiftest of wings, leaving her a bit dazed by the happenings about her. She had awakened early as usual but Milly had told her that today was to be her day off. She was not to come downstairs until she wished her breakfast, and then before the kind girl had left the room, she had also said that Mrs. Simmons had told her to tell Lisa that a carriage would be by just before the noon hour and that she was to be dressed and ready to go with Mr.

Rollins's servant.

On hearing this, Lisa had fairly flown from the covers. Craig Rollins had asked her the night before to come to his home for an afternoon, but she had never dared to think that she would be going there so soon.

Her excitement at its highest, she dressed in one of the riding habits she'd had made before leaving England. This outfit was black, but beneath the snug-fitting waist jacket she wore a shirt of the sheerest blue satin. Wishing to look her absolute best, she brushed her long, waist-length curls until they fairly gleamed. Then she wound them and pinned them at the nape of her neck, leaving only small tendrils of curls at her temples. To offset her coiffure she donned a smart-looking hat with a light blue feather jutting out, placing it at an angle upon her golden head. And looking into the mirror she smiled at her own reflection. She had not felt so excited in a long time, she thought. It was amazing that a visit with an elderly gentleman and an afternoon ride could so effect her. She realized she was acting strangely, but she didn't care. She wanted to shout in the empty room, to run down the stairs and hug Milly and laugh aloud. She was enjoying the sheer exuberance of finding herself free at last.

Only a short time later the Rollins carriage pulled up in front of the inn and Adam came into the common room to seek out Lisa. Having just finished her breakfast, she was eager to be off.

So now enjoying the delicious effect of the cool, fall air, Lisa gazed from the carriage window at all she passed. She had not noticed the countryside when she had come to her aunt's inn, but now, her senses attuned to all about her, she saw the red, orange, and gold of the trees and marked the grace of the birds swooping overhead. Everything seemed vital and alive and she, herself, felt her pulse race as though she were going to meet her long overdue destiny at the end of this ride.

After an hour the carriage pulled down a long tree-lined drive, and there before Lisa was the most beautiful view she had ever seen. The house was a large, stone manse, its towering heights fashioned in such a manner that from a distance it seemed to be built into the side of a large mountain, but as they pulled closer she could see that the mountain was indeed some distance from the manor itself.

When Adam pulled the carriage to a slow halt near the front steps, Lisa looked out to see if her host would be meeting her.

Adam hurriedly opened the door and helped her to the ground. "Come this way, miss." He started up the stone steps and opened the large, dark wood door for her to step through.

Lisa looked about herself as Adam led her to the front parlor. "If you will wait here, I will tell Mr. Rollins that you have arrived." Without waiting for her reply he left the room, leaving her to browse as she wished.

The large house was cool and decorated sparsely though with good taste. Each piece of furniture seemed to suit the room exactly and the colors of soft cream and gold struck a pleasurable mood.

In a moment Adam again entered the parlor. "I am afraid that Mr. Rollins will not be able to join you for some time." At her worried frown he reassured her. "He usually naps at this time and was bothered this morning by a headache. It is truly nothing. He suggests that you enjoy yourself with a ride about the estate while he rests."

"I had not expected this," Lisa spoke softly. "Are you sure that he is all right and does not mind my borrowing a mount?" She felt rather odd, having come all this way to visit the man only to be told that he was abed. Perhaps it would be better to go back to her aunt's, she thought with some hesitation.

"He insists that you do so," Adam enjoined her. "He shall be up and about by the time you return. And then you may have your visit with him."

Lisa thought this over for a moment before nodding her blond head. Had she not come to his home to spend an afternoon riding? What difference would there be if she visited with the man upon her return or now.

"The stables are in the back, if you will follow me I shall have a horse readied for you." Adam smiled and then started through the portal and toward the back of the house.

As they passed through the kitchen Lisa noted several women in this area cooking, but what stuck out in Lisa's mind was that these women were not white. They were dark skinned with long, black, braided hair. At her questioning look Adam only smiled.

Could the women be Indians, she wondered as the small man led her into the stables and ordered a young boy to saddle a spirited mare of a toffee color. But as she sat upon the animal all thoughts of Indians flew from her mind. "Thank you, Adam, I shall not be too long." She flung this remark over her shoulder as she urged the mare past the house and toward the drive they had entered in the carriage.

She did not know where she was going but with a horse beneath her she felt the power of being alive once more. She pulled the reins to the right and spying an open field she kicked the horse's sides and let her run.

It was with some reluctance that she reined her horse to a slower pace when she neared the edge of the field and a forest of some size lay before her. How beautiful everything about her was, she sighed. The earth seemed to be at peace in this place. She thought that it was too bad the man who owned this vast, beautiful piece of ground could not ride out and enjoy what was his. But perhaps that was why he had invited her. He may have wanted her to see that the ugly reality of her aunt's inn was not all there was to this area.

Slowly and carefully, she guided the horse into the cool fragrant forest. Not knowing her direction, she intended to go only a short way and she stayed to the barely discernible trail before her. She knew that she should not venture too far into this unknown place but something seemed to be beckoning her to press onward. Glancing about, her blue eyes saw only the quiet, peaceful forest.

Pulling the mare to a halt, she jumped to her feet, sinking a bit into the soft earth beneath her kid boots. Then in carefree abandon she twirled about, her arms wide, breathing the sweet, pleasant air. She had not felt so at ease since she had gone to the cliffs at Culbreth manor and watched the mighty sea below. She now felt the same sense of oneness with this forest that she had experienced in the past with the waves that washed upon the rocks. She forgot she was in a new country, far from all that she had ever known. She forgot about her aunt and the Pheasant's Inn. She roamed about, gathering a handful of flowers as her horse grazed peacefully on the thick, green grass.

Finally, as Lisa sat back against the mighty trunk of an oak tree and began to weave some of the colorful flowers into a garland to place upon her head, her eyes were drawn toward a clump of bushes in which she'd heard a twig snap. Then, as though appearing from thin air, an Indian stood before her. Lisa pinched her arm, thinking that she was again dreaming of Silver Fox. Perhaps this place had so calmed her that she had entered her dream world.

But all too quickly Lisa realized that this was no dream. Silver Fox was actually standing and looking at her with fathomless black eyes. Clutching her garland in a tight grip, her blue eyes went from the towering, vital frame of the man standing so near to her horse that grazed only yards away. She felt her breathing grow shallow from the panic that was overtaking her, and her pulse beat wildly, making her feel faint yet giddy at the same time. She could not move so she sat and stared, her mind telling her that this was no dream but reality. Then all of the horror stories she had heard about Indians came to her mind only to be banished by memories of the last time she had been with Silver Fox.

She could see herself in those strong arms on the moss bed, and she could hear the cries of passion she'd made that day. Despite her intentions she had been unable to put from her thoughts what had happened when he had taken her from the stage. Each time when she thought of the ransom she had paid she forced herself to burn his memory from her mind, telling herself over and over that it had only been a dream, that nothing had really taken place. But now he stood before her and she knew that she could no longer tell herself it had all been a dream.

Silver Fox stood tall and immobile, looking at

the girl before him, trying to seek out her inner feelings. He saw the fear and panic written upon her pale face but he wished to know more. Had she, too, been tormented by memories of the day he had taken her from the stage? Was her fear really due to the feelings elicited that day? Taking a step toward her, he took a deep breath. "Do not fear me, I but wish to speak with you." His voice was deep and clear, filling the area about them.

Lisa still could not move, but she watched each step he took toward her. He looked the same as he had on the first day he had appeared to her, the only difference now being that he wore no paint upon his handsome face and his black straight hair was pulled back with a leather thong.

Now, squatting down, the Indian was face to face with Lisa and without saying a word the pair looked searchingly into each other's eyes. Silver Fox desired this woman, but having followed her since she'd left the manor he simply wished to sit and look upon her wondrous face, making certain that she would not flee him.

Lisa was of a different mind. She had tried to block out what had happened once between them, and though she had heard stories about him that should frighten her, she was more frightened of herself. Could she so easily give herself to any man? Had this man not taken her and then ridden off and left her? Still, as she sat there looking up into his face, a feeling of comfort settled over her.

As though his black eyes could pierce to the

very core of her brain Silver Fox realized that her fear was lessening, so he waited a moment longer before he began to speak. "I did not mean to frighten you. I would not hurt you or anger you in any way. I have been following you and but wished to hear the soft music of your voice."

Lisa could not believe her ears. It was as though she were caught within her dreams. She felt herself losing control. Reality became hazy, and she could not tell where her dreams started and real life stopped.

But with shattering force she realized that this man was flesh and blood for Silver Fox reached out and took her into his iron-hewed arms, and his lips, the same she had nightly imagined touching upon her own, were now descending and softly, forcibly seeking her surrender.

Time seemed to stand still as the pair, dark-skinned Indian and golden, beautiful woman clung together under the massive oak tree. No distractions in their surroundings penetrated their hypnotic attraction. Lisa's knowledge that this man was forbidden to her and Silver Fox's that his people must come first, could not pull the couple apart.

They savored this moment, losing themselves in touch and delight—each exploring the other. Silver Fox slowly let his tongue probe the inner recess of Lisa's sweet mouth, feeling his passion flare at this simple act. And Lisa, aware of how this man had stirred her, gave her body to his keeping, trusting that he would not hurt her. She also released her feelings, hiding nothing as her small, slim arms went about this large man's neck and clung tightly.

Their bodies strained together hungrily, having once tasted of the draught of love and knowing that only together were they complete. Lisa moaned softly under the exploration of his practiced hands, responding freely and clinging to him as he led her into the depths of passion.

Silver Fox seemed to luxuriate in the splendor of the moment, rejoicing that she again was in his arms and that he could taste her lips.

As the gentle breezes stirred the trees overhead, Silver Fox made love to Lisa with a tenderness that belied any talk of savageness. He plied her body and lips with tender ministrations. Beyond reason, she was swept up and up until she thought herself able to touch the clouds.

Silver Fox drew on his passions to bring this woman to a pinnacle of pleasure, of shattering brilliance, and then with a large sigh he joined her, racing against all time and knowledge, propelled to a higher climax than he had ever experienced.

With some reluctance Silver Fox slowly returned to awareness of the earth about him, leaving the sweet sphere of satisfied desire. With a tender smile upon his features, he looked deep into the face before him. What he saw there went to his heart like a small penetrating dart. Her feelings were obvious to his dark eyes. She did not practice deceit. Nothing was kept secret. Bringing up a large, dark hand he slowly traced the outline of her fragile jawline.

"How is it that you have come into my life?" He spoke softly as though to himself, not expecting an answer but trying to understand what was happening to him.

Lisa was in a similar state of mind but her thoughts were not as troubled as those of the man next to her. She had not been brought up in these parts, and she did not know the depth of the prejudice the whites here had against the red man. She knew only what her heart told her and she thought of the nights she had dreamed of being held and soothed by this man. Her struggles had been different from those of Silver Fox.

Silver Fox looked into her trusting blue eyes and spoke softly, "You are like a newborn fawn, trusting beyond reason, but there are many troubles for us if we resist the prejudices of your people." For some reason he needed to hear her say that nothing else mattered but the two of them, that she did not care what anyone would think if she were to love him.

But Lisa, on hearing his words, saw the faces of her aunt and cousin. What would they say if they were to find out that she had made love with their enemy? What would they think if she were to tell them her true feelings. Their hatred for Indians came swiftly to her mind, as did the sounds of the many voices telling her different tales that revealed the horror and hatred they felt for the red man.

"My people are well known for taking that which they want and at this moment my heart cries out for me to take you upon the back of my horse and to keep you within the confines of my tepee, regardless of what anyone would say." He had sensed the worries brought to the forefront of her mind and so had put into words his own feelings. His steady gaze flooded her with a tender warmth as he went on. "I would prefer not to have you in this manner, where we must forever be watching for someone to discover us. I shall wait until your own heart shall lead you to me." Slowly he stood to his full height.

Lisa felt panic grip her. She could not let him leave. She might never see him again. On wobbly legs she also stood, and not truly knowing how to make her feelings understood, all she could do was to reach out a small white hand and touch his oak-ribbed chest as small diamondlike tears formed in the blueness of her eyes.

Seeing her dilemma and knowing the cause of her pain, for he also was feeling torn, Silver Fox wrapped his mighty arms about the woman before him. How precious she was. How sweet, innocent and naive she appeared, he thought, but as his lips once again lowered to enjoy the honey taste of those petal-soft lips, he knew that she was all he could ever wish for in a woman. And as his arms gathered her closer, he could feel a quick response building in her body, and it set his own limbs aflame.

"You had best leave now," he said huskily as he set her from him, depriving himself of the sweet nectar of her charms. "They shall be waiting for you at the manor." His black eyes probed her blue ones intensely, as though he were only saying the words because he knew he must, although some inner part of him wished her to stay.

Lisa shook herself, knowing that what he said was true. Mr. Rollins would have arisen from his rest by now, and he would start to worry if she were not at the manor soon. "But when will I see you again?" The words were out before she was aware of what she was saying.

Silver Fox smiled tenderly down at this golden beauty. How it tore his heart to send her from him, but he knew that for now it must be so. "Do not worry, little flower, I shall come to you."

"But you must be careful." Lisa felt an overpowering fear for the safety of this man for whom she was forbidden to care but who had come into her life so unexpectedly and forcefully that she was completely powerless to deny him her heart. "My aunt and Willie, my cousin, hate you and would see you dead." At this statement she again felt tears come to her eyes.

Reaching out with a long trim finger, Silver Fox wiped away a lone tear as it made a path down her cheek. "Do not fear for me. I shall not be harmed, and if possible, I would have it that you would never weep again." His words were tender, consoling love words spoken from the depths of his being.

"You shall be careful then?" Lisa knew that if something were to happen to this man a part of herself would die along with him.

"Aye. Nothing shall long keep me from you." With one last parting kiss, the Indian walked Lisa to her mare and helped her to remount. "I shall see you soon, my little golden flower." And with those words he disappeared through the bushes from which he had come.

Lisa did not move for a few moments longer, and then, knowing that Silver Fox had left her, she gently nudged the horse down the same path that had brought her to this isolated spot.

Her ride back to the manor was slow and contemplative. She had known when she had first left the manor that something was pulling her away from it, and now she knew what that force had been. No longer was she indulging in pleasant dreams. Her feelings were now much stronger. Lisa Culbreth, who had never loved before and who had never met a man capable of shattering her resistance, knew that now she was bound to Silver Fox with unbreakable cords. She was entrapped in a love that, at this moment, seemed hopeless and perhaps would always be so.

As the mare led her back to the large stone house, Lisa was lost in a world of her own, not truly paying any attention to where she was going until Adam came out from the stables and greeted her with a warm smile.

"I hope that you had a pleasant ride, ma'am. Mr. Rollins is awake now and awaiting you in the front parlor."

"Thank you, Adam," she mumbled, wishing that she could be allowed to return to the inn and lock herself in her chamber so she might be alone and free to think of this day. But she knew that she could not do this. She had come here to visit Mr. Rollins; she could not very well leave without even greeting him. Perhaps she could plead that the ride had tired her if he wished her to stay very long.

So, following behind the dark, small man, she entered the house by way of the kitchen as before and then headed for the parlor.

Craig Rollins sat, very relaxed, in a great wing-back chair, his head turned down toward a book. As he heard footsteps at the door he set the book down and smiled at the young woman entering the room. "Bring us some tea, Adam. I am sure that Miss Culbreth would like something to drink after her long ride."

As the small man left the room Mr. Rollins looked toward Lisa and pointed to a chair across from him. "Please sit down, Lisa." His voice projected the same scratchy, low sounds that Lisa had heard in the past.

"Thank you so much, Mr. Rollins. And thank you also for the loan of your horse. I did so enjoy my ride." As she said this, Lisa looked with new interest at this man across from her. He was watching her intently over the rim of his glasses, and his look touched off a warning in her. What is it? she wondered fleetingly. What should she know about Mr. Rollins that was hidden from view? But too much had happened on this day for her to worry overly much about anything except Silver Fox, so heaving a soft sigh, she settled into a chair.

"I am glad you enjoyed yourself. I hope you shall feel free to come again and ride the afternoon away. I only wish that I could partake of these outings with you."

Lisa smiled, revealing a touch of pity, for though she did not know exactly what this gentleman's problem was, the shawl that was always draped about his shoulders and his raspy voice indicated that something was wrong. But before she could voice any of her thoughts, Adam entered the room carrying a tray of cakes and tea.

"You may set it down there." Mr. Rollins pointed to a small table between the two chairs. "Miss Culbreth shall pour so you can go about your duties, Adam."

Lisa willingly poured the two cups of tea, glad to be doing something to keep her mind from the track it was wont to take.

"Did you ride over much of my land, Lisa?" Craig Rollins's black eyes sought Lisa's. And as she shook her head, he added, "You must not wander far from the manor. I hope that Adam told you this?"

Lisa felt as though she were choking. Did he know of her meeting with the Indian, Silver Fox? Had he somehow guessed by her appearance what had occurred on her outing?

"There are Indians in the forest that borders my property. I, myself, have never had trouble with them, but they are there."

He looked her full in the face as he said this. Feeling her hands begin to tremble, Lisa hurriedly set down the tea pot and, hanging her head, poured cream into the dark liquid in the cups.

"Aye, Indians," he rasped. "My grandfather rather liked them, that is why this house stands so close to their property. And as a lad when I would visit my grandfather upon occasion I even saw some of these Indians."

Lisa looked up from her chore, trying to decide whether this man was just talking to pass the time or if indeed he did know something about her and Silver Fox. But as he reached over and took his cup of tea, sipping at the warm liquid without saying anything further about Indians, she felt some relief.

Indians were not brought up again for the rest of their visit. Craig Rollins questioned Lisa on her impressions of Missouri, about her stay with her aunt, and also carefully, about her life in England.

Lisa felt herself on safer ground when dealing with these subjects, so she talked freely about her past life and the one she was now leading as servant-kin at the Pheasant's Inn.

It seemed to her only a short time later that Adam was once again driving her to her aunt's. The sun had already lowered in the sky, and feeling it safe in the dark carriage to indulge in her thoughts about Silver Fox, Lisa leaned back against the finely cushioned seat and shut her eyes, imagining once again the feel of those muscular arms about her.

With each passing day Lisa felt herself more in bondage here at the Pheasant's Inn. Rising early each morning she would begin another long day which finally ended at an hour when the steady drift of people finally thinned to a trickle and she was allowed to seek her chamber and her bed.

It had been a week since her visit to Craig Rollins's estate and her meeting with Silver Fox, yet her thoughts were constantly on that mighty warrior. And although her dreams had been pleasurable before she'd met Silver Fox that day near the Rollins estate, now they were filled with pain. In them, she could feel his hands and lips upon her, yet she was powerless when she awoke to do aught but weep into her pillow at her feeling of loss.

Nightly Craig Rollins ate his meal at the Pheasant's Inn, spending the better portion of the evening alone over a leisurely dinner. Lisa was delighted each time she saw the gentleman, and a closer friendship was beginning to grow between them. It did not matter to her that he was older. He had been kinder to her than her own kin and she valued his friendship.

This evening as in the past, finding a spare moment, Lisa made her way to his table. She still did not serve him for Brandy seemed always at hand whenever the wealthy older man entered the door.

"It is good to see you this evening, Lisa." He greeted her warmly as she stood before his table and smiled upon him. "I can see that it is a busy evening and also that you look a bit tired." He watched her features carefully, noticing how truly tired the girl really looked.

"It is good to see you too, Mr. Rollins. I trust that all is well with you?" She did not respond to his words about how tired she was, for she felt that if she were to admit the weariness that she felt she would more than likely collapse.

Suddenly, from across the room, a shout was directed at Lisa. "Get that pretty little bottom over here, girl, and bring me and my friend something to eat." It was Willie Simmons shouting, not as usual for Brandy to wait upon him but for his cousin.

Lisa sighed tiredly, knowing that because of this, more than likely there would be a scene between herself and Brandy. But seeing no way out, for now both Willie and his friend were glaring at her, she smiled toward Mr. Rollins and excused herself.

As Craig Rollins watched Lisa approach the table of the two loud-mouthed men, his features were as unreadable as a wintery sea. Only the tensing of a muscle in his jaw revealed the anger that consumed him. He had borne almost as much of this girl's suffering as he was able, and so with a resolute mind he beckoned Adam from the bar.

As Lisa approached Willie's table she could see that he had already had far too much to drink, and the evil glint in his eyes told her to be cautious. "What is it that you are wanting, Willie?" She looked from her cousin to his friend who seemed to be in need of a washing and a shave.

"What is it that we be wanting you ask?" Willie slurred out loudly. "First, my lovely little cousin"—he pronounced cousin as though it were an evil word. "Me and Charlie here shall be having something to fill our bellies, and then let's you and me get to know one another a bit better. It is a shame that we are cousins but do not even know what the other feels and thinks." He grinned wickedly as his companion laughed heartily at Lisa's embarrassment.

"I shall get you your dinner, Willie, but do not expect any more from me." Lisa pushed away the hand that reached out to encircle her waist.

"You had best wise up, my girl, and let yourself be treated kindly by me. There are plenty here who would not be as considerate as your own kin."

Lisa gasped from shock and then hurried away from the table, their loud guffawing laughter following her all the way into the kitchen. She could not believe that her own cousin could say such things to her. Yet he was typical of the men who stood here nightly at the Pheasant's Inn, talking about the savageness of the Indians, and about how filthy and foul they were. These men did not see themselves, how low and detestible they were.

Brandy had also seen the interplay at Willie's table, and this time she did not blame the girl. She had seen Willie try to touch Lisa, seen Lisa push him away, and she had also seen the girl's face turn to flame as she hurried away to the kitchen. For a moment Brandy chuckled to herself, letting her humor override her anger at Willie. This girl was a babe thrown into the midst of a den of wolves. Brandy would have welcomed the crude words that had come from Willie's mouth, and the feel of his hands upon her form. She laughed to herself. There was no accounting for taste. Leaving the table she was serving, Brandy went to the kitchen.

Ladling some gravy into a plate, Lisa looked up just as Brandy came through the door. With a sigh she faced the larger girl, knowing that those cat eyes of hers had seen everything and that she was not going to let it pass.

"I be taking those plates for you, girl." She reached and took the plates that Lisa was setting on the tray to help Hanna.

"Thank you, Brandy," Lisa said, surprised at the other's actions.

"Willie needs to be set back upon his heels every now and then, and I reckon that this is one of them nights." She hefted the tray up and started from the kitchen, leaving a shocked Lisa looking after her.

"There sure ain't no making out that there girl." Hanna shook her head back and forth at Brandy's retreating back.

Lisa was in full agreement. She did not understand what had come over the other girl. But with no time to turn the matter over further in her mind, she hurried back into the common room to serve her tables.

On the following day, as the evening hour approached, Milly gave Lisa a message from her aunt Adell. Lisa was instructed not to serve dinner in the common room but to help Hanna in the kitchen instead.

Lisa was jubilant at this news. Though she had been given good tips, to her no amount of money could compensate for the physical abuse—the pawing—to which she'd been exposed, nor for the insulting comments made by so many of the male customers.

Work in the kitchen was not easy, but Lisa found that she much preferred it to serving the men eating in the common room. So under Hanna's kind supervision, she helped to cook and clean.

Late that evening Hanna told her to take two buckets and fetch some water. Without delay Lisa did as she was bid. Once outside, she had to pause a moment before she could take her first step, it being so dark.

As she started in the direction of the well, a hand reached out and took hold of her waist.

She was about to scream out her indignation, thinking this to be one more of Willie's games, but as she turned about the scream died in her throat. In the dim light coming through the kitchen door she could make out the dark features and clothing of an Indian. "You," she gasped, hardly speaking above a whisper and barely daring to believe that Silver Fox was beside her.

A wide grin was her answer.

"What are you about?" Lisa hurriedly came to her senses and looked about now frantically, her large blue eyes exploring as best they could the dark shadows behind the inn, while a fiery warmth burned through the waist of her gown where his large hands held her. "You must leave. If you are found here they will hang you. Every man in the common room does nothing but talk of catching you!" She tried to push to the back of her mind the feeling those hands evoked in her.

She was frantic at the thought that his presence might be discovered. She could not bear the thought of harm coming to his large, fierce man.

"And you, golden moon glow? Are your thoughts, as theirs, also consumed with only me?"

Lisa could not speak, she seemed enraptured by his presence, his very voice filling her with warm desire. And her thoughts as he had just said were consumed with only him. She visualized the afternoon of their last meeting, felt his warm hands upon her body and his moist lips upon her own, seeking and plundering.

"Do you think of me during the day while you do the chores set out for you and during the night as you climb into your cold bed? Does your heart beat as though it will burst?" His hand rose from her waist, and boldly but with the lightest touch, it rested beneath her breast at that most tender spot he had just mentioned, feeling for himself the answer to his question. "Are your thoughts also of me? Can you put from your mind the delights your body experienced as you lay with me? Can you dismiss from your mind the passion that has been awakened in you and that needs my touch to come alive?"

Lisa felt his words enflame her to the core of her being. How he could describe her feelings so accurately was a mystery to her. She longed to tell him that what he said was true but an inner sense of protectiveness—she did not know what feelings her words would arouse in him—won out.

She shook off his hold upon her and, taking a step backward, remembered the pails. She knew she must hurry or someone might come looking for her. But she yearned for his touch. She craved to lose herself in their passion, to bask in their bodies' joys.

The Indian watched her retreat, and knowing her mind, he spoke softly, as though caressing the night air. "I would not have you carrying such a load." He reached out, took the buckets, and started to the well.

As Lisa followed him, he continued to speak. "I would not have you serve the men in the common room their dinner either. I think most of them, given the choice, would have you, my flower, upon that tray that is set before them, instead of the food that is served." His dark eyes rose to her face as he filled the buckets with cool water.

"What would you have of me?" Lisa breathed, her words coming softly.

For a moment longer his eyes continued to behold her and then with a large sigh the Indian hefted the buckets from the well and set them on the ground, his hands once again seeking out the woman before him and gently finding her waist. "I would have you as you should be. I would place you in a splendid prison of love and adoration, to be waited on hand and foot and pampered for my delight. You would do only things that pleased me and no other. No harsh or angry words would reach your ears, nor any foul abuse your tender flesh." His words were gently spoken as though half in jest, but something in his tone told Lisa of their truth.

Expelling a small sigh, Lisa murmured with some feeling, "If only it could be."

"You would welcome my love?" Silver Fox asked, as though wishing to be sure of her reply, while in his thoughts he remembered her body tightly pressed to his own and the soft cries of passion that came from her throat. He wished to be sure that what he had sensed about her feelings in those tender moments had not been created out of his own need but that she felt the same as he.

Not knowing how to be anything but truthful, Lisa nodded her head. "I do not see how that could be possible, though." She started to tell him her doubts and fears but was brought up short by his flaming lips upon her own and at this contact, driven beyond will, she glided into a world where only his touch mattered.

Silver Fox was elated at her confession. He had worried that with the passage of the days since last he had seen her she might have felt that their worlds were too different and not have dared to broach the gap between the two. Now he knew that her feelings were as deep as his own, too deep to be torn apart by the feelings of others. She was his and soon he would claim her.

Yet, Lisa still did not fully realize exactly what was at stake here. She did not know that loving this Indian would cause her white brothers and sisters to look upon her with hate-filled eyes and to regard her as the lowest of creatures for having been held within an Indian's arms. She only knew what lay within her heart and soul. Nothing could stem the feelings raging within her. And as she clung to this great warrior, knowing the full pleasure of his touch, she sealed her destiny.

After a moment, Silver Fox stepped back and looked into her eyes, those limpid blue pools. "It will not be much longer, my little flower, before I shall come for you."

"But why must it be so? Why can I not go away with you now?" For the first time she realized the depth of the love she felt for this man. She would throw all caution to the winds to be in his arms. She cared for nothing except him, and she was ready to prove this love.

But Silver Fox was not of the same mind. "Trust me." Gently he rubbed her cheek with his knuckle. "You shall be mine."

At that moment the back door opened and Hanna poked her head out into the darkness. "Lisa," she called loudly. "Are you all right?"

Recalling herself, Lisa realized the danger Silver Fox was in. "You must hurry, Silver Fox," she whispered and then called to the kind Hanna, "I am fine. The buckets are heavy." And hefting the buckets as best she could, she looked once more into the eyes of the man she loved.

Silver Fox stood near the well, watching her as she struggled to the back door with her load. How he wished to carry those two buckets for her, but he knew that it would be disastrous for him to be seen here about the inn. So as soon as she had reached the safety of the kitchen, with silent pantherlike strides he sought out his great black stallion and raced off through the darkness of the night.

Chapter Seven

After a fortnight had passed Lisa was once again ordered to appear before her aunt Adell. As on her last visit to the large woman's private chambers the summons came in the morning before the working day had started.

Lisa stood outside her aunt's door, wondering before knocking what she had done to deserve her recent treatment? Since the night she had seen Silver Fox outside the inn, she had been told to stay to the kitchen and she had, indeed, done just that, preferring this work to the rude insults she had faced in the common room. But as she prepared to enter her aunt's chamber she experienced a sense of doom. Yet, not understanding her feelings, she brought her hand up and boldly knocked.

"Come in." The command reached her through the door.

"You wished to see me, Aunt Adell?" Lisa remembered the first time she had viewed this same room, but then she had hoped for a loving home and kin that would make her feel welcome. Now she did not know what this large woman wished of her.

"Come over here, girl, and take a chair." Adell Simmons waved Lisa away from the door and toward the bed. "I have some things to discuss with you."

"What is it?" the girl asked with some concern as she sat on the edge of the chair and looked into the large features of her aunt.

"The only way to go about this is to grab the bull by the horns, so to speak." Her aunt spoke roughly. Then, with Lisa's questioning blue eyes upon her, she went on. "You do remember Mr. Leroy Moore?" She cocked a graying eyebrow at her niece.

Surprised, Lisa nodded her head. What could this conversation possibly have to do with the fat man from the coach? she wondered idly.

"Well, I have received a message only a few days ago from the good man, and he has asked for your hand in marriage."

As these words reached Lisa's ears, her features turned white. "Marriage? Mr. Moore?" she blurted aloud, as though the thought were impossible.

"Don't be acting so high and mighty, girl, and let me finish. As I said he wrote concerning you in marriage. Of course, I had some time to consider his request but as I was pondering this situation another man broached me on the same subject. It would seem that my niece is the most popular attraction here in Missouri." A lopsided grin appeared on her hard features.

Lisa sat as though in shock, not believing her own ears.

"To tell you the truth, girl, I was rather relieved when I was able to turn down Mr. Moore's offer. I do think that my dear sister Virginia would turn in her grave if I had been foolish enough to go ahead with allowing you to marry such a man. I think that the man does have some evil thoughts." Here she stopped and gave a loud guffaw of mirth. "But getting on with the matter at hand . . ." She saw that her niece was not in a very good humor so she thought it best to finish this interview quickly.

"You shall be married the day after tomorrow to Mr. Rollins."

Lisa rose from her chair, still not believing what she was hearing. She was to marry Craig Rollins on the day after tomorrow? But she could not marry the older man, she loved another. She felt her world shifting and as dizziness settled over her she sat back down in the chair.

"Are you all right, girl?" Adell Simmons demanded, seeing the pale features of her niece.

"I shall not marry Mr. Rollins, Aunt Adell. You must at once change the arrangements." She did not know what her aunt and the kindly older man had arranged, but she did know that she would have no part of it. She knew that Mr. Rollins was only trying to be kind. More than likely her aunt had gone to the poor man and told him of the offer she had had from Mr. Moore, thereby pressuring him to offer his hand in marriage to her niece. Well, she would have no part in such a farce. Besides she would marry no one but Silver Fox. Her heart was already taken, and she believed that soon he would be coming for her.

Adell Simmons grinned at her niece as though she were merely a child and did not know what she was saying. "Over there in that chair"—she pointed across the room to a comfortable-looking chair with a large box resting upon it—"is your wedding dress. Mr. Rollins himself sent it only last evening."

"No." Lisa clutched at her throat as her eyes probed the box upon the chair. It was true then. He was willing to marry her.

"I will play no games with you, Lisa. You shall do as you are told or you shall be thrown out with neither clothes nor lodgings."

Not knowing what to say to this formidable woman Lisa just stared.

"A preacher should be arriving here tomorrow and on the following morning the wedding will be held."

"No!" This time Lisa rose to her feet and glared at the woman upon the bed. No one had the right to tell her who she must marry. She would not be forced to do her aunt's bidding this lightly.

"I shall not argue with you any more, Lisa. Go to your chambers and think over what has been told to you. You shall not have to work anymore, seeing as how you shall be married to the wealthiest man in these parts in only two days."

Lisa hurried from the room and up the stairs, still hearing the laughter of the cruel woman who could claim to be her kin. Shutting the portal tightly behind her, she flung herself upon her small bed.

Marriage to Craig Rollins, she kept repeating to herself. But how could she marry this man? She did not love him. Of course, she liked him well enough as a friend, and she had no doubt that he was in some manner trying to protect her; but she could never go through with marrying him.

The image of Silver Fox's strong powerful features came to mind and tears coursed down her cheeks. He would somehow save her from the fate that was being thrust upon her. Although she had not seen him in two weeks she knew that somehow he was aware of her plight and would come to her aid.

As her tears streamed steadily, she heard dimly

the sound of a key turning in the lock of her door. Jumping from the bed she hurried to the portal, only to find that indeed she had been locked in. Pounding upon the hard wood door, she cried for release, but soon she wearied, not hearing anyone without.

Going to the window she looked out. Far off in the distance, she could barely see the mountains which bordered the forest where Silver Fox and his people lived. "Oh, my love, come to me quickly," she cried as her hands clutched the material of the curtains to her chest.

But neither Silver Fox nor release were to come soon to Lisa. The day turned to evening and another morning followed in its wake of night. Meanwhile Lisa was left to herself and her shattering thoughts, the only person to break her solitude being a boy who occasionally brought a tray of food. Lisa knew without checking that there was no escape, for she could hear the voices outside in the hallway each time the youth came and that meant that Adell had men guarding against any attempt she might make to escape.

So with the passage of time Lisa began to reflect on what would happen to her the following morning. And as the hours swept by, she began to fear that her Indian love would not come to her in time.

What would happen if Silver Fox did not

come? she cried over and over into her pillow. The first day she had stormed, saying to herself that there was no way her aunt could make her marry a man she did not love, but as time passed and she had nothing else to do but think the matter over, she was fast realizing that if she did not wed Craig Rollins she would be forced to submit to Leroy Moore. At the thought of the fat man having any claim upon her, she shuddered.

She would never submit to marrying Mr. Moore, but she now knew that where money was involved her aunt Adell would have her way. She might even sell her niece to the fat man as his servant, having no compunctions about doing this foul deed. Lisa knew that when the time came she would have to marry Craig Rollins. She had no delusions about being able to love the older man but she did in some ways care for him. He had become a friend and she knew that he, at least, would not force his attentions upon her and that she would live as she had in her past in England. But how she ached within. To finally have found that one most special love and to have had it ripped away as though it had never been.

She would be forever bound to Craig Rollins. She would never again be free to indulge the strong feelings she harbored for Silver Fox. She would have to pretend that she had never felt the deep, overwhelming desire that she had only known in his strong arms. She would have to assume a pretense of wifely devotion, for she knew that Craig Rollins had only offered marriage to save her from Leroy Moore. At this thought she felt the beginnings of loyalty to him growing within her. She could never, once the vows were spoken, betray the man who would go to such lengths to secure her safety. Then from deep in her mind arose a memory that she had, indeed, buried. It was Craig Rollins who was holding her tightly and his lips were touching her own that night aboard the *Sea Maid*. Quickly she pushed them aside. She could barely believe that such a scene had taken place. Not once since that time had Craig Rollins acted in any way other than as a true friend.

At daybreak the following morning, Lisa was awakened by the sound of someone turning the key in the lock on her door. To her surprise, Milly was entering her chamber with several boxes in her arms.

Sitting up quickly, the first thought going through Lisa's mind was that this girl whom she knew to be a friend might try to help her escape from this room which was now her prison. But the sad look upon Milly's features told her that these thoughts were futile.

"Good morn to you, Lisa." The girl set her bundles down upon a chair and started toward the bed nervously. "I do hope that you are doing well?" she ventured, imagining how badly this girl felt at being forced into a marriage not of her choosing and at being locked in this small, airless chamber for the past two days.

Lisa smiled at her friend, knowing that the girl had nothing to do with the trickery that was being played on her. "I am fine, Milly." She patted the bed, inviting the girl to sit for a moment. "Why did Aunt Adell let you come to me instead of that boy?"

"I have been trying from the first to be the one to bring you up your tray, but Mistress Simmons and her son Willie would not let me near your door until this morn. They said that if I wanted I could help you to prepare your toilet for the wedding."

Swift, stinging tears came to Lisa's blue eyes as the pity in the girl's tone touched her ears.

Noticing, Milly was quick to offer comfort. "I am the first to say that what your aunt be doing to you is foul, but I have had these days to think the matter over and I think that you will be better off than most with a man like Mr. Rollins." She spoke her mind, hoping that Lisa would not take offense at her words.

Lisa did not respond, but hung her head, trying to recapture some of her dignity.

"I know that it ain't my place to interfere, but last eve, when that Mr. Rollins came to dinner, I was the one to serve him. Brandy didn't object since I gave her the tip. But I told him the treatment your kin were dealing you, and the look on his face told me that he was angry. In fact I don't think I ever have seen such fury in a pair of eyes before. And as I be seeing it, girl, if'n he be angry at such rough treatment toward you he shall see that you are treated fairly when he weds you."

Lisa knew that the girl wished to be helpful so raising her blond head she smiled toward her. "I know that Mr. Rollins will only treat me with kindness. It is not he that I fear but myself."

Milly looked upon her, not understanding her words.

"I do not love him," Lisa finally got out.

A large grin came over the other's features. "Is that what be bothering you about this whole affair?" She had forgotten how young Lisa was, how innocent of the world about her. Did the girl think that one married only for love? Why most people did not even know what the word meant, and she was sure that this girl sitting opposite her was a novice to the word. She did not believe that Lisa had known any deep love in her life. "Why, luv, people don't always marry because they love each other," she tried to explain.

Lisa knew all of this, for she had known plenty of girls who had been forced into arranged marriages. But she had never been able to stand the thought that she might be one of them.

"You ain't never been in love, Lisa, so how do you know that you won't in time love this Mr. Rollins?" Milly tried to reason with the girl, but as she did the image of the man's shawl-draped body and his white wig came to the forefront of her mind. Still, even with this sight before her, she remembered how he had looked when she had told him that the woman he was to marry this very morn was locked in her room, a prisoner. The expression on his face had revealed a strength that no one would ever suspect. She had seen a different Mr. Rollins at that moment and the image would not leave her.

How Lisa wished that she could tell this girl or anyone else about her Indian love. How she wanted to shout to the world that she loved the mighty warrior Silver Fox. But she knew this was impossible. She would only bring about her downfall by saying these words. Even this girl would not understand her true feelings. Milly's people had too much hatred for the Indians, so Lisa had to remain silent about her feelings for the man she so desired. "I know of the devotion that others have shared. My own mother and father were deeply in love so I am aware it takes more than marriage vows to seal one's life forever." She tried to explain to this girl who was her friend some of her inner thoughts and feelings.

Milly only chuckled at her words. "If only it could be that simple. I am afraid that in Missouri we live a far different life from what you were used to. If this man, Mr. Rollins, does not claim you— he will treat you decently and you will live in a fine house, for I have heard the many stories of the mansion that his grandfather built—then your aunt will pawn you off to someone else. But, Lisa, you must be aware that all men will not treat you as this Mr. Rollins would. You shall have a chance at some happiness wed to this man. You may never know such joy if you marry some of the other men who have approached your aunt about you." The girl looked seriously into Lisa's blue eyes, hoping that somehow she was making herself clear and that the girl would use her brains and not fight this marriage, for if she did Milly was sure that things would go far worse for her.

Lisa nodded her golden head, her soft curls flying about her shoulders. "I have had time alone here in my room to think this all out and I know the truth of your words. I shall go through with this affair, though my heart and soul cry out against it." Slow, crystal tears clung to her cheeks.

Milly's own heart went out to this small, heart-stricken creature, and reaching out she held her tightly, for a moment treating her as though she were indeed her younger sister. She patted Lisa's hand gently and spoke kind, soothing words.

Lisa had needed comfort and in Milly's strong arms she gradually regained some of her composure. "You have been a dear friend, Milly, and I shall never forget all of your kindness." She placed a small kiss on the other girl's cheek.

Milly felt embarrassed, and rising from the bed, she scoffed. "You indeed are my friend but I be thinking that we had best start getting you ready for your wedding or that Mr. Rollins will be standing all by himself in front of that preacher."

Lisa smiled along with the girl and rose also. "What things are in the boxes that you brought with you, Milly?"

Milly's features spread into a large grin as she went and brought the boxes to the bed. Mr. Rollins sent these for your wedding, Lisa. Wait until you see what is inside." The girl excitedly pulled the strings wrapped about the boxes and opened the lids. Their contents drew both girls' eyes.

The larger box contained a gown of the purest white lace, the border of the bodice embroidered with tiny white pearls, the sleeves puffed at the shoulders and then tapering to a snug fit down the arms and at the wrists. Lisa's breath caught at seeing the gown's beauty.

Another box contained white slippers and the next, a veil and train. The last box, when it was opened, revealed the underclothing to be worn under the gown. Looking at it, Lisa felt her face flush. No detail had been left to chance, and as she held up the delicate chemise she knew that Mr. Rollins had a gentleman's eye for beauty and for a woman's size. The material in her hands was of the sheerest satin, trimmed with the same soft lace from which the gown was made. How fortunate for her, she thought with some ill humor, that her husband would be so generous as to clothe her in such a fashion and that he also possessed such an eye for style.

Milly held her breath as Lisa took the chemise

from the box. Never had she seen such a beautifully made article of underclothing. Her own had always been made of scratchy wool or the cheapest material that her few coins could manage. "Goodness, girl, that be heaven itself," she said aloud with a wistful breath.

Lisa smiled at the girl, knowing full well the beauty of the cloth. "It would seem that Mr. Rollins would have a bride who is dressed in a fitting manner."

"Aye, that he will too," Milly exclaimed as she spread out all of the articles from the boxes upon the bed.

As Lisa looked down she thought of her own clothing. She had not worn any color except black since leaving England and though she felt observing mourning was an obligation she owed her father she knew, as her fingers traced over the white material of the gown, that she would not be able to resist this white creation.

Setting to the job at hand, Milly ordered Lisa over to the chair and began to brush out her waist-length hair. "It shall be a pleasure to help you dress for this day, Lisa." She smiled as she began to twine curls about Lisa's blond head and to capture each of them with one of the tiny pearl hairpins that had been sent in the same box as the underclothing.

Lisa let herself relax and enjoy the attention paid her by the other girl. It had been some time since she had enjoyed luxuries, yet she was thankful that Milly was here. She could not imagine herself having the strength to get herself ready for the ordeal ahead.

A few hours later Lisa stood before the portal, her hand ready to turn the knob and her mind contemplating her destiny. Taking a long, deep breath she turned and one last time smiled her thanks to her friend, Milly, before leaving the chamber.

With slow, halting steps Lisa went down the hallway, her hands holding the white gown above her ankles so she would not trip. As she approached the stairs she heard voices coming from below. Milly had told her earlier that her aunt had shut the doors to the inn for the first time since she had worked there, so Lisa knew that the people below were here for her wedding.

As she began to descend the stairway the noise quieted and all below looked up with awestruck eyes.

Milly, following only a few steps away, smiled her pleasure as she, too, heard the voices halt and saw the looks of astonishment written on the faces of those standing below. The one most affected she thought was Mistress Simmons. If that one did not shut her gaping mouth, Milly laughingly thought, she would soon be housing a fly in that large opening.

Mr. Rollins stood off to the side of the small group, accompanied by his servant, but as his dark eyes filled with the vision of loveliness floating down the stairs, as though upon a white, sheer cloud, he hurriedly, with the aid of his gold-handled cane, made his way to the bottom of the staircase.

Lisa stopped for a fleeting moment to look at the faces below, but seeing Craig Rollins's shawl-draped form at the rail awaiting her descent, she again started down. She was startled, for upon seeing Mr. Rollins she thought of Silver Fox. Her marriage would signify the ending of their love. She wished that she had the strength to scream out her rage to this group of people, to tell them of her love and that she would never betray him. But as she felt a gloved hand take her own, she knew that she did not possess the strength this act would take. She knew, as she glanced about at the evil smiles of Willie Simmons and his friends, that she would not even make it to the front door before they would capture her. And such a move would cost her more than what was now being thrust upon her. She lowered her head, willing the tears not to come as she felt the small squeeze of the hand that was holding her own.

As Craig Rollins had viewed the descent of the woman he was to marry, he'd felt thunderstruck. He was aware of her beauty, for that had been what had first drawn him to her, but this woman possessed more than beauty. She was all that he desired in a woman, yet she seemed a vision as she made her way to his side. The gown that he had purchased for her only accented her own loveliness, bringing out all of her wondrous charms for all to see. He had never seen such exquisite perfection in any other woman, and he strove to control his emotions as he realized that she was finally to be his in name and reality.

The procedure was a blur to Lisa. She was only vaguely aware of the preacher who stood before her and Craig Rollins and began to read from a small black book. She realized that her aunt and cousin and their friends had formed a small circle about her, and sensing the steady pressure of the gloved hand, which had moved from her hand to her waist, she felt suffocated.

When the service was over, Craig Rollins turned to Lisa, and his black eyes struck a tiny spark of recognition in her. She felt caught in a tight trap, for his ebony orbs seemed to capture and hold her blue ones, projecting a magnetic force like those of only one other.

But the rough, hearty laughter of her heavyset aunt broke the spell. "Well, my sister's girl is married now," she chortled to the room in general. "I'll not have to lose my sleep any longer worrying over her."

Willie and his friends laughed as loudly as Adell Simmons at this remark, all knowing well the abuse Lisa had suffered at her aunt's hands and aware that thoughts of Lisa Culbreth's well-being had never affected Adell Simmons's sleep.

Craig Rollins shook himself, and taking hold of his wife's arm, he began to steer her toward the door of the large common room. "We must be on our way now, Mistress Simmons. I thank you for permitting us to use your home for the ceremony, but we must now leave."

Adell Simmons stood, mouth open wide. Surely the pair were not rushing off this quickly. She had hopes that now that the chit was married to this wealthy man they could all be on friendly terms. Lisa's wealthy husband could do a lot for her and her son. "Why now, Mr. Rollins, I had planned on you and your wife here staying for a small meal and a toast to your future." She hurried to the pair, loath to let them go through the door. "Why the vows haven't been uttered but a bare few minutes," she added as though she were surprised at his actions.

Craig Rollins, one hand upon his cane and the other on Lisa's arm, directed an angry glare at the woman in front of him. He had borne her foulness in the past in order to gain Lisa's hand, but now that he had won the prize that had led him to the Pheasant's Inn he was not about to pretend to be friendly to the Simmons family any longer. "My man Adam is now gathering my wife's belongings and taking them to my carriage, madam. I find the idea of eating under this roof distasteful."

Aware of his direct insult, Adell Simmons glared. "What of the dinners you have been eating under this roof each evening? It would seem that my inn isn't all that distasteful to you."

"Aye, madam, you are right there. But what

you are mistaken is in the reason for my nightly visits to your establishment. It was not the food that drew me but a much more valuable object." He again squeezed the tiny waist that lay beneath his hand.

Adell Simmons could not understand his meaning, but before she could say any more her son and his two friends approached the small group standing near the door.

"Where you be off to Mr. Rollins?" Willie questioned him with a large grin. "My friends and me were just saying that a small kiss from the bride would be in order for the occasion." Willie now reached out and, laying a large hand upon his cousin, began to pull her toward him. "Come along now, dear sweet cousin, I cannot let you be leaving without at least once having a taste of your charms. It is a shame that I did not do this sooner."

But as he drew Lisa to him he fell backward upon the floor. Craig Rollins stood over him, cane raised above his head as though he would again let the younger man taste his anger. "My wife is not to be mauled by the likes of you or any of your friends." His low rasping voice seemed to fill the room with deathlike sonorousness. "She is now Lisa Rollins and she belongs only to me. I shall tell all within this room that only once. What is mine I protect and hold most dear, so beware next time whose wife you lay hands upon."

Willie Simmons lay where he was, not believing that this quiet older man could have thrown him to the floor, nor that the man was threatening him as he was. He glanced about to see where his friends were but they, too, stood staring at the man, afraid to aid Willie for they, too, had seen the steely quality in the bewigged gentleman's dark eyes. They did not wish to challenge him and perhaps come out worse than their friend lying upon the floor.

"We shall wish you all a good day," Mr. Rollins said as though nothing had occurred, and turning to Lisa, he murmured, "If you are ready, my dear, we shall be on our way."

Adell Simmons bent down and helped her son to his feet. "Why the ungrateful beast," she whimpered as she took hold of Willie's arm. "Knocking my boy down like this after I let him have my own sister's daughter in marriage." Completely forgotten now in her anger was the fact that Craig Rollins had given her a most handsome amount of coin for her niece's hand.

Still, Lisa was the one who was most surprised by her new husband's outburst. He had been so quick that she had barely seen the movements that had knocked Willie off his feet. And with a new look of respect in her blue eyes, she let him help her up into the waiting carriage, where, displaying tender concern, he placed a warm fur lap robe over her legs.

"I am sorry to rush you like this, Lisa, from

your aunt's home but I am afraid I could not bear the lot of them a moment longer." He smiled into her anxious face as he settled his large frame back against the opposite seat.

"There is no need to apologize, sir. It is just as well that we leave." She shuddered at the thought of Willie and his friends. What torture she would have had to endure if not for this kind man opposite her. "Thank you, Mr. Rollins, for your protection in the inn," she added.

As Craig Rollins looked at this innocent, he experienced a tinge of regret. What this woman had had to suffer due to circumstances but through no fault of her own filled him with pain. "Please, Lisa, call me Craig. We are man and wife now and I think this should be proper." As color flooded her cheeks, he sighed and then added, "You are now under my protection and I shall see that no harm shall ever again befall you."

Lisa was most grateful to him. She knew at this moment that although she did love another, she would try her utmost to care for him as a wife should her husband. But on the other hand she thought of Silver Fox, just as at the inn she had been reminded of the large, handsome Indian when her husband had looked into her eyes after the ceremony had ended. She wished that she could give this kind man what he deserved, not a wife who would be forever thinking about another man.

"I hope that you will find my home to your

liking, Lisa," Craig Rollins said as he peered at her from beneath his spectacles.

"I am sure that all shall be fine, Mr. . . .I mean Craig," she murmured.

Craig Rollins smiled at her confusion. "I am afraid that I must leave you for several days." When she glanced at him questioningly, he continued. "I have business that is most important. It cannot be delayed. After we arrive I will not be staying, but Adam will be there to see to your needs. Also, the women of my house are aware that you shall be arriving and they will do anything that you wish."

"But . . ." Lisa could not believe that she had married this man in the morning and that he would leave her in the afternoon.

"I would not leave you so soon but it cannot be helped."

Adam returned before Craig could say any more and with a nod of his head to his master he unloaded Lisa's possessions and drove the pair of horses to the stable.

"Perhaps this separation will allow you the time you need to adjust to the fact that you are married," he added, hoping to put her at her ease.

Lisa could only nod her head, not wishing to argue the subject with him. She did not wish to appear so soon to be pressuring him. So instead she looked out the window at the scenery, and Craig Rollins sensing her mood remained quiet. However, his dark eyes did not watch the opposite greenery. Instead he enjoyed the view within, his black eyes going over the beautiful profile of the woman who now shared his name.

Soon the vehicle pulled up in front of the monstrous stone mansion.

Craig looked toward Lisa, pity in his dark eyes. He could well imagine her despair. She was being thrust here and there, deprived of her own will. She would have to make a new life for herself here at his home, and though he realized her thoughts were bleak now, he hoped sincerely that in time she would be able to sing with happiness and to live the type of life she well deserved.

Lisa sat up in the carriage, waiting for Adam to open the door and help her down the short steps. As she looked out the window at the cold stone Rollins fortress, she gave a small shudder. She was now mistress of this place that she had only visited once before. How would the servants react to her coming and upsetting their lives? Would there be resentment and would she have more problems than she had had in the past? She let out a soft sigh, as though the entire world rested on her shoulders.

Craig's keen eyes noted her slight shudder and he sensed the meaning of her sigh. She was nervous about this change in her life. How vulnerable she appeared to him at this moment. His heart seemed to constrict with pain. Reaching over he laid a gloved hand upon her own. "You have no reason to worry here, Lisa. Everyone at my home will see that you are made comfortable." This was the only thing that he could think to say, and seeing her soft smile directed toward him, he knew that he had said what she needed to hear.

As the pair made their way up the stone steps, the large front door was thrown wide and standing before the portal, huge grins upon their features, were the same two women Lisa had seen on the day she had passed through the kitchen of this house.

Craig Rollins smiled and, stepping into the house after his young bride, greeted the women. Then he said, "Lisa, these are the only servants in this house. If you find more would be desirable you need only mention it. However, they keep the house in fine order. I call them Ruby and Pearl and you will realize what gems they are, given time."

Lisa smiled back at the grinning pair. "I am sure that they will be fine," she said shyly but already feeling at her ease with the two dark women.

"You may go then and fetch your mistress something cool to drink. I am sure that she is quite thirsty after the long ride." Throwing carefree giggles over their shoulders the two left the foyer and headed back to the kitchen.

"Are they Indians?" Lisa asked, thinking of the darkness of their skins and of the way both women wore their black hair pulled back and braided. Actually, she had no way of knowing, for the only other Indian women she had seen since being in this country were those in the towns. They were usually filthy and skinny, and were either begging for a crust of bread or doing a white man's bidding.

"Does it matter to you, Lisa, if they be of Indian blood?" Craig responded to her question with one of his own, his black eyes looking deeply into hers.

Lisa felt her face flush from the heat of his gaze. "Why, of course not. I but mentioned it because I have not heard of anyone else hereabout having Indian help in the home." She tried to defend herself, not wishing for him to think that she would in any way think badly of Indians.

"They have been here since my grandfather was alive. Yes, they are Indians. But they are good and trusting, not as others would have you believe. They see to my comfort, and now that you are my wife, they shall do the same for you."

"I did not mean to imply anything, Craig. I myself have met Indians that seem most friendly." She did not say that she had met one Indian that was more than a friend to her, but her heart ached for Silver Fox.

With slow, halting steps Craig Rollins made his way to the front parlor, and as though he had not heard her words, he relaxed in a comfortable chair, motioning with his hand to indicate that she should take the one opposite him. "Tell me more, Lisa," he murmured as she settled herself.

At her questioning look, he added, "What were these Indians like that you found so friendly?"

Lisa felt desperate. What was she to tell this man who was now her husband? She could not possibly tell him of Silver Fox. She sensed that if any person would be able to understand her feelings it would be this man sitting across from her, but she also knew that no man wished to hear of the past love of his bride only hours after the wedding. Still, she must tell him something, she thought, searching her wits. "I have only met them in passing, sir," she lied, thinking that he would leave it at this.

But Craig Rollins was not one to leave anything half finished. "Yes?" he responded, his dark eyebrows slanting as he waited for her to continue.

"It was at my aunt's inn," she blurted and rose from her chair. Feeling the need to be active so that he could not so easily tell that lies were coming from her mouth, she walked about the large beautiful room.

Craig Rollins knew she was not telling the truth, so with a small grin he let the subject drop. "I imagine that you would like to see your room, Lisa?" So abruptly did he change the subject that Lisa turned from regarding the porcelain figurines resting on a table and looked at her husband. "Why that would be nice," she got out, relieved that the subject had been changed.

"After Ruby brings the tea I shall have her

show you to your room, then I am afraid that I must be leaving you. Business must, after all, be tended."

Lisa sat back in the chair and within a few seconds one of the Indian women entered the room with a small tray of tea and cakes.

Before the woman could leave the parlor, though, Craig Rollins halted her. "Ruby, will you show Mrs. Rollins to the master chambers after we are finished with our tea?"

The dark woman smiled and nodded her head, indicating that she would be happy to do his bidding. "I shall be back soon," she said before leaving the room.

Lisa felt a small knot forming in the pit of her stomach as her mind turned his words over and over. He had said the master chamber. She had hoped that in this marriage she would not be forced to fulfill that part of wifedom that she most dreaded. She had come to the conclusion, as she had been held prisoner in her room at the inn, that this man would not force himself upon her. He being older and a gentleman, she could not envision his desire being that of the other men she had found in this country. But suddenly she remembered that one kiss aboard the *Sea Maid*. Perhaps she had not thought long enough upon the matter.

"I would, myself, show you to your room, Lisa, but I am afraid that the long climb up the stairs is too much for me." As he spoke a soft smile touched his features, and Lisa felt her face begin to flush at her absurd feeling that this man had somehow read her mind.

When they finished the tea, Ruby again entered the parlor and cleared away the tray, telling Craig that she would be back shortly to show his young wife to her chambers.

Rising to his feet, Craig Rollins slowly made his way before Lisa, and bending down, he took one of her hands within his own. "I hope you will not be too upset at my leavetaking. If I could change this meeting in any way I would postpone it, but alas, it has been arranged for some time now." He apologized, hoping that she would not be too angry.

Actually, Lisa was relieved that he would be gone for a time. Now she would have a few days to orient herself to the situation. Being the wife of this older man was new to her. She wanted to be the best wife she could, but she would need time to subject her other feelings to her will. "I am sorry that you have to leave, but I shall try to get on until your return." She smiled up into Craig's kind face and for a second she was again reminded of another as she had been this morning, but as he turned his gray wigged head the thought flew from her. Silver Fox was forever lost to her, she realized, yet she would need this short reprieve from her husband to clear her thoughts of the man she loved.

"Then I shall leave you. I shall be leaving Adam

here since you might have need of him. He will be glad to take you for a ride in the carriage, if that is your wish and mounts are available if you would rather ride astride. Just tell him what you would like." Bending his head he brushed his lips against the back of her wrist. Then he turned and left the room, moving slowly.

Lisa sat there in the parlor until Ruby came a few moments later. So much was happening to her. She was now the wife of Craig Rollins and mistress of this huge mansion. She had only been in this country for a few short weeks, yet already her life had changed drastically. She could scarcely believe her position. For a moment her thoughts went back to her sister's slyly grinning features. If she did not know better she would think that Sylvia had arranged all that had transpired since she'd arrived in America. But she knew her sister had had no dealings with Craig Rollins. For some reason she could not discern, he had taken it upon himself to be her protector.

"If you are ready, ma'am, I shall show you to your room." Ruby brought Lisa out of her reflections.

"Oh yes, thank you." Lisa hurriedly rose to her feet, not wishing the woman Craig had spoken of so highly to find fault with her.

She was led up the spiral staircase and down a long, lighted hall. The woman opened a door at the end of the passage. "These are the master chambers and I hope that everything shall be to your liking. If you wish anything changed, you only have to tell me or Pearl and we shall see that it is done as soon as possible." Ruby entered the room and pulled the velvet-trimmed, wine-colored drapes apart, to let the sunlight in.

Lisa looked around the room with some awe. Never had she had a chamber of such magnitude. And off to a side, a door was ajar. Through it she could see another room which boasted a small love seat and chair and she knew that this was the small parlor of the master chambers.

Her blue eyes glanced at the huge bed positioned in the middle of the room, then at a small desk to the side, upon which rested several books and pen and parchment. Across the room was a wall-length hearth and she realized how warm she would be when the weather turned chill. On the opposite wall from that was a dressing table and a bureau, both pieces made of a deep warm wood that richly enhanced the burgundy carpet and the matching floral drapes. "It is beautiful," she exclaimed aloud as she went about the room.

Ruby smiled proudly at this young, beautiful woman. "The old master bought everything in here before he died to please Mr. Craig. But the younger master has not used these chambers much. There is a small sitting room off here." She went to the adjoining door and waited for Lisa to follow. "It is much brighter in here for sewing and reading."

That room was decorated in lighter shades,

mostly gold and white and Lisa found it to her liking.

"I shall leave you now and let you settle yourself. Pearl shall come up shortly to prepare your bath and bring you a tray. Your clothes have not yet been brought up to your chambers, but you shall find all that you might need now in the armoire." Ruby's words were very businesslike, but she directed a small caring smile toward the young girl.

Lisa looked about the small sitting room a moment longer and then turned again to the bed chamber. She felt at home in this large room, and as she walked about she came to the desk. Picking up the books there, she found that she had read several of them aboard the *Sea Maid*. Opening their covers she found the same bold script flourishing across the first page of each proclaiming ownership. Craig Rollins must have had these books placed here for her pleasure she thought, but as she heard the door open she set them neatly back into place.

As Pearl entered, pulling behind her a large brass tub, her dark eyes saw the movements of the young woman. With a large smile she set the tub in front of the hearth and softly said, "Mr. Rollins has a fine library, just filled with books of every variety. Perhaps you would like to go there and find something that you might rather read?" Her eyes went to the desk where the books rested.

"Thank you, Pearl, but I think that these shall

suffice for the time being." Lisa went to the tub and watched as the woman poured a rich, pink liquid into it. "The water shall be up in a moment. Perhaps you would care to disrobe while I go downstairs."

Lisa looked about the room for a second at the woman's words.

Grinning, the Indian woman nodded to the tall armoire across the room. "You will find a robe and slippers within." Having said this, she went about her business.

Lisa was surprised, when she pulled the gold handles of the armoire and it opened, to view the wealth of clothing within. Gowns of every description and color greeted her eyes, and pulling one out, she found by holding it up to her form that it would indeed fit her. Something was strange here, she thought as her hands slipped over first one gown and then the other. Had these been meant for her, she wondered as she came across a satin blue dressing robe with flounced-lace sleeves. She had only been told about her marriage a few short days ago, had Craig Rollins known about it sooner? Had he had these gowns and other articles made up and brought to his house? She thought of her wedding gown, the one she now wore. It fit as though she had stood and been measured for it, but until now she had been so rushed that she had not thought about it. Her confusion was plainly written on her features.

As Pearl entered the chamber carrying two

large buckets of steaming water, she saw what was bothering the young girl. "Mr. Rollins had those made up and brought to the house. Only yesterday did they arrive, and I know that he paid a fair price to have them here in time for your own arrival." The woman's voice reflected the pride and love that she felt for the man she worked for. It was a rare man who would have such costly gowns made up for the woman he was to marry, she thought as she added water to the tub and the pink liquid sent a fragrant, flowered scent about the large room.

Lisa quickly shut the doors and took the dressing gown across to the bed. "It was most kind of him, but I do have my own things." She did not wish to be thought of as a poor waif who had married this woman's employer for what he could give her. "If Adam would bring my things up I would be most grateful," she added, thinking of all the gowns she had had made for her before leaving England. But as her hand lingered on the blue satin dress she was reminded that all of her clothing was black and she was not as eager to wear it as she wished to appear.

"Your things shall be brought up in time. Adam is a very busy man and must tend to other matters first. Perhaps by morning your cases will be in your chambers." Pearl left the room again to bring more water.

Alone, Lisa took off her wedding gown and, tenderly placing it upon the bed, eyed the beauty of its material once more. Certainly her husband had an eye for beauty. Even the cut of his own clothing, at least from what she had seen beneath his shawl, told her of his good taste. He had always been superbly tailored, wearing only the most fashionable and expensive suits, and now she could only think that he wished the same for the woman who bore his name.

"Your bath is ready now," Pearl announced as she again entered the room and, pouring the contents of her buckets into the tub, left to fetch more water. "I shall be back to help you in a moment," she threw over her shoulder as she started from the room.

Lisa relaxed against the rim of the tub, letting the deliciously soft and sweet-smelling water enfold her body. Not since she had been at Culbreth manor had she been afforded such luxury. Aboard the ship and at her aunt's inn, she had been allotted no more than a sponge bath each evening, so now she felt herself sink with sheer delight into the water that encircled her and rose under her chin.

Shutting her blue eyes, she tried as best she could to go over this past day. This was a day she should remember for the rest of her life, it being her wedding day, but with so much happening she could barely remember what the pastor who had performed the ceremony looked like. Still, she could vividly remember the faces of her kin and their friends. With a soft smile she recalled Willie upon his back on the floor, and her husband standing over his prone body. She had never expected such an action from Craig Rollins. She would never have imagined such a gentle and kind man standing up to anyone as strong and healthy as her cousin. She had been surprised by the man who was now her husband. He had shown the strength that he harbored in his elderly form, and she could well imagine the hatred that her kin now harbored for her spouse.

However, she did not care what either her aunt or her cousin thought. She was only thankful that she no longer had to be under their roof.

Pushing these thoughts of her kin to the back of her mind she tried to think of her husband. She could remember how frightened of him she had been aboard the *Sea Maid*. She would never have believed that one day she would be married to this older man who had once filled her dreams with terror. But she had learned that he was not what she had thought. Indeed, quite the opposite was true of Craig Rollins. He had singled her out to be the recipient of his kindness. Even by marrying her he had proved that he had a kind and concerned heart, and did not wish her to suffer at the hands of a man such as Leroy Moore. To save her pain he had taken her for the rest of his life as his bride.

Even though the deed was done Lisa could still not believe that any man would offer to do such a thing for a woman he barely knew. Certainly

Craig Rollins with all of his wealth could have any woman he wanted for his wife. Yet he had chosen her, and though she was most grateful, she could not help wondering what could have influenced him to take such a gigantic step.

She had no more time for such thoughts, for Pearl entered the chamber and, taking the young woman into her skilled hands, lathered a sponge with pink liquid and proceded to scrub Lisa from head to toe.

Lisa had never undergone such intense personal care, but not wishing to offend Pearl, she gritted her teeth and let her have her way.

Once the bath was done, the woman held up a large, fleecy towel and enfolded Lisa's frame. Then leading her to the bed, she told her to lie back as she took up a scented perfume and proceeded to rub this over Lisa's golden form.

Lisa felt her eyes droop as the woman massaged her tired muscles with slow deliberate motions that went from head to foot. "You rest here for a time and I shall bring you a tray for dinner. You need your rest so do not get up."

To Lisa the woman's order seemed very wise. She had no desire to rise and destroy the soft drowsy feeling which had closed in about her. So closing her dark silky lashes, she did as bid.

It seemed to Lisa that she had slept but a moment when she heard a soft voice coming to her ears. "Here is your dinner. You must wake and gain your strength."

Raising her head and seeing the kind Indian woman, she noticed that it was dark in the room. She must have slept for some time.

"I shall leave the tray here on the bed table and shall come again to take it back downstairs." The woman lit a small candle and then started from the room as soon as she saw Lisa wrap herself in the dressing gown and start to eat.

Lisa was starving. It seemed that she had not eaten in days. She did remember that she had eaten little since yesterday. So attacking the food upon her plate, she promptly finished it and, rising from the bed, went to the armoire to select a soft nightgown. It would not be wise to sleep nude as she had this past afternoon, she thought with a slight flush, remembering that she had not even thought of dressing when the Indian woman had left her after the massage.

However, as Lisa made her way back to the large, soft bed she found that she was not as tired as she had been earlier, so taking one of the books from the desk, she started to read by the candle light coming from the bed table.

Pearl was of a different mind, though, when she came to reclaim the tray. "You had best try to get to sleep now, Mrs. Rollins. You have had a hard day, and we want you to be well rested when Mr. Rollins returns." The kind Indian woman would not accept any excuse, and as she reached over and took the book from Lisa's hand, she also blew out the candle. Then leaving the room, she shut the door softly behind her.

Lisa lay in bed for a time, trying to sleep, but instead her mind reviewed the past and when it touched upon the Indian, Silver Fox, she sighed aloud. She did not wish to think of this man any further. She must put him from her mind and think only of her husband. But she could not. Even though she knew it was a betrayal of Craig Rollins to think of Silver Fox as she was doing, the image of the strong, bronzed warrior haunted her.

It was no use, she realized, and then letting herself respond to her cravings she finally found the slumber that she sought by dreaming that she was in the arms of her Indian love.

Chapter Eight

In the soft, hazy nether recess of her mind Lisa dreamed that her love held and caressed her, whispered soft love words in her ears and placed feather-light kisses upon her face and neck. With a sigh she relinquished all hold upon reality and let herself be swept into this maelstrom of pleasure.

She envisioned herself and her Indian wrapped in a golden cocoon of rapture, that no one could enter—just the two of them. She felt his gentle hands upon her and knew, if only in her dreams, what it meant to be a woman. But as she heard her name whispered over and over, she somehow pulled herself from the depths of her imaginings to reality. With a sharp gasp she sat up in bed, finding that some of her dreaming had been fact, for beside her upon the bed was Silver Fox.

Silver Fox had stolen into the room by the window and seeing his desire upon the bed he had approached her to find that she was as tormented as he had been since meeting her. He knew when she reached out and pulled him to her that she had been dreaming about him, and he smiled with pleasure, though he tried to awaken her. She was like the softness of the dew after a scented rain. Her tenderness left him blinded to all but her. But calling her name, he pulled himself from her soft lips, wishing to draw her from her dream world and to possess her aware mind and body.

Lisa sat up, her blue eyes rounded. "What are you doing?" she got out before she remembered that this was her husband's house and that she could not allow this man to be here. Great tears came to her eyes at this thought.

Even in the dark Silver Fox's sharp eyes could see the shining tears streaming down her creamy cheeks, and he reached out a large gentle hand to wipe them away as he pulled her into the fold of his warm embrace. "I have come for you, my little golden flower, as I promised."

Shaking her golden head, Lisa knew that it was too late for them. She belonged to another; she could never be his.

Stilling her head by putting his palms upon her cheeks, Silver Fox placed his strong lips over her petal-soft ones, and drinking of them, he sealed his possession of her. "Have no doubt you are mine," he whispered as he pulled his lips from hers and slowly rose to the side of the bed, Lisa still wrapped in his arms.

Lisa knew she should break away but nothing seemed to matter at the moment but this man holding her. So relinquishing all and giving herself into his strong, capable hands, she gave a soft sigh and laid her head upon his oak-ribbed chest.

As he started toward the door Lisa pulled herself from her stupor. "What of my clothes?" she asked, looking down at the flimsy nightgown that adorned her body.

"I shall clothe you, my little flower." He smiled into her face and she had no choice but to trust him.

Noiselessly he carried her down the staircase and out of the stone mansion, toward the back of the house. He gave a soft, piercing whistle. Seemingly from nowhere his large black stallion appeared and with little difficulty Silver Fox placed Lisa upon his back. Then in one quick, graceful motion he was behind her.

For a moment, with his strong arms gone from around her, Lisa realized what she was about to do. Here she was married only a day, yet she was running away with her Indian lover. How could she do this to the man who had saved her from the life she was leading? "Silver Fox, we must not do this," she finally got out as he mounted behind her. "I was married today. How can I do this thing to my husband?" She wished him to somehow make it possible for her to go with him.

For a second Silver Fox did not move his horse. He just sat and looked deep into her blue eyes. "I cannot take you by force, Lisa. You are my life now and you have been from the moment that I first met you. I can but tell you of the deep, burning feeling within my chest. My life is empty except when my mind if filled with a vision of you. My heart sings at the sound of your voice. I am only a man but one who will forever keep you from all harm." His words were soft and heartfelt, reaching into the very depths of Lisa's soul with their intensity.

"But Craig?" she said desperately, knowing that she owed the kind older man at least this much.

"Your husband will always love you. But what of you, Lisa. Who do you love?" his voice came softly to her ears, and with a small cry she clung to his neck, not caring about anything except the feel of him beneath her hands.

"Let us forget everything but ourselves," he whispered into her golden curls as he urged his stallion on with a gentle kick.

The night was dark, only a sliver of moon shining down upon the land, and as the couple rode through the forest, the stallion seeming to know the way, they spoke of their newfound love for each other. It was as though all that existed stood still for the blond woman and her bronze warrior. They seemed wrapped in a world of their own as they kissed and touched, delighting in the freedom allowed them.

"I shall take you to my home and my people. You shall share my tepee as my woman. All that I own shall be laid at your feet, Lisa." His ebony eyes sought her own, trying to see her reaction to his words.

The cold air made Lisa shiver, so she snuggled closer into the warmth of this arms and finally responded, "But what of your people, Silver Fox? Will they accept me as you do?" Until this moment she had not thought about anyone else but now reality had to be faced.

"Many say that I am chief of our tribe, mostly stupid white men who know no better. I am not chief, but I love my people and they love me. As they love me, they shall love you. You are my golden flower and I have chosen you above all others." His lips silenced her further questioning. He wished her to know that he would take care of her and not let even a single word hurt her.

Deep in the night, the barking of a lone dog warned the Indian village that all were not abed as the black stallion took his master to a large tepee and stood, waiting for the couple to leave his back.

Silver Fox looked at Lisa, and with a soft grin he hefted her to the ground. Then, jumping to his feet, he stood large and strong, his woman held tightly in his embrace. "Go to your own woman." He lightly patted the large black horse upon its rump and the animal, as though understanding all the Indian said, turned and headed to the back of the tepee.

Lisa felt nervous as Silver Fox carried her toward the towering structure he said was his home. Pulling back a flap, he stooped and went in.

Lisa looked about when Silver Fox set her down on a soft pile of furs at one side of the room, noting a small fire in the center of the interior.

"I shall warm the place for you, Lisa." He spoke over his shoulder as he went to the center and began to build up the small fire that was already blazing.

Lisa's blue eyes took in nothing but the towering man squatting before her. She had wished to be his and now she would be. How impossible this all seemed, but she knew she wished to be with him and no other. She wanted only to feel his tender touch and to be lost to all but the feelings that he could provoke in her.

Rising to his massive height, Silver Fox turned to the woman within his home, looking with a keen eye at her silhouetted form upon the pelts. He had envisioned this sight so many times in the past that now he could barely believe his eyes. Her golden curls were wrapped about her down to her waist, and the sapphire pools of her eyes spoke of her feelings far better than any words could. She was his now and forever. He went to her gently, not wishing to frighten her for he knew that this evening had taken a different turn from the one she had expected and he wished this night to be beautiful for her and himself. The other times that they had shared their love had been rapturous, but this night he wished to feast upon their passions, to lay all obstacles aside and to find total, all-consuming delight with her. At this thought his hands reached out, and he tenderly stroked the golden hair that drew them.

Her sultry blue eyes ignited at his touch. Since the first day she had met this man she had wished for nothing except his touch. Instinctively, she wrapped her arms about his strong shoulders.

The pair soon were consumed by the fierceness of the smoldering fires that had lain dormant since first they had met. "My golden flower," Silver Fox whispered over and over as he lay beside her and kissed her searchingly. His passion-filled kiss left her breathless and giddy.

Then this strong, overpowering man brought Lisa to a pinnacle of rapture. She was lost to all but his passionate touch, his kiss, his strong body seeking her own. And as she found herself feeling the total pleasure of being a woman, she found her blood coursing at a frantic pace, her heart beating at a rapid tempo. Now she was in the arms of the man she loved.

Never again would she have to dream of his

touch or yearn for the pleasure she had shared with him in days past.

As Silver Fox looked down into her soft, limpid eyes, he was overwhelmed by a yearning that he could not express. When his flesh touched hers, he caught his breath at the feeling of wonder that was storming through him. This woman had, indeed, been brought to him by a stroke of fate. He wooed her, softly, caressingly, lovingly. He whispered love words, letting her know his innermost thoughts, and at the moment of their joining they came together as one, their passions igniting. Their souls touched, and Silver Fox lost himself to all but the woman within his arms, knowing that he had what other men searched a lifetime to find.

As they slipped, by degrees, back to reality, Silver Fox tasted Lisa's soft, pliant lips. Their sweet ambrosia was hers alone. "You are my heart, Lisa," he stated seriously, looking at her with tender concern in his eyes.

Lisa, though this was not the first time she had lain with this man, felt some shyness now that she was here in his home. And for a moment she turned her golden head from his bold look.

Silver Fox, seeing her response, took her chin and gently brought it up to his gaze. "Our love is beautiful. Do you turn from this? I would have you know my heart, Lisa. I have found in you a world more rich than one I could have imagined. You have made me complete."

Soft tears gently escaped Lisa's eyes at these words. How well he had captured her own true feelings.

"You are my strength and my weakness, my golden flower. You are my all, my own." Again his lips sought hers and again they indulged in that delicious course that only they could share. They were driven to search each other's depths, and to draw out what lay hidden there. So with gentle strength Silver Fox consumed Lisa, transporting her, thereby, to a soft, dreamy limbo where only he and she could survive.

Lisa's body quivered at his every touch, and her needs as great as his own, she strove to attain the peak of gratification. Silver Fox felt her desire building and he took her, bringing her to smoldering heights of rapture.

The splendor of their lovemaking brought their souls forth and laid them bare. And so borne beyond any hindrance they lay amid the embers of their union, each knowing total bliss.

Having been lost to everything but their pleasure in each other, their return to earth was as unsettling as an afternoon thunderstorm.

With fevered protectiveness Silver Fox wrapped his strong arms about the slender girl upon his bed. "You are mine," he proclaimed, wanting no doubt to linger between them.

"Yes, yours," Lisa softly murmured, laying her face against his sturdy chest, but deep in her mind were thoughts of another, the man who had dared much to afford her protection. What she had done to the older man lay heavy on her heart though she knew that at this moment she was where she should be. Then, her attention returning to Silver Fox, she considered questioning him about his manner of speech. For although he was called a savage, he spoke better than most of the white men here in Missouri. But despite her desire to know the answer, her blue eyes grew so heavy that she could only snuggle close to the man next to her.

Pulling the furs closer, Silver Fox wrapped them in a cozy cocoon of warmth, and then pillowing Lisa's head upon his shoulder, he lay waiting for sleep. But even when he heard the easy breathing of the woman next to him, sleep would not come.

He had thought all would be well when he brought her to his tepee but there was still a part of herself that she kept hidden from him. He knew her sense of honor was strong, and though she would not speak it, she thought she was betraying the man who had married her. A small grin came over his strong features. It was hard to find a woman with such loyalty, especially for an older man with little appeal. For a moment he wanted to wake her and tell her what should be said between them—perhaps then he would know the fullness of her inner being—but something stopped him. He had to be sure that she was not merely enamored of him because revealing the truth could affect the well-being of his people. No. He could not risk revealing everything to her until he was completely sure that she would not have a change of heart.

A vision of her kin came to his mind and for a moment a black cloud seemed to envelope his brain. What ruthless, scheming people her aunt and cousin were. To treat an innocent as they had, selling their own flesh and blood and working her like a slave. As he again visualized Willie Simmons's crude features, Silver Fox doubled his fists. How he wanted to smash that one's chin. He would kill that man if he ever laid a hand on Lisa again. Cousin or not this girl-woman was his. He looked at Lisa, then tucked a fur beneath her chin. Just gazing on her gentle features cooled his anger. He would be glad when everything could be settled and brought into the open. Where she was concerned, duplicity was almost more than he could bear.

Finally sleep came to Silver Fox and with it a contentment that he had not known in the past. He snuggled his large body close to Lisa.

When the everyday noises of the Indian village signaled that morning had broken, Silver Fox stretched his long, lithe body and this movement reminded him of the one beside him. Looking over at Lisa's still, sleeping form he smiled with pleasure. How beautiful she looks in the morning light, he thought, and bending over her, he lightly kissed her small slightly upturned nose, then her

251

closed lids, and then her soft, giving lips.

His first tender kiss woke Lisa, but keeping her eyes closed, she enjoyed his attentions until his lips touched her own. Then the power they exerted made her respond. Bringing her sleek arms up she wrapped them about his neck, bringing him ever closer to her.

"I thought you were sleeping, my flower," he murmured gently against her cheek.

His only answer was a smile as Lisa pulled him back to her mouth.

Now that they had shared the joys of their bodies it was only natural that they should once again delve into that most special portion of their love. They gave and took, each caressing the other with tenderness and adoration, their innermost feelings surfacing and being shared.

Silver Fox's whispered words of love, mingled with tender touches and caresses, had Lisa's senses reeling and left her completely at his mercy.

He brought the two of them to the peak of pleasure and then to a shattering climax. On its crest they rode their passion to the end, rejoicing in their union.

Then he looked down into her face and the sheer heat of his gaze left Lisa feeling helpless and breathless.

Never had Silver Fox been so enraptured with a woman and bringing his large hand up he traced the softness of her lips. "You have found a place within my heart that no other has ever touched."

Lisa felt her own heart skip a beat at his confession. But seeing the seriousness of his mood, she lightly quipped, "Surely such a brave, handsome warrior as yourself has had any number of women running after you?" She smiled up into his dark handsome face and waited for him to respond.

"I speak the truth, Lisa." His look was serious as he gazed down upon her. "I have never before thought of any other woman as I do of you. There is a love burning within me that craves you night and day when you are not with me. I am powerless to still my thoughts of you. You are my all, you are my heart, my sun, my moon. Truly you are my very breath."

"Oh, Silver Fox, within me are these same feelings," she cried clinging to him with all of her strength. "But I am so afraid now that I have tasted of this most splendid joy something will happen to destroy it."

He drew her from his chest and looked into her moist, blue eyes. "What could ever destroy this love that burns so strongly within us?"

"I do not know, I only feel . . . Oh, hold me, Silver Fox." She wept openly, overcome by fear of some danger ahead.

Silver Fox's strong arms held her tightly against him, one hand stroking her golden curls lovingly. "I would protect you with my very life. You know this?" Again he held her from him so that he could see her face, and at the slow nodding of her head, he sighed. "My strength is great. That is why I am called the Fox. Not many have ever been able to best me either in body or mind. You are my life and I shall protect you as though you are a part of my own body. So still your fear. It does not belong in my home." He brushed away the tears that were making a path down Lisa's chin.

She tried to quiet her weeping, embarrassed by it. Why was she suddenly possessed by this feeling of doom? she wondered fleetingly. Then knowing that she was only upsetting the man she loved, she tried to smile, a soft sob escaping at the attempt. "I am sorry. I did not mean to upset you, Silver Fox."

"You have nothing to be sorry for, little one. You must always tell me about your feelings so that we can share them. I want all of you, not just a small portion."

How could any man be this wonderful? Lisa asked herself as she kissed him. Never had anyone behaved so gently and lovingly toward her.

Silver Fox rose from the warmth of the furs and, stretching his arms up and over his head, he smiled down at Lisa. He loved the sight of her snuggled warm and delicate upon his pallet. "The weather is getting cooler. Stay put until I get the fire going." The look that he sent over her form left her warmer than any fire ever could.

It only took Silver Fox a few moments to stoke the coals in the small pit that held the fire for his tepee. By adding more wood upon the licking flames he soon had warmth encircling the room and was once more squatting down at Lisa's side.

Bending down, he touched her lips with a lingering, slow kiss of love, and Lisa, with a single motion, turned into his sturdy arms. "I fear your intentions are to stay hidden in this cozy lair forever." He chuckled as he pulled his lips free.

Lisa's cheeks flooded with color at his light banter. "Is it your wish that I should go about with nothing more than my thin nightgown for clothing?" She had to remind him that he had taken her from her husband's home with only her nightgown upon her body.

Silver Fox was in no way put off by her reference to what had happened last night. Instead, pulling the covers from her form with a greedy leer, he grinned. "Ah, what a pleasant thought you do put in my mind." He stroked her upper arm. "But I am afraid that the sight of you walking about my village with only this sheer material for covering might cause some problems. I think my Indian brothers would be hard pressed to contain themselves at the sight of your beauty. I might be able to fend for you for a short time, but something tells me that it would not be for long and you would be taken from me."

Lisa also smiled at his playfulness. "I have full confidence in you, sir. If you wish I shall rise." She moved to pull back the warm furs.

"Do not tempt me, little one. I would love

nothing more than for you to wear only what you now have on. But then I would also have to keep you here within my tepee so that no other eyes might see what pleases me so." Laughing he stood to his full height and went across the small space of the tepee. When he returned to her side, he held a leather bag.

"I have thought of your needs most carefully." He bent and pulled from the satchel a fine embroidered, doeskin Indian dress. As Lisa sat admiring this garment, he also pulled a pair of matching moccasins and a tortoise shell comb from his cache of treasure.

"Oh, how lovely." Lisa's hands went over the soft hide of the garment.

Silver Fox smiled with pleasure, happy that she enjoyed his gifts.

"Oh, thank you so much," she exclaimed as she clutched the dress to her bosom and looked into the Indian's handsome face.

"You are my woman now, and I shall tend to all of your needs." He reached out and stroked the lock that rudely curled away from her golden mane. "I love you, little flower."

Never had Lisa felt so happy. Though the gifts he was giving her were simple, she felt her heart sing in response to this expression of his wish to care for her. Jumping to her feet she did not speak but hurriedly pulled the nightgown from her body and drew the Indian dress over her head, letting it slide smoothly over her naked form.

Silver Fox now sat in the simple tribal position. As his coal black eyes watched the young woman with an admiring stare, his heartbeat accelerated. The carefree abandon with which she enjoyed his gift pleased him.

Straining this way and that, Lisa turned her head trying to see every angle of the dress upon her body. All of her gowns had always left her body completely covered, but this alien garment she now wore rose to mid calf and left her with a feeling of newfound freedom that she relished.

"The moccasins will cover your legs." Silver Fox spoke up, grinning because he understood how she must feel at this moment. White women wore so much clothing under their gowns. Even in the gowns themselves he did not know how they could draw breath. But Indian women wore simple garments and did their work comfortably. Not that he wished his golden flower to do that kind of labor, just the opposite. She had worked hard enough at her aunt's inn. He wished only to pamper her and let her enjoy life.

After Lisa had pulled the moccasins on, she stood, trying to see how she looked in them. Then Silver Fox called her to him. "Come and let me comb out your hair, my flower. The tangles of last night's sleep are still apparent." He spread his legs, waiting for her to come and sit between them.

Complying willingly to his suggestion Lisa did as bid, placing herself between his strong, muscular legs and relaxing back against his chest.

Silver Fox took up the comb and gently stroked the soft, fragrant gold before him. Touching the satiny texture of her hair brought a soft sigh to his lips. "Your beauty confounds my senses, love." He continued combing, but now his mind began to wander to other aspects of her beauty. Her lips came boldly to mind, leaving him desperate for the taste of their sweetness, and not being a man to resist that which was within easy reach, he pulled her around and, lying upon his back, pulled her atop him.

"I thought you were going to comb out my hair?" Lisa lightly submitted to his play, just as willing as he to have done with the comb and to again feel this man's power overcome her.

Her long golden hair formed a silken curtain about them, shutting out the outside world and creating for the two of them a sheltered spot which only they could share.

"Your hair is beautiful, just as you are." Silver Fox whispered in a husky tone before pulling her face to his own and drawing out all that was hers as he spiraled them both to dizzy heights of passion.

With a soft sigh, he pulled his mouth from hers. "If we do not stop now, your dressing shall have been in vain." He smiled, and then with a hearty whack upon her buttocks, he pulled himself and Lisa to their feet. "It is far past the rising of the sun and if we linger much longer here in my tepee someone will be sure to spot my horse and come to find me. Whoever comes would surely be surprised to find a golden beauty in my arms." He laughed good-naturedly as he turned her about and once again ran the comb through her long, silken tresses. This time, though, he did not let his mind wander and he soon finished the pleasant job.

Lisa felt a knot of nervous apprehension forming in her throat. How would his people receive her? she wondered as the time drew near when she would have to step out and meet them. In this man's tepee only she and he existed. She would have to face this village of people foreign to her. Although after the past night in Silver Fox's arms, she knew that she could face anything at his side, she wondered if they would resent her for not being of their race. She was sure that she could bear this, too, but what of Silver Fox? Would she be able to stand the pain of knowing that he was being hurt by her presence at his side? With a long sigh she felt the full weight of what was happening. Here she was in an Indian village, having spent the night in an Indian warrior's arms yet she was another man's wife. If these people were cruel to her, had she the right to expect anything else?

Silver Fox understood the meaning of the sigh that escaped her lips, and pulling her small body tightly into his embrace, he lightly stroked the cheek that lay against his chest. Then, a small smile forming on his lips, he bent his head and kissed the top of her golden curls. "I am strong and can deal with anyone who might try to hinder us, beloved. Nothing shall keep us apart. I have searched a full lifetime for you. Our spirits are joined, and that bond is strong. Nothing will separate us."

"Oh, Silver Fox." Lisa clutched at him, burying her head upon his thick chest. "It is not only for the moment? You will not tire of me and then set me from you?" She finally had spoken aloud the fear that had been tormenting her. "I can bear all things as long as I know that you will be near." She broke down and wept.

Pulling her chin up so that he could look boldly into her blue eyes, Silver Fox stopped her tears with a look. "I am a worthy warrior, one that my people have trusted since my early boyhood, and the reason for this is that I am bound by the words that leave my lips. I do not go back on that which I proclaim. I say I love you and I do. I tell you that our spirits are joined and they are. I promise you that I shall care for you as though you are a part of my own flesh and I shall. You are my golden flower and my heart did not stir until the first time my eyes looked upon you. Do not doubt that which I speak, or you will only be sad for no reason. I shall let nothing stand between us."

Lisa drank in his words, digesting them as if starved for them. No longer was there room for doubt. Silver Fox had set all her fears aside. She knew now that he was truly hers and she had no cause to doubt him. She was totally open to his love and whatever else the future might bring. "Never have I known such love as you speak of," she softly said, her thoughts going over the people she had known in the past—her stepsister and her kin here in America. None had treated her with a fraction of the love that this Indian standing before her now offered.

Silver Fox smiled down upon her. "The passage of time shall only increase the love I hold for you. We shall share the pleasure of many long winters together."

Briefly, the image of Craig Rollins came to Lisa's mind but she was pulled from her thoughts when she looked into the handsome face of Silver Fox.

"Let us go now and I will show you the village. There are those I would have you meet." Silver Fox kissed Lisa briefly upon the forehead before taking her hand and starting toward the flap that barred the outside world from the tepee.

After the dimness of the tepee, the bright sunlight caused Lisa to blink, but as the glare went away, she looked about. She had seen little the night before when she had ridden into the village upon Silver Fox's horse, but now she could see the tranquil activities carried on in the large camp and the other tepees set about at different angles. She turned once more and looked at Silver Fox's tepee. It seemed to be one of the largest in the village, and the drawings and different paintings upon it seemed to signify some degree of power.

Awareness was evident in Silver Fox's black eyes as he watched Lisa's every movement. "My tepee is larger than the others because at one time it belonged to my grandfather Black Hawk." At Lisa's wondering look, he added, "It is not usual that one takes another's lodgings but my grandfather on his deathbed ordered that his lodge was not to be destroyed as is the custom of my people but that it should be handed to me. He felt that I would need the strength that he had acquired over the years, and he thought that if I lived within the boundaries of his home of many years I would feel close to him and be better able to solve any problems that would come before me. Black Hawk had been a mighty chief of my people and he held great wisdom."

Lisa could imagine this tall, bronzed warrior standing next to her as a child sitting at the knee of the older Indian chief. He must have taught many things to his grandson for Silver Fox to be so kind and knowing. "You must have had a wonderful childhood," she said quietly but with a touch of envy, remembering her own with some distaste.

A fleeting cloud darkened Silver Fox's conscience for a second as he looked down at the woman he loved, knowing from all that she had ever told him of her own past that his childhood had not been what she would think it. There had been times as a boy when he had wondered if he would ever again see his beloved Indian village and his great-grandfather. "The past is better left behind. Look to the future." He squeezed Lisa's hand as he started her toward a smaller tepee.

Lisa thought he was trying to soothe her own past hurts, and she smiled at his kindness, following willingly anywhere he led.

"My cousin lives here and his wife Singing Bird will welcome you as my woman." They hesitated briefly outside of the tepee, then a small, dark-skinned woman appeared holding a small infant to her breasts. As she looked at her visitors, she directed a warm, friendly smile at Silver Fox. "It has been many days since last we have seen you, Silver Fox. Would you care to enter my husband's home? Though he is out hunting, I could fix you something to drink or eat?"

Silver Fox grinned at the woman, and reaching out, he lightly patted her babe upon its buttocks. "I came only for you to meet Lisa, Singing Bird." Silver Fox's black eyes went from the Indian woman to the golden beauty at his side.

"I am indeed honored, Silver Fox, that you would bring this lovely woman to me. I am most grateful to meet you, Lisa." She held out a hand and grasped Lisa's tightly within her own. She had seen the look that her husband's cousin had bestowed upon this woman, so she knew that Lisa must possess some special quality. All of the young maidens of the village had tried at one time or another to catch the eye of this most handsome warrior, but none had succeeded in capturing his heart. Yet with a single brief look, Singing Bird knew that this woman had gained all of Silver Fox.

Lisa smiled broadly and, with a sigh of relief at being accepted, replied, "It is also a pleasure to meet you, Singing Bird." Then she added, as a touch of friendliness, "Your baby is lovely."

Singing Bird grinned at the other's words and looked at the small bundle in her arms. This was Light Path's first born. She had given him a son, and proud of this creation of theirs, they were both delighted whenever anyone made mention of the infant. "You must bring Lisa back to visit with me, Silver Fox," she told her husband's cousin as she saw that he wished to be off. "Perhaps, next time Light Path shall be here and the two of you can keep busy while we women talk and become friends."

Both Lisa and Silver Fox smiled with pleasure at this woman's kind words, and promising to do as bid, Silver Fox led Lisa away.

"You shall find many kind friends here in my village, Lisa. But there shall be time enough to meet them all. I wish to show you about, so if you need to get water or wood for our fire you will know where to go."

So far, Lisa was delighted with the Indian village, thinking that everyone would be as kind as Singing Bird. She felt that her life here with

Silver Fox's people would be a pleasant one and that she could put the past from her mind.

But soon she was to witness another side to the dark-skinned people she had so recently met. As they went through the village, more and more people looked in their direction, wondering about the golden beauty who stood so proudly at Silver Fox's side. The Indians were used to white people being captured by raiding parties and used as slaves or sold to other Indian tribes. But hardly ever did they see a sight like the one that greeted them now. The woman walked at the warrior's side, and Silver Fox held her hand. The looks he directed at her were tender and not those of master to slave.

Everyone in the village knew that Silver Fox was different from most of the Indians in the village. But he had shown his strength and daring time and again on raiding parties and had been the favorite of his grandfather Black Hawk. Everyone respected Silver Fox for his strength and knowledge. Yet few knew anything about his personal life which seemed a mystery, for he came and went to and from the village as was his wont. Still, everyone thought of him as one of the tribe, so now most thought it odd that he would so favor a white woman.

Silver Fox felt the eyes watching Lisa and him as they made their way through the village, but he held his form straight knowing that only a fool would dare to question him about his feelings for the white woman at his side.

As the pair neared the edge of the encampment, Lisa saw a stream of sparkling water in the distance. At its edge were several Indian girls filling buckets with water and laughing companionably.

Lisa envied them their freedom and their closeness as she approached and heard their friendly voices shouting to each other. She had missed this as a young girl, never having had anyone that she could truly call her friend.

The laughter and talk quieted as Silver Fox and Lisa came into view along the bank of the stream. "The women get their water here, along this stream where they are close to the village. Usually there is a guard watching over them in case there is someone about who might do them harm."

Lisa could not imagine any harm coming to anyone in this village. Who would dare to broach a warrior like the one who stood at her side?

"The women also gather twigs and small logs for their fires as they walk the paths back and forth from the stream to the village. But you, my flower, shall not labor so. I shall gather our wood and water." He bent and lightly kissed her on the brow, not noticing anyone but this woman who so filled his heart.

The Indian girls, though, were an audience for the caresses he gave to the white woman before them. And with dark looks, they glared in the direction of Silver Fox and the woman at his side.

Almost all of the girls at the stream this morning were unmarried maidens, fetching water and gathering wood for their families' homes. This time of the morning, they usually gathered to talk and laugh as the young are wont to do, so it was with some malice that they watched the pair before them.

"Silver Fox, is this another white slave you have brought to our village for our braves to fight over, or is she to be sold as most of the others?" a brave-hearted maiden spoke out, not being able to endure the sight of this man for whom she had harbored tender thoughts standing before her and kissing another. "Why do you dress her in the clothes of our people when she will only too soon have them stripped from her back?" Morning Lily shouted, provoking giggles in those about her.

Silver Fox's features clouded with anger at the girl's words. He felt Lisa drawing back at this abuse. "Your bitterness bites needlessly, Morning Lily. This woman is no slave unless one would call heart ties enslaving. She is not for any other besides myself and shall not find her clothing taken from her form or another buying her." He wanted to make it clear to these simpering young girls that he would not permit their harsh tongues to again attack his woman. He was aware that Morning Lily and several of the other girls had wished to bind him. But he had promised no one what he had offered freely to Lisa. Though at times he had been tempted by the soft curves of these Indian girls, he had told none of them that he loved her.

Morning Lily was remembering other times, too, and she could still feel Silver Fox's strong hands upon her body, recall the soft caresses that she had known only from Silver Fox. Feeling her face turn bright at his insult, she turned in the direction of the village and fled.

The other girls stood for a second longer, then they, too, gathered their buckets of water and hurried toward the village, their chattering voices following some distance behind them.

Lisa had felt the Indian girls' words as if they had been physical blows, and though she had heard Silver Fox's declaration of protection and love, she still could not help the slow tears that came from not being wanted.

"Ah sweet, sweet love," Silver Fox whispered, pulling her up into his arms, feeling her pain as if it were his own. "I would never have you hurt. Those were only stupid, jealous girls. Pay them no heed. They do not understand what they are about." He softly stroked her golden curls, trying to bring her a measure of comfort.

Lisa could not speak, but she tried to stifle her sobs, knowing that she was bringing discomfort to the man she loved. However, she was not able to put the harsh words of that girl from her mind. She had thought her a slave to be bought and sold. How could she endure staying here in this village when everyone—well not quite everyone,

Singing Bird had seemed genuinely kind—of those girls had looked at her with black hate. Would she be able to overlook those glances if she saw them again? She knew that she could do nothing about them, for to leave here would mean to leave the man who now held her in the protection of his arms and his love. "Hold me tight," she whispered aloud and feeling his arms grow tighter about her, she began to regain some reason.

Reaching down, Silver Fox gathered Lisa into his arms, not caring if there were probing eyes watching his actions or if the two of them were, indeed, alone. "Those girls are nothing to us. Only you and I matter, my flower." He began to walk with her in his arms, taking Lisa to the stream bank and holding her until her sobbing quieted.

Silver Fox wondered if she had fallen asleep, but seeing her blue eyes looking up thoughtfully, he pulled her to his chest and smiled into her beautiful face. "Let us share the rest of the day in this quiet spot." Gently, he stood her on her feet and waited for her to look about at the lovely area to which he had brought her.

Lisa was thrilled by the place, and a quiet peace settled over her as she saw the beauty about her and the love in Silver Fox's eyes. What did anything else matter as long as she was able to see the shining love he had for her? she asked herself. And rising on tiptoe, she planted a kiss upon his chin.

Grabbing her up, Silver Fox swung her about in a small circle, feeling his pulses soar as he saw that her hurt was gone. "Can you swim, golden flower?" he lightly asked as he pulled her tighter into his arms.

"Why, yes," Lisa answered, looking farther about them and seeing that the small stream they had been following ran into a pond at this spot. From the cliffs overhead showers of water cascaded down into the large pond. "I can swim indeed. I learned as a child in England, but I am afraid that I have nothing to wear." She looked down at her buckskin dress and wondered if he had brought some other clothing that she had not seen.

Silver Fox grinned slyly as he, too, looked at the dress adorning her body. "I thought that perhaps we could take a swift dip without the comforts of our clothing," he stated, experiencing no qualms of modesty.

Lisa looked at him as though he had taken leave of his senses. It was easy for him to say this, for he wore only a simple breechcloth which left most of his torso bare. But she was a lady, and ladies did not strip and jump into the water.

Hearty laughter filled the area and settled about the cliffs. "Are you shy then, my flower? I would not have thought so while you were lying upon my pallet."

"That was different." Lisa felt her features flame. "We were alone."

"But we are alone here." Silver Fox reached out and began to unlace the leather string that held the upper portion of her dress together. "No eyes shall ever gaze upon your beauty but my own."

"What if someone were to happen upon us?"

"No one would dare to do this thing. Trust me."

Lisa was lost to the black orbs before her. Letting all self-control go and wishing only to please him, she pulled the gown from her head and next the moccasins, but before he could reach out and pull her into his hungry arms, Lisa turned and dove into the water, coming up sputtering and gasping from its cold depths.

Within seconds Silver Fox had shed his own simple clothing and was diving into the clear water beside her. As he ascended his arms encircled her waist. Grinning, he noticed that her teeth were chattering. "The water is cold, but it will warm your blood."

"Warm my blood." Lisa laughed and, pushing against his chest, set herself free. She swam off in the opposite direction from him.

Silver Fox grinned, and pleased by her play, he let her go some distance from him as he watched her sure strokes and the pleasant picture of her silken curves which every now and then rose above the water.

But when she neared the other side of the pond, he dove into the water and with swift strokes he pulled her by the ankles down to the depths and into his arms.

271

"You thought you could flee from me, but there is no escape." He laughed as they rose to the surface.

"I have no wish to flee you," Lisa whispered, not finding any amusement in his words, but only wishing to let him know how much he meant to her.

"Nor would I let you, my golden flower." He rose to his full height with Lisa's arms still wrapped about his neck and drew her to the water's edge, their bodies molded together and the pond's water still clinging to their forms as he lowered her onto the soft grass and whispered words of love. They touched and caressed until their ravening hunger for each other had to be quenched.

Responding to his gentle hands and to his words of love, Lisa succumbed to the feelings abounding in her. His fingers elicited a rapturous trail of fire, as he caressed her full firm breasts. And when his tongue followed the same path, scorching her flesh with endless kisses, she knew this man was hers, for now and forever. Whether time stood still or was borne on wings, there would be no changing her fate. Her very life and breath depended on this warrior. He alone could seal her fate with a harsh word or a shattering look. Nothing else mattered but the simple words of love that he was now speaking into her ear.

Her senses pulled her deeper and deeper into the realms of feeling that he was awakening in her, and soon she responded hungrily.

Her touch, like molten liquid, seared his flesh, awakening every cell until his entire body was attuned to her wants and desires.

His physical expressions of this awareness brought Lisa to the pinnacle of passion and then drew her into an all-consuming cauldron of desire. A maelstrom of the senses sealed their love. Then, lips meeting and hearts beating wildly, they softly floated back to reality.

Against a background of soft, green grass, their coloring was in vibrant contrast, her skin like a translucent pearl, his like copper. But, hidden from view, their hearts were the same, love flowing from one to the other without restraint.

Lifting a wet, golden strand of hair from her shoulder, Silver Fox kissed its softness. "The great spirit looked with favor upon me when he sent you," he whispered gently.

"My life, until I met you, was merely a bad dream, Silver Fox. I love you." As Lisa spoke she felt the sting of tears come to her eyes.

"And I, golden flower, love you also." He kissed her soft lips. Then pulling himself up, he drew her to the water's edge and dove once again into the cold depths. "Let us swim for a moment before I find us something to eat. The day grows long with nothing to sustain us."

Lisa realized that she had not even thought of food until now, having had an appetite only for love. But as she entered the water a more ordinary hunger overtook her.

Late in the afternoon the Indian warrior and his golden woman again made their way through the Indian village, this time, though, their passage was marked with only slight glances that were followed by hurried looks in the opposite direction. The Indian girls who had been at the water's edge that morning had hurried back to the village and had spread the word that Silver Fox considered the white woman his own. And though some thought this foolish, none dared to speak of that.

As Lisa and Silver Fox approached his tepee, a small group of warriors returning from a hunting trip saw Silver Fox and pulled abreast of him and the woman at his side.

"Well, my cousin, I see that you are once more with us and I see that you have brought something with you." The man's black eyes went to Lisa, but kept hidden any true feelings he might harbor toward her.

"It is good to see you, Light Path. I went this morning to your home, but Singing Bird told me that you were off hunting. I hope the trip was worthy of your efforts?" Silver Fox talked lightly with this dark Indian who was a cousin from his great-great-grandmother's bloodline.

A large grin split Light Path's features when he remembered the huge deer that he had shot that afternoon, and he forgot about the woman that stood to Silver Fox's side. "Small Sparrow, bring up the horses so that my cousin can see the fine kill we have made this day," he shouted to one of the riders behind him. These men had been listening with some curiosity to the words of the two warriors, but now their glances were lustful, looking to the white woman at Silver Fox's side.

A tall, overly thin Indian brought up the packhorse bearing the deer. As he came closer to the small group his eyes were drawn again to the woman. She was even lovelier up close, he thought.

While the cousins talked about the fine kill, Small Sparrow silently calculated the worth of the woman who stood silently by. She was lovelier than any white woman he had ever seen, and he knew that he would give everything he now possessed to gain her. She would bring him great pleasure for a time and when he tired of her he could sell her for an even larger price to another tribe who had not grown accustomed to her beauty. The problem was, how much must he offer for her. If Silver Fox wanted her as his slave he would demand quite a bit. But in the past he had never known Silver Fox to own a white slave, so he thought perhaps he had a chance. At least he could ask what it would take to gain her, and if he did not now have what was needed, perhaps he could acquire it. "I do not wish to disturb the two of you, Silver Fox, but I wonder about the woman at your side?" Small Sparrow ventured.

Silver Fox's dark head turned in the direction of Small Sparrow, his black eyes easily reading the other man's thoughts.

Not receiving an answer to his question Small Sparrow added, "She is a white woman of little worth, but I would give you five of my best ponies for her. I could make a good profit and you will be much richer."

For a moment Silver Fox had to restrain the urge to drag Small Sparrow from his horse and thrash him for what he had dared to say. But remembering the customs of these people, his mind cleared somewhat. "The woman is mine and she is not for sale."

"If it is a higher price that you wish—perhaps I was a bit low—surely you will tell me what it is that you would take for her?" Small Sparrow looked again at the golden woman, knowing that he had to possess her, but he did not see the anger that flashed upon Silver Fox's features as Lisa, feeling the greedy eyes of the brave upon her, stepped behind Silver Fox.

Reaching out, Silver Fox took hold of Lisa's hand, wishing to give her some small comfort. "I have told you once, Small Sparrow, this woman is mine. No price can take her from my side."

Light Path saw the anger contorting his cousin's features. Realizing the other man was thinking only of possessing the woman at Silver

Fox's side, he placed his hand upon Small Sparrow's arm. "My cousin wishes to keep this woman, for the time, to himself. Leave it at that."

As Small Sparrow was about to speak, something in the way Light Path looked at him warned him that he was in danger. Looking directly into the eyes of Silver Fox, he saw where the danger lay. Silver Fox was well known in this village and in all the Indian villages nearby for his strength and daring and here he was, Small Sparrow, who was a worthy warrior but not one to stand up to Silver Fox, becoming the object of his wrath. "I will take the deer to your tepee," he said hurriedly and kicking his horse's sides, led him away from Silver Fox and the woman at his side. No woman was worth his life, he told himself as he realized that this would be exactly what he would have paid if he had persisted in his wish to buy Silver Fox's slave. Perhaps at another time he would have his chance.

"You and your woman are welcome to come to my lodge and take the evening meal with Singing Bird and myself." Light Path turned to Silver Fox, acting as though the incident with Small Sparrow had never taken place. He had seen the deadly glare in his cousin's eyes when the other brave had expressed his interest in the girl. He had known this man, his cousin, since early childhood and in all of this time he had never known Silver Fox to reveal such feeling in front of others as he had only a few moments ago—and for a mere white girl. He knew that his cousin was different from the other Indians in the village, and he even knew some of what Silver Fox did with his days. One day he had followed closely behind as Silver Fox had left the village and he had discovered where he had gone. However, he would guard that secret with his life, knowing that the blood that ran through Silver Fox's veins was the same as that which ran through his own.

He had always thought Silver Fox would have made a good chief for their village, but he had also known that this was impossible. For in his cousin's veins white blood ran with that of his own people. Light Path could not remember ever feeling anything but love and respect for his cousin. He had grown up with Silver Fox who had spent his summers in this village, and the old chief, Black Hawk, had always been near at hand to instruct the young child. Perhaps this was the reason Light Path had always accepted him. But now having seen him show weakness where a white woman was concerned, Light Path was relieved that this man had not become their chief. Their tribe needed a man who was all Indian and who would not bend toward any white. Though he loved his cousin well, he knew that he was but a man and part of his blood was mixed with that of the enemy.

Silver Fox read some of the thoughts going through Light Path's head, but he was aware that his cousin and all the braves in his village knew him well and would not question what he wished. "Lisa and I are tired this evening. Perhaps another time we shall share a meal with you."

Light Path smiled at the other as though in agreement, he knew well the ways of those in love. "My wife will be glad that you have found yourself a woman to care for you, my cousin. She has long fretted that you would never find yourself one." He chuckled fondly remembering the times that his Singing Bird had had him invite his cousin to their tepee while she had a young girl there.

"Your wife is kind in her concern for my welfare." Silver Fox also grinned. He had been aware of Singing Bird's fondness for matchmaking. "Tell her I hope that she and Lisa will be friends."

"I am sure that they will be, my cousin." Light Path turned and jumped to the back of his horse. "Perhaps tomorrow when you are well rested we may talk longer." Giving a slap to his horse's flank, he started off toward his own tepee.

Lisa did not say anything as Silver Fox pulled the flap aside and allowed her to enter his home. Again she had been made aware of the ambivalence of her position in this Indian village, but Silver Fox had been protective. Still she knew the other Indian had offered to buy her and she had seen on his face the realization that he had angered Silver Fox. She wondered what would happen if everyone in his village turned on Silver

Fox. Then, crossing the tepee, she sat down upon the pallet that she had shared only the night before with this man.

Silver Fox did not speak either but went to the fire and stoked up the coals to arouse them to flames and drive the chill from the large room.

Rising, he saw Lisa upon the pallet and thought how beautiful she looked sitting atop the lush, multicolored furs, her golden hair cascading about her in disarray and her features so thoughtful. He knew that she was upset by the day's turn of events. He wished again that he could strangle Small Sparrow. He could well imagine her frightened thoughts at being considered an object which could be purchased. But she also must know, he thought, that he would never let anything happen to her. No man could ever take her from him.

"I will go and get some water and then make us a stew," he said, rising to his full height and looking toward Lisa. Perhaps she was in need of some time to herself, he thought.

Lisa did not speak. She merely nodded her head and watched his large frame leave the confines of the single large room. She sat for a few moments until a cold chill seemed to overtake her. Then wrapping her arms about herself, she made her way closer to the fire. The room seemed so empty without Silver Fox's sturdy frame in it. For a second she thought of leaving his tepee and running down to the stream just to get a glimpse of him and to assure herself that she was not alone and that he was real. She had a strong need to belong, to have someone to care for. Silver Fox was fulfilling this need.

A small smile came over her features at this realization. And as she watched the shifting, dancing flames before her, she realized that he felt the same as she. Out of the millions of people upon the face of the earth, they had found each other and nothing could ever separate them. She had left her people and her husband for this man, and she knew now that his own people would not stand between them. Silver Fox was too strong and would never let this happen.

She looked up as Silver Fox came through the flap. Seeing the smile upon the face of the woman he loved his heart began to take flight. He had been right to give her time alone. Nothing he could have said would have brought this happiness to her. She had to find in herself the trust she needed to feel for him.

"I have brought the water," he said and went to the fire.

Lisa looked up with love-filled eyes. "I shall help you with dinner. Though I know little about cooking I am willing to learn."

"No, my little golden flower. You sit there and watch. There is time enough for you to do this job. I have long been alone and am used to cooking for myself. Though I have never had the enjoyment of watching a beautiful woman as I prepared my meal." He bent down and, setting the water off to the side, lightly kissed Lisa's parted lips. "I think I shall enjoy preparing this meal." He grinned and then went to fetch his cooking pots and food stuffs.

Lisa watched his back as he turned from her, her eyes going over his large but trim form with delicate care. He was all that a woman could ever ask for in a man, his features most pleasant to look upon and his ways tender and caring. She had known little love in her past, and now her heart nearly burst at the full realization of what she felt.

"It will only take a short time for the stew." Silver Fox placed a pot upon the fire. "Let us relax upon my pallet until it is ready." He held a hand out toward her to help her to her feet, and as she rose he swooped her into his arms and carried her the short distance to his bed of furs.

"What is it that you do to occupy yourself when you are alone here?" Lisa asked aloud as he set her down upon the pelts.

Silver Fox smiled at her curiosity. "Usually I am not here alone." At the widening of her gaze he laughed aloud, and falling down next to her, he added, "Most of the time I am gone with a group of other braves, either hunting meat or seeing what the whites are about." His large fingers lightly played with a lock of her hair which had turned about his arm.

"Oh," Lisa responded, feeling her face flush.

Her thoughts had flown to other woman and for the first time she had felt a taste of jealousy.

"Does it bother you that the whites are my enemies?" He rose upon his elbow and looked down into her face.

Shaking her head Lisa truthfully replied, "I care not who are your enemies as long as you love me."

Silver Fox bent and kissed the soft lips before him. Then pulling free, he added, "There may come a day that I shall have to fight your people, even your kin."

An image of Willie and Adell Simmons came to her mind, but pushing it from her, Lisa softly said, "You are my kin. The only concern I have is for you. I would not wish to live if you were to be killed or taken from me." Again she was reminded of the bounty that the people of her own race had offered for this man she loved. Trembling slightly, she clutched him to her side, wishing that she could keep him next to her forever and let no harm touch him.

"Ah, lovely one, nothing shall happen to me as long as I know you are mine. No force could keep me from you." He held her tightly against his chest, wishing to bestow some of his strength on her.

"I have but one regret," Lisa softly said after a few moments.

"And what is that, love?"

"That I have deceived Craig Rollins. He was

the only person who wished to aid me in my time of need." She pictured the older man. All day she had not even thought of him—the man with whom she had stood before a preacher to take vows of devotion and honor. She wished to erase the memory of her wedding to that kind man and her subsequent departure from his house with another man.

A light smile lingered upon Silver Fox's lips. "Do not let it distress you, golden flower. I know this Craig Rollins well and he would not wish you to be unhappy. He would want you to find the happiness that you deserve."

"You know him?" Lisa sat up and looked into his darkly handsome face. "But how? He never once mentioned that he knew you." She searched her mind, trying to recall if she had forgotten something Craig Rollins had said to her but she was sure that they had never talked about Silver Fox.

"I know him and well. But for now, let it be enough that I tell you he will be happy for you. In time you shall learn more and understand."

"But what are you—"

Her words were cut short by Silver Fox's lips.

At the feel of those lips Lisa was lost to a dreamy limbo. Forgotten were all other thoughts but those touching her at this moment.

Silver Fox pulled away and stood to his feet. "I had best check the stew. It would seem that we are drawn to things that have little to do with the care of our bellies." He looked down at Lisa. Her lips were still parted and her dark blue eyes still held the expression of one being loved. "Still, I must make sure that you do not take ill. You must eat and stay healthy." He went to the fire, and taking the bowls he had set out, he filled them with the delicious-smelling venison stew.

Lisa rose from the pallet, the aroma that filled the tepee arousing pangs of hunger in her belly. All this pair had had all day to sustain them had been some plump wild berries that Silver Fox had found near the pond's edge. At the time Lisa had been only slightly hungry, so consumed was she by love. Now as she felt the growling of her belly, she knew that she had abused herself long enough.

"Mmm . . . 'tis delicious," she exclaimed at the first bite.

Silver Fox smiled his appreciation of Lisa and of the meal that he was eating. "If you are good, I shall teach you how to cook as well."

Lisa laughed and, between bites, said, "You may keep your secrets to yourself if you so desire. I rather enjoy being waited on hand and foot."

"You are an enticing beauty, golden flower, first you bind me with your love and now you hold me as your slave."

"I am the slave."

Silver Fox immediately looked intently at her.

Upon seeing his look she finished, "I did not mean to imply that I am truly a slave." She thought of Small Sparrow's bid for her but this had not been what she had meant. She had been so busy eating that she had not made herself clear. "I am truly your slave but only in the heart. I wish to please you in all things, and I would do whatever you would wish but not for the reasons of most slaves. I love you." With misted eyes, she looked at him.

A grin appeared on his handsome face. "I like my slaves happy." He leaned over and kissed her moist lips.

After this kiss they hastily finished the meal, and placing the bowls near the pot of stew, once more expressed their newfound love. This time their union was special, as though the shared hurts and cares of this day had brought them closer together, and so with tender ministrations they both endeavored to express their love.

Silver Fox was gentle, desiring only to give and to share. As his hands roamed freely over Lisa's body, his touch set her afire. Igniting her to a fevered pitch, he orchestrated her pulsating movements, luring her to respond to his every touch and movement. Then when Silver Fox felt her inner restraint melt, his own blood raged. This woman in his arms was all his. His very heart and life were entrusted to her keeping.

Their souls joined this night, and their bodies, blending in sweet passion, soared upon the wings of phantomlike silken clouds while their hearts entwined. Each knew and loved the other.

As the fire burned low, the coolness of the night filled the tepee, but the couple upon the pallet did not notice. They were immersed in their love-making, aware only of each other.

Chapter Nine

A tranquil sphere of unreality prevailed in the large tepee of Silver Fox for the next two days. The pair, discovering and enjoying so much about each other, gloried in the delight that they shared. They spent most of their days walking through the forest or swimming in the pond that only they seemed to seek out. Their evenings were spent alone in the shelter of their large tepee, always in each other's arms.

Lisa found that in her short life she had never met a man like the one she loved. He seemed wise beyond his years, knowing just what to say in every instance, instinctively knowing when she was bothered by some worry. Not only did he have a quick mind, his strength and ability pleased her too. She thought him invincible, and with him always at her side was not disturbed by thoughts of him leaving her to fight the whites who hated the might of Silver Fox.

Time flew for the young lovers, one moment hurrying into the next. Nothing mattered to them but the feel of their young bodies, each seeking the other, and the taste of ambrosia which their moist lips imbibed freely.

Thinking herself very fortunate, Lisa smiled. To her it seemed she was the first to have found such a wondrous love, and as she put the tepee into some order after the evening meal, she thought over the past few days. Not once had Silver Fox shown a side of himself that had been displeasing to her. No matter what he was doing his eyes shone with love and desire for her. How lucky she was, she sighed as she put the bowls in their places.

Even at this moment as he was going about the village and talking with some of the other braves, she knew that his mind was really back here in the tepee with her. She felt like singing with joy, so happy was she. As she puttered about putting things away, she came upon the leather bag that Silver Fox had opened that first morning—the one from which he'd brought forth her clothing. Picking this satchel up and placing it neatly to the side, she felt it's full weight, and opening the leather ties, she peered within.

Then reaching her hand into it, she drew forth a book. What would a book be doing in Silver Fox's satchel? she wondered, and turning it over in her hand, she marveled at the leather binding and gold print. It was a book of sonnets, a richly appointed one, and it made her wonder where an Indian would gain such a treasure.

Taking a deep breath and squatting down upon her knees, she slowly opened the front cover. There before her astonished blue eyes was the name she had feared to see. Craig Rollins was scrawled boldly upon the first page. But how had Silver Fox obtained one of her husband's books? She tried to remember the night he'd come for her, yet she could not remember him picking up a book. What was this doing in his possessions? Rising to her feet she went nearer to the fire, trying to arrive at some answers to her questions as she idly thumbed through the pages.

But achieving nothing by this simple act, she stopped and stood, involved with her own thoughts, as the flap of the tepee opened and Silver Fox stepped into his home.

His black eyes saw at once what she had found, and unconcernedly he silently made his way to her side. "What is it that you have, Lisa?" he asked.

With a guilty gasp Lisa swung about, trying to hide the book behind her back.

"Do not be silly, love. What do you have?"

"I did not mean to pry into your things." She fully realized her mistake in not putting the book back in its place. But she had been so shocked to find it that she had not thought of the consequences if she were found with it.

"What is mine is also yours," Silver Fox stated softly at her outburst of apology. "I keep nothing secret from you."

With slow movements Lisa brought forth the book, and looking down at the deep, brown leather of its cover, she felt her face flush with shame. "How is it that you came by this book, Silver Fox?" she ventured, haltingly.

Silver Fox smiled fully into her face, and reaching out, he took the book from her. Opening the cover, he looked down at the name written before him. "I took it from the manor, golden flower," he answered, watching her features as he did.

Lisa did not know what she had expected him to say, but she felt her breath leave her lungs as though she had been holding it for a long time. Of course he had taken it from the manor the night he'd come for her, she had just not seen his actions. She thought again of that night and knew that she would not have noticed if he had carried half of the things in her chamber with him. All that had truly filled her vision was the sight of him.

"I told you that I know Craig Rollins, and I do not think that he will mind my borrowing this book from him," Silver Fox said lightly as he took hold of Lisa's arm. "Come and let us rest upon my pallet. I shall read you a love sonnet." He kissed her lightly upon the shoulder.

"You are able to read?" Lisa asked, surprise written upon her features. She had supposed that he had taken the book because it had attracted him in some manner, she would never have thought that an Indian could read.

Hearty, loud laughter filled the tepee at her words. "My grandfather made sure that I could well accomplish that simple skill." He pulled her toward the pallet and, lying back, pulled her down beside him.

"Perhaps that is why you seem so different from the others of your village," Lisa said, not quite aware that she was speaking aloud.

Again he laughed. "Am I so different, my flower?" At the slight nod of her head, he added, "Perhaps it is because I come from two different worlds and am only happy in the one I have now."

Lisa immediately asked, "From two different worlds? Is that why even your skin is not the same as that of the others in this village?"

He rose up on an elbow, and one fine, dark eyebrow rose too.

"I thought so the first time I saw you, the day you and your group stopped the carriage. You appeared to be lighter than the others, your skin more of a bronze color, as though you had been long in the sun. I was surprised, for I had heard that an Indian's skin was of a darker shade."

"You have found me out then." He looked at her seriously. "I am not a full-blooded Indian. My grandfather was a white man who married an Indian princess and she bore my father." He was quiet for a moment as Lisa digested this knowledge. "I grew up seeing the simple way of life that my Indian brothers had, as well as the cruelty and greed of the other side of my family."

"But how is this?" Lisa could not believe what he was telling her. "Why did your grandfather marry an Indian? And why has no one told me this before?"

"Not many know my story." Lightly he stroked her chin. "You shall learn all in time, golden flower, but for now let us return to our love for each other." Bending over, he took her lips with his own, making her forget everything but the moment at hand.

Then he settled back and opened the book of poems as Lisa sighed.

His strong voice settled about the pair as he read the love sonnets with such understanding that he might easily be their author.

Lisa listened with dreamy thoughts. How like her own feelings were those expressed on these pages.

"My love, my own, when darkness cloaks this land, again, and lovers seek the hands of their beloved . . ." Silver Fox also seemed wrapped up in the words before him as his deep husky voice rolled on.

But when he finished the sonnet, with a sigh of pleasure he set the book from him and turned to the woman upon his bed. Their eyes locked in silent agreement; depths of blue and black saying what their mouths could not. The sonnet expressed their feelings better than their own words which sounded simple by comparison. Although their pulses raced at a mere glance or smile, each felt unable to lay bare what was in his or her soul and to place it before the other, but here in this tepee, upon the fur pallet, the lovers in the night found a way to communicate their deepest feelings. Their glances revealed all. So needing no words, their hands reached out, their lips clung and searched. In their joining they felt complete; in their passion they were as one. For them this was inevitable.

Then in a shattering collision of passion they were triumphantly pulled to the very heights of feeling, from which they slowly descended, their mutual fire of delight dissolving to leave both with a feeling of satisfaction.

To Silver Fox this draught of love was the finest elixir, and with whispered words he told Lisa of his feelings, wishing to bind her to him even more fully. "I love you as though there had never been a yesterday; you have always been within my heart. I recoil and feel tortured at the thought that you would leave my side."

"I love you also and shall forever be next to

you." Lisa kissed his neck and tightly molded her body to his.

"You have been here in my village for some days now, and it is time that we talk of the future."

Cold fear gripped her heart and she shut her eyes tightly, willing him not to say what was in his mind. She held no knowledge of what was to come, but for some unexplainable reason she knew his words would somehow determine her fate. The picture of her older husband came to her mind, but this time it was not so easily put from her. She had committed a terrible sin, and having been raised with the knowledge that one was always punished sooner or later, some inner sense told her that the moment was now at hand.

Not aware of her fear, Silver Fox was in a high mood as he drew her closer in his arms, and turning to look her full in the face, he began to explain what he wished of her. "Your husband shall be returning in only two days from his trip. I want you to go back to the manor and await him."

The blue eyes before him revealed more of her feelings than words ever could. The betrayal she felt was obvious, and as her silent, crystal tears coursed down he realized the full extent of her hurt.

"Trust me, golden flower," he soothed her gently, brushing at her tears, but she could bear no more. With a sob she buried her face upon his chest, and his heart plunged because of his feelings for her. "I will take care of you, but it is time that all comes out into the open. Is it your wish that we hide ourselves away here in this village for the rest of our days? Do you not wish to face this Craig Rollins with our love?"

Lisa could not speak. Instead she shook her head from side to side, her pain too great to bear. She thought she was going to lose this great love that she had found. How could her husband calmly understand what had passed between his wife and her Indian lover? Did Silver Fox think Craig would so easily walk away after speaking the wedding vows with her? She did not want to leave this village. She wanted to spend the rest of her life here in this tepee with the man she loved—but she would do as she was bid, she knew. She was unable to refuse this man. Her need to belong and her need of him were too great. Whatever he would have her do, she would dare. But her pain was unspeakable. She felt as though a piercing blade were finding its way between her ribs and into the spot that most felt for this man. What if she were forced to stay at the manor and was unable to see him again? This fear deep within her, she pulled her head up and looked into the handsome, tender face before her.

"I will do as you wish," she whispered between sobs. "I would rather that we not go to my husband for I fear your loss."

"Ah, my heart." He gently brushed the back of his knuckles against the wetness of her cheek. "I would never let harm befall you nor would I ever let anything part you from me. But I am a man of honor and cannot let this thing lie at rest. You must face your husband and tell him of your love for me." Silver Fox watched her closely as he spoke these words, trying to gauge the depths of her love.

Lisa saw the intent look that he directed toward her, and she knew that she could tell anyone of her love for this man. "I will do this thing, Silver Fox, though I fear that no good will come of it. Still, whatever you wish I shall dare. I know that as long as you will be there with me I have no reason to fear."

Silver Fox looked down into the blue orbs before him, seeing all of her love written plainly in their depths and a great joy bubbled up in his chest. Pulling her tightly to him, he prepared to tell her everything, but before he could speak her lips touched his own and sent such thoughts from his mind. And as her touch ignited him into further action both were drawn into the spell of their lovemaking.

Small Sparrow's dark eyes watched closely as the golden woman made her way down the path that would take her to the water's edge. For days he had been waiting for her to venture from the mighty Silver Fox's tepee by herself, and this morning with the first rays of sunlight she had made her way from her lover's tepee.

The village was just coming to life, a dog barking occasionally and muted sounds coming from tepees indicating that their occupants were just starting to move about. Small Sparrow had awakened much earlier and had been drawn to Silver Fox's tent as he had each morning since first setting eyes on the golden woman who belonged to the other warrior.

He stood behind a tall tree, his thin, dark frame concealed by it, but early as it was, he knew that only a few were about. He wondered if the golden woman was going to gather wood and water. In days past he had seen the brave Silver Fox doing this woman's job, so he thought that she now must have risen early and left her man to rest while she did this task. A large grin came over his intent features. Silver Fox would learn to watch more closely over the treasure he had in his possession.

When, at the water's edge, Lisa bent to dip her bucket into the crystal-clear depths, Small Sparrow with silent, pantherlike steps gained her side, and as Lisa turned on her bent legs she looked up into the grinning features of the Indian who had offered to purchase her from Silver Fox.

Rising slowly to her feet, she looked with fright at the hard features of the man before her. "I have come to get water for Silver Fox's tepee," she said in a choked voice, knowing that her fear was showing. Gazing about, she realized she could not get away from this man although she wanted only to return to Silver Fox. She had awakened early this morning and, on an impulse, had thought to save Silver Fox the duties of gathering wood and water before breakfast. Now she knew that she had made a mistake and she could only hope to be able to handle the situation. "Silver Fox is awaiting me. I must hurry." She bent once again and took hold of the handle of the bucket, taking a step away from the Indian next to her.

In the next instant Lisa felt her breath leave her lungs as the bucket was knocked from her grasp. She was pulled against the man's thin frame, her mouth covered by a large hand and her body pinned tightly to Small Sparrow's.

"You must hurry? To the arms of your lover?" His face was inches from her own and his leer was sly and crafty. "You are a white woman and of little value to the mighty Silver Fox. He will thank me when he finds you missing. Perhaps I shall even give him the ponies that I talked with him about the other day. That day he was too enamored with your golden beauty, but by this time I am sure his passions have waned and he will not mind sharing his good fortune. After all you are only a white woman." His free hand reached up and touched her golden curls with some awe. He had been waiting for this moment for some days now, and the very feel of her in his arms left him weak and light-headed.

Experiencing the frantic fear of one who is captured, with all her strength Lisa tried to break his grasp. The look in his black eyes bespoke his evil intent, and as he touched her hair, she glimpsed the depth of his insanity. She tried to scream, but his hand was held too tightly over her mouth. No sound came, and with a light jerk he pulled her even tighter into his embrace, forcing her to stop struggling.

Looking about with a hurried eye, Small Sparrow pulled Lisa from the water's edge and toward a group of trees where his horse was waiting. With one last look about him he put Lisa atop the beast and, with a swift movement, jumped behind her, kicking the animal's sides and starting through the forest.

Lisa's fear was deeper than any she had ever experienced before or she knew could exist. Her captor's hands were about her and she could feel his excited breath on her cheek as he pushed his mount faster and faster.

Small Sparrow was headed for another village, one where he had traded before and was well liked. He intended to reach it before Silver Fox could find them. He was sure that he would be able to find help in this village once he promised them that they could have the golden woman when he had finished with her. So he pushed his horse harder and harder, knowing that even at this pace it would take a full day to reach his destination. Still, with luck on his side, Silver Fox would not know what had become of the golden woman until it was too late.

*   *   *

Silver Fox awoke. Stretching, he opened his black eyes to see that Lisa was not upon his pallet. Smiling as her vision came to his mind, he pulled himself up on his elbows and looked about the tepee. Seeing her nowhere in view, he noticed that the water bucket was gone too, and with a grin he realized what she was about. Her thoughts were ever to please him and she knew that the gathering of wood and water was a task that she should be doing. Laying his head back down upon the furs he let his mind fill with thoughts of his golden flower. Since she had come into his life he had changed completely. No longer were his thoughts filled with bitterness and hatred of the whites. Now he had no time for such unimportant matters. His thoughts were constantly on ways to please his love.

And loved she was; never had he felt such a sweet piercing pain in his chest at the mere look of a woman. But from the first moment his eyes had rested upon her he had known that she would be his. And for the rest of his days he wished nothing more than to live a life of trying to please her.

He lay there for a while longer, awaiting her return, and then finally, remembering the first day when he had shown her the area where the women gathered and got their water, thoughts of the younger women came to his mind and their angry words again pierced his ears. Rising to his feet, he started from his tepee. He would not allow Lisa to be hurt, and if any were at this moment abusing her in any way, they would have to pay and pay dearly. His stance was angry as he walked through the Indian village, his mind set on protecting his golden flower.

But as he neared the water's edge, his dark eyes scanned the scene and saw only a few of the older women of the village doing their daily work. Suddenly the grip of fear caught Silver Fox and all but brought him to his knees.

Where was Lisa, his mind screamed, as he tried to control his emotions and make sense of the happenings about him. He had not passed her on the path nor had he seen her in the village. He had even passed his cousin's tepee and had heard no noise coming from within, so he knew that she had not gone to Singing Bird's. She had to be here at the water. But even as he thought this, he knew that something was very wrong.

Taking a deep breath of the fresh, cool air he made himself draw nearer to the water, his eyes checking the grass around the area. Off to the side along the creek's edge something caught his attention, and looking down in the tall grass, he saw a water bucket. He knew instantly that this bucket was the one that belonged in his own tepee, and bending down he grasped it in his strong grip while his black eyes roved over the area. He wished his golden flower would step out from the group of trees nearby. He pictured her doing so, an inviting smile on her face as she walked in his direction. But this was not to be.

Silver Fox knew she would not appear, knew with a dreadful certainty that the fates were dealing him a blow that was meant to shatter him.

He felt within his very depths an emptiness that he had never before known, his very being seemed to be screaming out that what he was seeing was devastating. His lips formed the name Lisa, and he felt the burning sting of painful tears. But as the urge to scream came to him, his eyes caught a small glittering object on the ground near the spot where he had picked up the bucket. Stilling all movement and letting his senses respond only to that object, he felt the breath leave his lungs in a loud hiss. Picking up the piece of jewelry, he clenched it tightly in his grip. His black eyes now held the frozen gaze of one looking upon death.

With long strides Silver Fox went to the group of trees near at hand. Then in a moment he was hurrying back to the village.

The never-ending pace kept Lisa in a state of pain and exhaustion, her body abused at each movement of the horse beneath her and her flesh painfully crushed by the arms that tightly bound her.

Small Sparrow had not stopped, not even to eat or drink, but had kept his horse moving ever onward, trying to put as much distance as possible between himself and the Indian village. With each mile that he traveled, he felt safer. He envisioned Silver Fox looking for his woman and not knowing the reason for her disappearance. He felt a tingle of delight over his trickery. He had always felt small compared to the mighty Silver Fox, and he had never, in all of his years, thought that he could better the larger warrior in anything. But now, feeling this soft woman in his arms, he knew that he had bested Silver Fox, and each time that he enjoyed this golden woman, he would be reminded of his great feat.

It was dusk when Small Sparrow pulled his horse to a halt near a small stream of water. "We shall stay here this night," he stated, jumping from his mount's back and pulling Lisa behind him. "I shall start a fire and get some water. Look in that bag on my horse's back and you will find food to prepare." Leaving her no choice but to do as he said, he walked away from her and cleared a small spot in which to start a fire.

Lisa looked about, but with night descending, most of the trees and underbrush lay in darkness. Her thoughts were only of escape. She had to get back to Silver Fox. She had no idea what this Indian intended to do with her, but she knew that his intent was evil and that if she did not get away from him, she would soon be lost.

She stood there a moment, undecided what to do, until she felt Small Sparrow's eyes upon her. Knowing that he was well able to force her to do as he bid, she went to the horse and began to take the leather bag from its back.

Small Sparrow seemed pleased by her actions, and after starting a blazing fire, he started to the stream.

Lisa knew that her chances to escape would be few. So as she watched him walk toward the water's edge, she noiselessly set down the leather pouch and silently but hurriedly left the small campsite, heading in the direction from which they had come.

For a moment she considered going back to get his horse but she thought better of this idea when she remembered that Silver Fox had only to whistle for his large black stallion to come to his side. Perhaps Small Sparrow's own beast was as well trained.

No longer thinking, she increased her pace, each step faster than the next until she was running as fast as she could. She had to get away from this man who held her captive. She had to get back to Silver Fox and reclaim the love they had shared. She continually reminded herself of her need for speed. And as she frantically raced through the dark forest, her thoughts were also occupied with her fear of being recaptured.

By now darkness had set in so Lisa had to slow her pace somewhat as only a small sliver of a moon shown through the dense trees. At any rate, the pain in her lungs and side would not let her run farther.

For a moment Lisa squatted down, trying to gain her bearings and to figure out which way to go. But as she gasped for breath and tried to still her racing pulses, she heard a noise, and before she could jump to her feet and try to get away an arm reached out and grabbed her forearm.

"So you thought to escape me did you?" Small Sparrow's voice was soft and low, but at this moment the moonlight revealed his features and Lisa gasped aloud as she saw the ugly look he directed toward her. "There are ways to control slaves that do not wish to obey." He jerked her tightly against his chest, his large hand digging deeply into the tender flesh of her arm.

Lisa cried out at the pain. "Let me go. When Silver Fox finds you he will make you pay for so treating me."

Harsh laughter was her only answer as the tall, thin Indian began to pull her behind him, back toward his camp. "You are wrong, golden woman," he finally said. "Silver Fox will not waste his time trying to find you. He has never cared for any woman and I am sure that he has had his fill of you."

Hot tears ran down Lisa's cheeks, but despite her fear of what he might do to her, his words provoked an angry response. "Silver Fox loves me and he will come for me."

Again laughter filled the forest. "I have known the Fox for years; he will not waste his time. But if there is some truth in your words, white woman, think on this matter: how will Silver Fox know of your whereabouts? Can he know the direction that I have taken or even that I took you?"

Lisa realized that what he said was true. Silver Fox had been asleep on his pallet when she had left. By the time he awakened to find her gone, how could he know in which direction to look for her? Again tears flowed from her eyes. It would seem that her life was destined to be of pain and suffering. First she had been cast from her home and sent to kin who abused her, then she had been married off to an old man, and finally when she'd thought all would be right because she had found the love for whom her heart had yearned, she was torn from that love to be the captive of a man who cared only for himself.

When they reached the camp, Small Sparrow shoved Lisa down beside the fire. "Do not move or I shall tie you to that tree." He nodded his head toward a nearby oak. "I shall fix something to eat this night. But do not think there shall be many nights such as these. You are only a woman and a white one at that." He spit a long line of saliva into the blazing flames as though disgusted by this subject.

Lisa, seeing the angry look in the eyes that blazed across the fire at her, scarcely dared breathe, lest he vent more of his hostility on her. She still felt pain in her arm from his rough handling. She had never been physically abused and the thoughts that were now going through her mind made her cringe with terror.

The aroma of the simple fare that Small

Sparrow prepared struck Lisa's nostrils with the force of a bolt of lightning. Her stomach growled and her mouth watered in anticipation of food. It had been a full day since she had eaten, and though she fought the temptation to accept anything that this vile man would give her, she also realized that she must keep her strength up. So when Small Sparrow held out her portion of the food she reached out hurriedly and took the bowl.

Small Sparrow smiled thinly at her reaction to the food. This woman would be easy to bring to heel. In a small amount of time he would have her begging him for favors. "Hurry with your meal. We must get some rest, for we ride again early in the morning."

Lisa looked sharply at this Indian, sensing that he was thinking of the night that lay ahead of them. Swallowing hard, she set the bowl down upon the ground, losing all appetite at the thought of what must be going through Small Sparrow's mind.

Silver Fox, she silently cried. How was she to endure the torture that lay ahead of her? How could she prevent this repulsive man from coming near her and using her body as if she were a thing. She thought of what she and Silver Fox had shared during their nights of love and she shuddered uncontrollably.

Searching, ebony eyes watched the small fire and the occupants of the makeshift camp.

Thoughtfully, they took in every movement of the pair, the stance of the intruder one of alertness, like that of an animal ready to spring. Hot anger rose from the depths of his belly as Small Sparrow's words carried easily over the night air and reached his ears.

"Are you so quickly finished with your meal and so willing to come to my pallet?" Small Sparrow spoke slyly when he saw the golden woman put her bow down. "I can understand why Silver Fox was so anxious to keep you and not to share you now. It is a pleasure to find a woman, even if she is white, who so willingly wishes to please a man."

Lisa could not believe her ears. With mouth agape, she rose to her feet, finally able to speak out her indignation at such an insult. "How dare you mention Silver Fox's name? You are not fit to speak of him. If you think that I shall easily give myself to you, you are mistaken. I love Silver Fox, and he loves me. Our love is strong and has a purpose. But you are lower than an animal. I would rather be dead than let you lay a hand upon me."

Small Sparrow also had risen to his feet, and watching her rage, he felt a tightening in his depths. Indeed, she was a rare woman, her beauty unsurpassed by any he had ever seen before. But her temper would have to be tamed. He was a warrior and would not stand for any woman to talk to him in this manner. He had taught other women how to behave and he would again. This time, though, perhaps he would find even more enjoyment in doing so than in days past. He could barely wait to have this golden woman in his arms.

"You shall not speak of Silver Fox again to me." His tone was harsh and commanding.

Hearing the harshness in his voice, Lisa thought only of fleeing, getting as far away from him as she could, but after she'd taken only a few steps, Small Sparrow imprisoned her in his arms.

Bracing herself, Lisa decided she would fight as hard as she could and would not give him any satisfaction. She would give nothing freely. So reaching up, she raked her nails across his face, leaving deep bloody lines upon his cheeks and a look of fierce hatred on his features.

Lisa knew that she would not get away with what she had done, so knowing that she was lost, before he could react she kicked out, trying to hurt him in any way she could. Again she brought her arms up and struck out at him.

This was too much for the Indian warrior. He had fought men and killed them, so when this woman hit out at him, a searing anger consumed his body. Screaming like an animal in torment, he raised his fist and then drove down upon the golden head below him.

Lisa reeled, and her thoughts going blank as a dark cloud descended upon her, she crumpled into a heap at Small Sparrow's feet.

Silver Fox had started toward the couple when he had first seen Small Sparrow take hold of Lisa, but everything had happened so quickly that Small Sparrow had swung at Lisa before he could reach him. With a roar, he leaped at the other brave's throat, thinking only of snuffing out the life of this man who had dared to lay hold of the woman he loved.

Eyes bulging with fear, Small Sparrow was thrown off his feet. He landed upon the ground near where the woman lay, and immediately his breath was cut off by Silver Fox's hands. His own hands reached up to break the hold upon his throat but all was to no avail. He could not free himself from Silver Fox's strangle hold.

"You dared to take my woman? To take her from the protection of our village, to lay in wait for her like a common thief and to take hold of her and steal her from my arms?" Silver Fox's words barely made any sense to Small Sparrow who now felt his life's breath slipping from him.

"You shall not again have the chance to commit such an act. Our fathers cry out from their place of rest for me to have done with the life of such a one as you." Silver Fox applied more pressure to the throat under his hands.

But just then, in the deepest recesses of his mind, Silver Fox became aware of the faint whimper of the woman beside him. Without a second thought he jumped from his position over

312

the prone Indian and went to Lisa's side, gathering her up tenderly into his arms.

"Ah, my golden flower," he said soothingly, his large hands, which could so quickly kill, now gently stroking her bruised cheek.

Lisa still felt dazed by the brutal blow that had felled her, but her senses responded to the tender words he spoke. Forcing her blue eyes open, she saw the man she had been calling for. "Silver Fox." She wept, tears of relief and thankfulness.

Her tears more than anything else touched off a quick response in Silver Fox, and with a light brush of his knuckles, he wiped them from her cheeks. "You are safe now, my love. No more harm shall touch you. Rest easy in my arms and let me care for you."

His words of tender consolation brought instant relief to Lisa who gave a soft sigh and shut her eyes as she lay her head against his chest.

Going to the stream nearby, Silver Fox filled his cupped hands with water and then tenderly moistened Lisa's bruised cheek, his anger once again overcoming him as he pictured Small Sparrow striking this woman who was so precious to him.

Looking back to the spot where he had left Small Sparrow, he noticed that the brave was gone. For a moment his thoughts shouted out for revenge, but he knew that he could not leave Lisa to search for the other Indian. So, after a few moments his thoughts cooled, for he knew that

Small Sparrow would never harm him or his again. The other brave would more than likely never show his face back in Silver Fox's village, the act of stealing another's woman being considered one so low that none of the other Indians would wish him about if they knew.

Again he directed his full attention toward the woman in his arms and, with a gentle movement, kissed her forehead, his senses aroused by the feel of her once again in his arms. Taking a deep breath, he reassured himself that he did have her once again. She was all that mattered to him. As he had ridden through the forest trying to catch up with Small Sparrow, he had gone over all the feelings that he harbored for her. She was his life, for on this day he had discovered that he had no desire to live without her. He had felt empty, unable to bear knowing that she had been taken from him, and so he had determined that he would move heaven and earth to have her back at his side.

Now rising and going back to the fire, Silver Fox whistled loudly. Within a few seconds his stallion was stomping his front feet impatiently before Silver Fox. Silver Fox climbed onto his horse's back and lifted Lisa up before him.

Lisa was soon lost to the throes of deep slumber, her mind wishing only to bury itself in the dark safety that only sleep could bring.

Silver Fox knew that he could not ride throughout the rest of the night, but he wished to put some distance between him and Small Sparrow's camp. He doubted that the brave would come back to brave his anger, but he wished to take no chances since Lisa was in his care.

It was not long before Silver Fox pulled his horse to a stop. Dismounting with Lisa in his arms, he pulled a pack from the back of the stallion, headed toward a large oak tree, and gently set Lisa down.

Lisa had awakened as the horse had been pulled to a halt but she had stayed still, loving the feel of Silver Fox's arms about her. When she had first opened her eyes, she had not known where she was, but his tender movements had quickly told her that she was in the arms of the man she loved, that this past day was over, and that nothing could hurt her now.

"Sit here for just a moment." Silver Fox kissed her lightly upon the lips. Then he took the pack and, pulling out the contents, made a fur bed for himself and the woman he loved.

"Come, golden flower. Let us find some rest and let me hold you in my arms." His words were so soft and full of meaning that Lisa felt her heart skip a beat.

At the small nod of her head, he reached down to scoop her back up into his arms and then started to the fur bed. "I thought that my very heart would stop its beating when I found you gone this morning." He spoke softly as he set her down and pulled the furs up about her chin. "I did not want to think of living with you away from me."

When Lisa looked up, in the moonlight she could see the tiny, sparkling tears that were lingering in his dark eyes. Reaching up, she lightly caressed his strong, handsome face. "I wish never to be away from you again. I would rather be killed than be separated from you."

Her words about death cut into Silver Fox sharply. With a small moan he took her gently in his arms, their lips meeting and drinking in the nectar that would reassure them they were, indeed, together again.

"How could I ever go on in this life without you?" Silver Fox whispered close to her lips.

Lisa could not speak, so captivated by the touch and closeness of this man was she. She had thought that she would never again feel his strong arms about her. "I love you, Silver Fox. I love you." She wept.

Their lovemaking, there in the starless night, was filled with tender consideration. Knowledge of their near loss brought a new depth to their passion.

With each touch Silver Fox strove to create a golden web of love where only the two of them existed. He wanted to shut out the outside world, to make her forget the hurts inflicted there. His tender love words fell lightly upon her ears, enhancing the sensual bliss of his caresses.

They were driven by a need to erase all that happened on this day, to know only the touch, feel, and scent of each other. Their movements were slow and lingering, leaving nothing to be desired but enjoying each other fully and melting away any lingering resistance.

As they lay in the folds of their soft fur bed, a cocoon of sheer love, their passion drew them on into flaming abandon and then slowly drew them into an upward spiral of utter pleasure.

Silver Fox was the first to speak. Over and over again he whispered softly into the golden curls about his face, "Lisa, Lisa." Then feeling his strong love for this woman, Silver Fox held her tightly against him, vowing silently never to let harm befall her, never to let anything separate them again. "You are my heart, my golden flower. My life would be lost and bare if you were not within my arms to share with me my simplest joys. I shudder to think of another taking you from my side, and I vow it shall never happen again."

Looking down into her eyes, he saw her glistening tears, and reaching out, he wiped them away, smiling tenderly meanwhile. Then he kissed her petal-soft lips. "You are my all."

Chapter Ten

The next few days seemed to fly by. Lisa wished to draw out each moment, not wanting Silver Fox to leave her side or to stray from her sight. They had returned to Silver Fox's village the next morning. Still feeling the sweet aftermath of the night's loving, neither was willing to destroy the mood with talk of Small Sparrow, so they banished thoughts of the day before from their minds.

Silver Fox, though, was still determined, as he told Lisa on the ride home, to venture to her husband's manor so that they might set aside the past and be reassured about their future.

Knowing they would soon take this step, Lisa

was worried about leaving this safe village to confront her husband with her foul deceit. She knew that Silver Fox would be at her side, but each time she pictured her husband, her heart was torn by the memory of his kindness in her time of need.

Would this man who had so kindly taken her into his life become angry and try to hurt Silver Fox or even herself? Or would her lover out of the need to protect himself or her do some harm to the older man? she wondered. Craig Rollins had always been kind to her, but could any man easily swallow the thought that his bride, upon their wedding night, had fled his home for the arms of her lover? And what of the fact that the man she loved was an Indian—Silver Fox, the most dreaded Indian in Missouri? Would Craig Rollins turn a blind eye upon this and let her leave with her love, or would he try to keep her? Would he perhaps hurt Silver Fox?

Why Silver Fox would not consider this matter further was a mystery to her. But since the night when he had first brought the subject up, he had not said another word about it until this morning. When she had tried to change his mind by telling him of her fears for him, he had brushed her with his lips. Then he had said that they would no longer talk on the subject. He had made up his mind that they would see this thing through.

Now Lisa wanted to weep but she restrained herself, not wishing to waste the small amount of time they had before leaving the village. Instead she wrapped her arms tightly about his form and tried to put fearful thoughts from her mind.

But that was hard to do. The uncertainty of her future disturbed her. What would happen when they left this Indian village? It had been a nightmare when she had been taken away from her love by Small Sparrow. Would it be any different if she were taken away from Silver Fox by the man who had the legal right to call her wife?

The evening before they were to leave for the manor house she tried once more to change his mind. After they had eaten a hearty meal, she had cleaned the bowls and put them away, then she had gone to Silver Fox as he lay relaxing upon his pallet.

"Would you like me to read to you from the book of sonnets?" she asked softly, standing over him and ready to obtain the book if he so wished.

Silver Fox looked up and again was struck by the beauty that this woman possessed. How lucky he was that she was his, he told himself now as he had with each passing day. He wished to spend his life—indeed, eternity—with this woman. She was his golden flower. Shaking himself, he sat up. Then, with a tender smile, he replied to her question. "I wish nothing more than to hear your soft, singing voice filling my ears with the tender love words upon those pages." Having said this, he watched her turn and get the book.

She was so small and perfect, he thought, watching the swing to her hips as she walked away from him. She was all that any man could ever desire, and his heart sung with the knowledge that tomorrow, though she might be angry at first, she would find that nothing would ever separate them.

Book in hand, Lisa stretched out beside Silver Fox, and opening the binding to her favorite page, she began to read to her lover.

When she had finished the sonnet, she knew his own heart must be open to the full knowledge of thier love as hers was. She slowly turned toward him, and as she looked into his handsome face she softly spoke from her heart. "Can we not stay here in your village? I have never known such happiness as I have come to find in these days we have shared. My love for you is so real; why must we take a chance that something foul might touch it? I would do all that you would ask of me. I would clean your tepee and cook your meals. I would stay in your home while you went with the other braves hunting or scouting. If you fear for me I would give you no reason. Please Silver Fox let us not go to my husband's home tomorrow. Let us forget that either of us ever knew Craig Rollins." At last tears formed and she could go no further.

"Why is it that you torture yourself so, golden flower?" He pulled her chin up so that she was forced to look him directly in the eyes. "Do you not know that all will be set aright by the finish of tomorrow? I want nothing to stand between us so there is a need that this thing be done." Tenderly he kissed her upon the forehead, knowing the fear that was in her heart. "You must bear with me, for I love you. Nothing has ever touched me as deeply as this love. You have entered my soul and nothing can cast you from me. Have I not proven this to you? I would be like a man dying in the desert who craves just a drop of water if you were taken from me. Do you think that I would chance such a fate as this?" His touching question demanded an answer, so she shook her golden head. He sighed and continued.

"Our life should have no shadows in it and after tomorrow all will be set right."

How silly she was being, Lisa told herself. Of course, Silver Fox would stand at her side and face her husband with her. He would never leave her to her own fate. Still, in the deep recesses of her mind she experienced a warning of danger, but pushing it from her she pulled the dark, strong form closer to her own. Her lips revealed her trust more than any words could as in the magic of the moment she molded her body to his, her heart beating urgently against his own, her hands reaching out for his strong lean fingers.

There was a fiery urgency to their lovemaking this evening. It was as though neither could delve deeply enough into the other. Their kisses explored and plundered. Their entire bodies were attuned and receptive, as though this were a special moment they had awaited. No soft words of love and devotion were whispered. Their feelings were too strong for this added inducement of love. Everything they felt was expressed through their bodies.

Aroused by Lisa's passion and his own, Silver Fox slowly began to bring them to a fiery climax. They strove only for what lay ahead, fulfillment, completion. Slowly they climbed toward it until they were overwhelmed by desire and lost to all but the overpowering pull of their bodies' passions.

The sweet sensual bliss of their union was complete. Silver Fox's hands and mouth plied Lisa's beautiful form, eliciting soft moans of ecstasy from her and attuning her body to his every movement. They were man and woman fulfilling all that their senses could desire. Their bodies blended and molded, each movement matched. They were heart to heart, mouth to mouth, thigh to thigh. They knew only their craving for each other. And as they neared fulfillment they came together with trembling expectancy. Blue eyes met those of the deepest black with shuddering force, and awed by this intense knowledge of her total senses, Lisa clung to her Indian lover as tears of joy trickled from her eyes. From her lips his name came forth, as her deepest vitals exploded in a gradually diminishing burst of pleasure from which she slowly descended to reality.

With a soft smile, Silver Fox looked down into her gentle face, knowing that the tears upon her cheeks were caused by the pleasure of their love. He desired no other happiness than that he now enjoyed as he, in turn, was drawn on to the peak of his passion.

Catching their breaths as they slowly drifted back to earth, Silver Fox snuggled Lisa tightly into his embrace. "Never have I known such pleasure." He sighed aloud. "Golden flower, never doubt my love."

Lisa drowsily smiled into his handsome features. "Never, my heart," she whispered and then sleep claimed her, leaving Silver Fox alone with his thoughts.

As he lay there, his protective arms still about the woman he loved, he thought ahead to the next day. What would that day bring? he idly wondered. All would come out as he knew it must, but how would this woman receive his tidings? He knew now, after this time spent with her, that she truly loved him, but just how strong that love was he was not sure. Nonetheless, he was certain he would not let her part from him. Even if she responded angrily to what she would learn, he would keep her at his side. Her anger would be better than nothing of her at all. Turning he looked at her sleeping face, her beauty touching him deeply. For a moment the sharp pain of imagined loss struck him. But no. He would never lose her. He had tasted a small draught of what that would mean when Small Sparrow had taken her. Immediately his thoughts of the other Indian filled him with a fiery anger. But regarding Lisa's gentle features, he softened, and reaching out, he gently stroked the softness of her cheek. She was his very being, and if she were to flee him he would be mindless. Life would have no meaning for him.

With a soft caress he kissed her tender brow, breathing in her sweet fragrance and assuring himself that all would be well.

After a hurried breakfast Silver Fox left the warmth of his tepee and fetched his large, black stallion and a small cream-colored mare for Lisa.

Lisa stood outside the home of the man she loved, shivering despite the fur jacket that Silver Fox had given her. She burrowed deeper into its warmth, and sighed, wishing that she would be riding his horse with him. It had begun to drizzle this morning and there was a cold chill in the air. Lisa reflected that the weather barely bothered this large man, who, other than having dressed in leather jacket and breeches, acted as though it were a fine day. Thinking of the coldness of the day's ride ahead of her, Lisa knew she would prefer to have the shelter of his large arms about her than to straddle the mare. But holding her tongue, she did as he wished and mounted the horse, also adjusting her jacket to obtain the maximum warmth and to allow little of the rain to penetrate.

Silver Fox smiled with some sympathy, but telling himself that this trip was necessary, he jumped upon his own horse's back. He had been told by Light Path that several of the scouts had spotted signs of trappers in the forest. Though he doubted that they would run into them, he did not wish to endanger Lisa should they come upon the white men.

With danger about, he would need all of his keen senses and abilities to see them to safety. With her in his arms he might grow careless.

With a tender smile in her direction, he watched her squirm deeper into the warmth of the fur jacket and then kicked the sides of his stallion which trotted through the Indian village with Lisa following closely behind.

Lisa gazed about attentively as they rode through the village. Most of the people who lived in the tall tepees were still within the warm walls of their homes; only a few were going about their everyday duties. As they passed by Singing Bird's and Light Path's tepee Lisa felt a pang of regret, as though she would not again see the kind face of this woman she had grown to know in the past few days.

A part of her rejected this feeling as nonsense, for her heart told her that after today, the confrontation between her husband and her lover over with, she and Silver Fox would return and she would spend her life here in this village. But though she told herself this, she still was haunted by an uncomfortable fear of the unknown.

Wishing somehow that she could impart her thoughts to Silver Fox and make him see that they should not leave the village, she drew abreast of him. "Perhaps we should put off our going to the manor until a more pleasant day," she called to him.

Silver Fox grinned broadly toward her, knowing her fear at having to face her husband. "We would have but to worry another day. The rain will stop by midday. I wish to have an end to all that stands between us."

"But . . ."

His next words silenced her. "Let us not talk anymore on the matter. The time shall be upon us soon enough and then we shall face it." He again pushed his stallion before her as they left the Indian village behind them and started into the forest.

Lisa remained silent for the rest of the morning as her mare followed the steps of the larger animal before her. It was useless to try to sway Silver Fox's decision, she knew. He would not change his mind about his intention to confront Craig Rollins, for himself but also for her—so that she would not live with the fear of a husband left behind and of her past. But still she had no idea how he intended to settle the matter. She was married in the eyes of the law and God to Craig

Rollins, and nothing either one of them could do would ever change this fact.

The rain let up just as Silver Fox had predicted, and pulling his horse to a halt, he jumped from the large beast's back. Taking a leather sack and a water canteen, he approached Lisa. "We shall rest for a few moments and eat. Are you hungry?" He smiled up at her as he extended his strong arms to help her from the back of her mare.

Lisa felt little hunger. In fact her stomach seemed tied in knots by her nervous thoughts about what lay ahead. "No, Silver Fox, I am not hungry," she got out as he set her to the ground in front of him.

"Golden Flower, your sadness greatly touches my heart." He pulled her close and took her lips with his own.

Lisa found the strength she had been needing all morning in his kiss. In his arms she was unafraid. His presence encircled her.

"I have told you before that I would let no harm befall you. Why is it that you so fear what needs to be done?" He stepped away, and opening the sack, he pulled forth some dried venison meat and held a piece out to her.

Lisa took what was offered obediently but her answer was not so obedient. "I do not wish to go back to the manor. I wish to stay here with you and never to see any of those people again," she blurted out, all the faces from her past appearing before her.

Silver Fox smiled as though to a child of little understanding. "But they are your people. They bear the same color skin as you and one that you speak of is your husband. You yourself told me of his care for you and his concern for your welfare. Would you wish to leave him with no word that you are well and loved?"

To this Lisa had no answer. She knew what he said made sense, but still the idea of being in the white world again disturbed her. Nodding her head she bit into the food that she had been given. "You are right of course and I am sorry that I have caused you such concern."

Silver Fox laughed aloud. "You will always cause me concern, my flower. But I shall dine with the knowledge that I bear this concern for the one I love so greatly."

Lisa felt a flush grace her cheeks, but his words fed her needs more than the simple fare she was now chewing. How she loved him and how well he expressed the feelings in her own heart. With a smile toward him she finished the venison and then took a drink from the canteen.

In a short time they were once again upon their horses, but now Lisa's mood was much more jovial. Her heart was lighter after the words Silver Fox had spoken. Of course she could not let Craig Rollins wonder where she was, whether she was dead or hurt somewhere. That man had been kinder to her than any other and she knew that, at the very least, she owed him some explanation.

Seeing her features, which had been pensive and clouded, become relaxed and almost carefree, Silver Fox became lively and talkative. He told Lisa about the forest, answering all of her questions about the different plants and the small animals that they saw. And as they rode side by side over the worn trail that wound through the massive trees, at times he would bend from his horse's back and plant light kisses upon her face, delighting in the way this simple act lit up her features and brought a smile of pleasure to her lips. She was his sun, her joy bringing brightness into his heart.

As their horses stepped from the forest into the open field that bordered the Rollins property, the whistling screech of a bird alerted Silver Fox some form of danger was about. His black eyes, trained from childhood, looked about as he pulled his stallion up, but before he could call out to Lisa, a roaring sound filled his ears and a piercing pain burned through his chest.

Lisa had noticed nothing unusual. Her attention had been directed at the man at her side. When he'd pulled his horse up, she had turned, thinking this strange, and in the next instant the booming of a rifle filled her ears. Her horse bolted and began to run across the field. With all of her strength she strove to bring the mare under control, while at the same time her mind cried with dreadful finality that Silver Fox had been shot. Turning as best she could upon the mare's back, she tried to see what was happening. She could not see Silver Fox nor his stallion, but from the corner of her eye she saw two riders approaching her at a fast gallop.

Now knowing it was dangerous to stop her horse, Lisa kicked the mare's sides, hoping to push her to a faster pace but still she could see her pursuers gaining upon her.

Turning about once more, she let out a scream as she was clamped about the waist by one of the riders.

"I got her Willie, I got her," the man shouted across the field, and as Lisa focused her eyes she saw for the first time that one of the riders was her cousin Willie Simmons.

"Aye, I see that you have, Joby boy, I see that you have." Willie pulled abreast of his friend and looked at the girl clutched in the man's filthy hands. "I knew that if I waited long enough I would be seeing you, my fine little cousin." His expression was not that of one glad to see lost kin. Quite the contrary, his look was evil as he took in her Indian dress and pictured his cousin and the Indian as they had ridden out of the forest. He had viewed for a fraction of a moment the love and joy upon their features, and his anger increased by the seconds.

Lisa saw the anger upon his features, but as she caught her breath her thoughts went to Silver Fox. What had happened to him? Had he been hurt? She knew he must have been shot, for he would never have let her be taken by these men if he could help it. "Silver Fox," she whispered aloud as she felt a piercing pain fill her chest.

Willie laughed cruelly as that name came from her lips. "Your Indian lover is probably out there somewhere waiting for a hungry animal to feast upon him, my sweet cousin. He is dead. I shot him in the heart. I do not miss my target."

The words—he is dead—seemed to overwhelm Lisa, and as she looked with horror at the thin, smirking features before her, she felt unable to breathe. She wanted to die herself, to join her love. And so unable to stand the pain of reality any longer she surrendered to the blackness of her emotions and fainted in the arms of the man called Joby.

"Pull her up tighter in your arms, Joby. But be sure that you don't hurt her in any way," Willie called out to the other man. For a moment he thought that perhaps he should carry her, but the thought of her in the arms of that stinking Indian made him shudder, so kicking his horse he started across the field with Joby and Lisa following behind.

"The carriage should be waiting at the inn. Can you carry her that far?" he called over his shoulder and receiving an affirmative answer he kept his pace up.

Lisa awoke in the darkness of night, and as she

opened her eyes they took in her cousin Willie who was sitting across from her in the interior of a carriage of some sort.

"I have been awaiting your presence, dear cousin." He grinned.

Lisa shook her head, hoping that she was dreaming and that this afternoon's scene had been nothing but a nightmare. "Where are you taking me?" she finally got out, feeling the lurching motion of the vehicle as it careened swiftly down a bumpy roadway.

"In time, dear cousin, in time," Willie responded and stretching out his long legs he relaxed against the cushion of the seat. "First I wish to have some answers to my own questions."

With her questioning blue eyes upon him, he began. "What were you doing with that Indian?"

At the mention of Silver Fox, swift tears came to Lisa's blue eyes and began to make a path down her cheeks. He is dead. The words filled her mind over and over. She wanted to faint again—to forget what had occurred. But her cousin would not allow this and reaching over he slapped her across the face. "Answer my question," he ground out from between clenched teeth.

But shaking her head Lisa wept aloud, releasing the pain she now was feeling. Silver Fox was dead and she was still alive to bear the pain of her loss. How was she to survive without his tender voice and gentle caress?

Willie sat back against the cushion once more,

watching intently the pain-filled visage of the woman before him. "You do not have to answer then if you do not wish to say the words. I already know what you were doing with that stinking savage. He was your lover."

Still Lisa could do nothing but weep. She did not care what he said; she was consumed by her own grief.

"I came to the manor to seek you out, to give you news of your stepsister, and I was told that you were not there. I was also told by one of the stable hands that your husband had left the afternoon of your wedding to attend to business, but I never would have guessed that you, sweet cousin, would so soon seek out a lover and be such a lowly creature as to crawl upon the pallet of a stinking redskin. Your husband would be quite astonished at such news, I am sure, if he were to hear of it. Isn't that so?"

Lisa sat back against the seat, her eyes shut as she tried to still her thoughts of Silver Fox and to concentrate upon Willie's words.

"Yes, indeed. I do think that your gentleman of a husband would not take too kindly to being cuckolded by one of them red devils. I am sure that he would thank me for my concern for you if given the chance. But I doubt that he will get this chance." Willie paused for a moment, aware that he now had his cousin's full attention.

"I doubt that your husband will care one way or the other about your fate when he returns from his trip and hears that you have gone off with an Indian lover. He will, I am quite sure, be glad to have done with such a cheap baggage as yourself."

Still Lisa did not respond other than to remain quiet and to listen to his words. Nothing could hurt her any more than she was already hurting.

"As I said, I brought word from England to the manor for my kin, only to find her gone off with her Indian lover. I intended to tell you, Lisa, of the death of your stepsister, Sylvia. There seems to have been some kind of fever in London, and she died some weeks ago of it. You, my dear, sweet cousin are now full owner of all the Culbreth riches."

Sylvia was dead. The thought washed over Lisa provoking little response. She had cared little for the other woman, always having been treated harshly by her. So, with Silver Fox on her mind, she could not even weep for her stepsister.

"I said that you were the full owner, but I forgot to add that you will be having help in the handling of your affairs."

Lisa's eyes opened wide for a moment. As she looked at Willie, she wondered briefly what new form of torture he planned for her.

"You see, dear cousin, my mother and myself have decided that being your only kin we should take control of your dealings. Having found that you are not as stable as one would wish, we have thought the matter over at great length and have decided that I should go to England with you and claim your inheritance. Of course, you shall have little to say on the matter of either Culbreth manor or the wealth that goes with it."

"What makes you think that I shall agree to this?" Lisa looked at her cousin, hating him for having killed the only person she had ever loved.

"Why, my dear, I care little whether you agree or not. If you do not do as you are told, I can easily see that you are disposed of as your lover was. You would be wise to realize here and now that you mean little to me. If you are out of the way, the entire Culbreth fortune will sooner or later come to my mother and myself anyway. But if you are pleasant, you will be able to stay alive and we shall gain all that we wish through you."

Willie and Adell had, indeed, talked the matter over at great length and the best idea they had come up with was to make Lisa a prisoner subject to their control. Willie thought himself quite capable of handling that job. If they were to kill her now, it might be years before they would be able to get their hands on any of the Culbreth wealth. Adell was not sure whether Richard had had any kin. She, being a distant relative, did not want to see the estate bound up in court for a great while before anyone was granted anything from it. So the best approach, Adell and Willie agreed, was to control Lisa, by threats and force.

But now as Willie studied the girl, he thought that controlling her would be much easier than they had expected. It had been a great stroke of luck to find her with the Indian. He would be able to keep her where he wanted by threatening to expose her to the public for what she was, an Indian's white woman.

Lisa did not give a thought to wealth or possession. She had only cared for Silver Fox and he had been taken from her. Whatever this horrible man wanted was of no real concern to her. At some point death would overtake her and she would be with her love. Nothing else mattered but her thoughts of the man who had held her heart. And knowing that they could not be taken from her, she withdrew into her thoughts.

Chapter Eleven

The inner recesses of his brain screamed a silent warning to Silver Fox. But as he pulled his stallion in and his black eyes searched the area, his senses told him the warning had come too late. He was about to call out to Lisa for the hawk overhead was screeching an alarm he knew he should heed. But as his mouth formed to call her name, another noise filled his ears, that of a gunshot. No longer able to react he was pitched across the back of his horse, his chest burning with a fiery pain.

Blackness seemed to cloud his mind but with a

last effort he pulled his head up. In a blur, he saw Lisa and her horse racing across the field before him. Then, he sighed painfully and was lost to total blackness. As his stallion felt the weight upon his back grow slack, he turned and started back in the direction that they had come.

When Silver Fox's horse walked into camp late that day its master slumped over its back, Light Path first took notice of the animal and he ran to his cousin, his hands quickly searching for a heartbeat. Finding a barely discernible beat, he hurriedly took Silver Fox to his own tepee and made a pallet. Then his wife, Singing Bird, tended the wounded man's body as tenderly as she would have her own husband's.

For several days Silver Fox hung on the brink of death. The tribal shaman stayed at his side, his low, deep voice singing and chanting to the bygone fathers of their tribe, and sending up a plea that would surely touch upon the great father to spare this man's life.

Light Path was outraged that such a thing could happen to his strong, invincible cousin, and taking several braves he followed the tracks left by Silver Fox's horse.

On the following morning Light Path and his followers came back to the village. Light Path immediately entered his tepee to see if his cousin had survived the night.

Singing Bird hurriedly made her way to her husband's side and in whispers told him of the wound, expressing her concern for his cousin's condition.

Light Path agreed with his wife that if his cousin's life was spared it would be for some reason that only the great father knew. He also had seen the wound, though yesterday he had not fully taken the time to examine his cousin, his anger being so great that this thing could happen. But he knew that Silver Fox had taken a bullet in his chest and that it had exited through his back.

His dark eyes followed the shaman as he went about his chanting and with a steady rhythm tapped upon a small drum. Nodding his head toward Singing Bird, Light Path gently reached out and caressed her cheek. "Tend him well for he is a strong man and will survive." He said this though he doubted his own words.

Singing Bird smiled wearily. She had been up all night, combating the fever that had overtaken Silver Fox shortly after he had been brought to their tepee. "Our son is at my father's home. Soon he shall need his meal. Would you go and bring him to me?"

Light Path smiled at the thought of his child. "Watch over Silver Fox. I shall be back shortly." With this he turned and left the tepee, the coolness of the outside world hitting him fully in the face.

His thoughts were angry but he also felt a deep loss. He had never thought that Silver Fox would be brought so low. He had always thought the other warrior above such hurt. His insides churned with rage. For if such a one as Silver Fox could be lying thusly upon a pallet, what of himself? He had found the spot where Silver Fox had been injured and the one where the two men had lain in wait. He knew that all the white man in the area wanted to kill his cousin, but he had never realized that such a thing could happen. Light Path remembered the golden dove that had meant so much to Silver Fox. Perhaps the woman had drained his cousin of his caution and his senses. Perhaps her white blood had made him unable to sense danger.

Besides having seen where Silver Fox had been shot, he had also spotted the tracks of the horses that had gone across the field, and following them he had been able to deduce the happenings of the previous day. Whoever the two men were, they had taken the woman Silver Fox had kept in the village for the past days. He could well imagine the force they had used upon her, knowing how white men treated a woman who had been with an Indian. Still, he did not intend to try to find her. He had seen the weakness his cousin displayed because of the golden dove. He had witnessed Silver Fox turning upon one of his own because of the woman, and now, as he went to get his son, he blamed the woman for what had happened to Silver Fox. She had been bad for him, and perhaps if his cousin lived, he would see the wisdom of his cousin's counsel.

*   *   *

The days passed with slow, frightening unreality. Silver Fox lingered in limbo, struggling to keep a hold upon life. At his every breath his chest heaved with pain, and at times his fever would storm so high that Singing Bird would weep from fear that he would not make it through another hour.

But somehow the crushed herbs in her warm broth had a soothing effect that left Silver Fox lying very still, except for the slight breaths coming from his mouth.

The shaman stayed in the tepee as long as the man upon the pallet lingered between life and death, and he offered the knowledge he possessed to Singing Bird to help her in the struggle to save Silver Fox's life.

The first sign that Silver Fox was improving came some days later when, for a moment, he sat up on the pallet and, looking about, saw Singing Bird and his cousin Light Path sitting near their small fire and eating their meal.

The shaman was the first to spot Silver Fox's movement, and his chanting stopped as his dark eyes filled with happiness.

Singing Bird and Light Path both heard the old man's halting voice. Quickly they turned, fearing that Silver Fox had finally died. But upon seeing Silver Fox sitting up, they both hurried to his side.

"You must lie back down," Singing Bird called, fearing that he would again open his wound and that the bleeding would begin once more.

Silver Fox looked about and then let them push him back upon the pallet. "Lisa." He forced the name from his lips as though it were being torn from inside him, and indeed, the pain in his chest was so unbearable that he lapsed back into unconsciousness.

It was two days before Silver Fox again opened his eyes. Yet his fever had gone from him on the day he had sat up on the pallet, so those caring for him had felt somewhat assured that he would in time regain his strength.

Upon awakening this time Silver Fox lay still, letting his senses tell him all that he needed to know. Feeling pain in his chest, he realized that he had been injured in some fashion, and as he lay there it came back to him. He had been shot while taking Lisa back to the manor. His thoughts filled with the golden vision of the woman he loved. Turning his head from one side to the other he tried to make out her form, but he could only see Singing Bird tending to her young son. Cautiously he tried to call out to the woman across the room. "Singing Bird, where is my cousin?"

Singing Bird jumped as she heard his voice, and setting her child in his basket, she hurried to Silver Fox's side. "You are all right?" she asked cautiously, remembering the first time he had sat up and spoken and how his exertion had left him then. "Light Path is gathering some wood. He did not wish me to leave your side so he has been doing my chores." She smiled into Silver Fox's

344

darkly, handsome face, noting that he was somewhat gaunt after his days of illness.

In response, a small smile lightly touched Silver Fox's features. He was amused by the thought of his cousin doing woman's work so that he would be watched after. With a sigh he relaxed and shut his eyes for a second before opening them to look at the woman above him. "Where is Lisa?" He again turned his head, wishing to search all of the dark corners of his cousin's home. Then he realized that Lisa should be the one tending him and, if she were, Singing Bird would be able to tend to the needs of her own household. His large black eyes turned back to the woman, and then bracing himself, he tried to rise to a sitting position. The pain in his chest left him panting and sweating but finally he was up.

"Do not get up," Singing Bird called and tried to push him back down. "You shall tear the wound open again. You do not know how sick you have been." Rising to her feet as she realized she was not going to be able to do anything with this large, determined man, she started to the flap of the tepee. "Stay where you are, Silver Fox. I shall go and get my husband, and he shall tell you what you wish to know. He went to the place where you were shot and tried to discover who had done this thing to you." Stepping out into the light, Singing Bird ran toward the end of the village, hoping to catch a glimpse of her husband, and there on his way back, his arms laden with wood, was Light Path. Seeing his wife running toward him, he hurried in her direction.

"You must hurry. Silver Fox wishes to know of the girl and is trying to get up. I fear that he will do himself more injury," she called out as her husband gained upon her. Then she turned and started back to their tepee as Light Path reached her side.

They found Silver Fox trying to stand up.

"You must lie down until you regain your strength." Light Path dropped the armload of wood and went to his cousin's side.

Silver Fox looked at the other man, pain contorting his features. "Where is my wife?"

Light Path regarded his cousin with greater understanding. Silver Fox had said wife, so he thought of the girl as his own. Light Path had known his cousin loved her but he had not realized his feelings for her were as serious as this. "Lie back down and I shall tell you all that I have learned."

As Silver Fox rose to his towering height and glared at the other man, Light Path shook his head.

"I will not tell you until you show good sense and lie still. It will do no one any good if your wound opens and you lose more blood."

Silver Fox saw that he would get nowhere if he did not do as his cousin wished, and the pain in his chest was now so unbearable that he expected to fall down at any moment. So with the help of

Light Path's strong hands, he lay back down upon the fur pallet. "Tell me of her now," he breathed.

These few words filled Light Path with some dread. He did not wish his cousin to jump from his bed and storm off to look for a white woman. That would surely be the cause of his death. In his condition he would be unable to ward off any attack. "There is little to tell," he began, but with Silver Fox's penetrating black eyes upon him he continued. "I went to where I found the forest trail ending and found the place where you had been shot. There were signs of two men. They had been hiding in some brush and waiting."

"And Lisa?" Silver Fox asked, holding his breath because of the pain that now consumed his heart. She was dead. She also had been shot but had not survived her injuries. This was why his cousin was reluctant to tell him of her.

"The golden dove was taken by the men."

To Silver Fox these words were like a reprieve from a death sentence. He would not have wished to live knowing she was dead, but if what his cousin told him was true, there was a chance.

"The two men—they were white?" Silver Fox now felt that somehow everything would be all right.

"Yes. Their sign showed that they were white men," Light Path added, sensing his cousin's feelings. "You must not seek her out until you are well."

"I must find her before some harm comes to

her." Silver Fox tried to sit back up, but he found that he had already done too much and with each movement of his body a sharp pain pierced his upper torso.

"A few more days shall not matter. If the whites have her, they will not kill her." Light Path looked at Singing Bird who was bringing a bowl of broth to Silver Fox.

"How many days have I been here?" Silver Fox reluctantly lay back upon the pallet.

"The sun has passed overhead seven times since I brought you to my lodge."

Silver Fox could not believe that he had been unconscious for so long. There was no telling what had happened to his woman in that time. He could only hope that she had been able to find some help. Perhaps she had found her way back to her kin, he speculated. Perhaps she was with her aunt. But no. She would be at the manor if she had been able to get to her aunt's inn, for her kin would see that she got back to her husband's house.

"You must eat as much of this as you can." Singing Bird bent down next to her husband's cousin and held out the bowl of broth. "You have lost much weight in the past days and must regain your strength."

Silver Fox did not argue, knowing the truth of her words. If he wished to be able to find Lisa, he would need all of his strength. So lying back he let his cousin's wife feed him with the life-giving broth.

It was a fortnight before Silver Fox was on his feet and able to walk about without experiencing the pain that bent his body. Each day he had lain upon his pallet he had done exercises to strengthen his body for the time when he would be able to stand and leave his cousin's tepee, and now that day had come.

He had told Light Path that he would not rush off in search of Lisa, but would go back to his own tepee until he was sure that he would be able to sit upon his horse's back for the duration of the trip he must make to find his golden flower. However, after only one night alone in the confines of his own home, he was ready to try to ride.

That night, time had dragged. He had been unable to shut his black eyes without thoughts of Lisa filling his mind. He imagined her moving about his tepee. And then, finally, not being able to bear the pain of his loss any longer, he rose from the pallet he had shared with her and started to pack the few items that he would need.

In the early hours of the morning, he again tried to get some rest, but as he lay looking into the flames of the fire, the image of his grandfather came to him. Black Hawk seemed to be standing beside him as he had in his youth, giving him strength and encouragement.

"Your blood flows with the redness of many great warriors and of the princess Slender Petal. You shall be lifted up and strengthened in your times of need. I have watched over you while you lay sick and dying and I shall continue to be by your side my son."

Silver Fox jerked himself awake at these words, and rising to his feet, he took deep breaths of air, knowing that his dream had made him feel stronger and had assured him that he would triumph.

Striding out into the dark of night, he filled his lungs with fresh, cool air. He would not bid his cousin and his wife a goodbye. Though he knew that he owed them this and much more because they had saved his life, he also knew that Light Path would try to sway him from leaving the village for a few days.

Silver Fox knew that the only immediate danger he faced was that he might not be able to sit his horse for the time it would take him to reach the Rollins manorhouse. But there, he knew all would be right and that he would find Lisa. So exerting a painful effort he mounted his stallion and at a slow pace began the journey that would take him to his love.

The trip was indeed a painful one, but Silver Fox endured it determinedly, telling himself that every hour he had stayed at the village had delayed his search for Lisa. He was obsessed by thoughts of her. Was she all right? Would he find her at the manor waiting for him to come to her? Or would she be at her aunt's? These same questions had haunted him during the long night.

Finally, at the first touch of sunlight, he found himself sitting his horse and looking down at the Rollins manor. Kicking the stallion's sides, he urged him into a gallop, hoping to make a quick approach.

That same evening Craig Rollins, with the aid of his cane and his manservant Adam, made his way to the Pheasant's Inn. As he entered that establishment, his dark spectacle-encased eyes scanned the busy interior.

Going to a seat on the far side of the large common room, he watched the busy traffic of the serving girls who shuttled to and from the kitchen until finally Brandy spotted him. Remembering his fine tipping, she hurried to his side.

"Why if'n I ain't some surprised to be seeing ye here, Mr. Rollins. Why we ain't been a-seeing ye since ye and the mistress's niece got married." Brandy smiled down at the older man and batted her lashes in an attempt to flatter him with her beauty.

"Yes. It's been some time, Brandy. How have you been faring?" he asked the talkative girl, hoping to find out some information.

"Me? I reckon I been well enough. I ain't

though got me no man." She winked at him and added, "If'n you know what I be a-meaning." She had not thought of spending any time with this older man before, but now that Willie was no longer about she figured that a girl must make a living so why not with this man who was probably easy to manipulate.

"Where is Willie?" Craig Rollins sipped at the drink she placed upon the table and watched the girl.

"Why that no good, two-faced rogue—he done left."

"Left? I thought that the two of you had a good thing going. Where would he have gone with such a beauty like yourself here at his mother's inn?"

Brandy preened herself at the compliment and then lowering her voice she went on. "I think that he left for England. Though the mistress wouldn't be telling me, I did overhear her telling one of her gentlemen that she and her boy is going to be rich soon and that Willie is gone to England to ensure that fact."

"Is that all you overheard?" Craig Rollins looked with some interest at the girl.

"Yes, only I be thinking that Willie done gone and took another woman with him. Not that I really be caring. The bum was starting to knock me about pretty good and I was glad to be shed of him." She didn't want this man to think that she had been doing nothing but mooning for Willie and that she could not put forth her best effort to entertain him.

"Another woman you say?" A dark brow rose in her direction.

"One of his friends was into his cups the other night and he said he saw Willie and Joby with some blond-haired wench. I don't know if they took her with them but I know that Joby went with Willie."

Craig Rollins's face did not reveal any of the black thoughts that were going through his mind. Instead he continued to make small talk with the serving girl until Brandy noticed Adell Simmons coming toward the table. Then the girl hurriedly took his order and headed toward the kitchen.

Adell Simmons, having noticed Craig Rollins talking to Brandy, hurried toward his table, taking quick steps despite her heavy form. She did not want the girl telling Craig Rollins too much. Though she thought the girl knew very little, still she did not want to take any chances. "How is it that you find your way here to my inn, Mr. Rollins? I did not expect to find you leaving your bride so soon after your marriage?" Her ponderous form loomed over the older man's table.

"I am afraid that I have some bad news, Mrs. Simmons."

"Oh?" She looked down at him with some interest, already knowing what he was going to say but pretending to be eager to learn what he was about to tell her.

"Yes indeed. I am afraid that my young bride

has somehow disappeared." He studied her features for a reaction to his words.

"Disappeared? But how can this be? Where would the girl go?" Adell Simmons tried her best to act the part of an aunt who was worried over a lost niece.

"I am afraid that I have been away on some business, and upon my return I have learned of her disappearance. I was hoping that you would have some information."

"I am afraid not. I have not seen Lisa since the day of her wedding. Perhaps she has been stolen by Indians," she rejoined, planting her huge bulk in the chair opposite Craig Rollins. "Or perhaps the chit just up and ran off. I am afraid that you did not know too much about my niece before you married her. In fact, I feel some guilt because I did not warn you about her disobedience upon a number of occasions. I would not find it hard to believe that she ran off, and I would not be surprised to hear that she left with another man." Adell Simmons looked him full in the face.

"You think my wife capable of such an act?" Craig Rollins asked.

"I am afraid so. You see her mother and she are both alike in that respect. My sister was a fine beauty too, but under the appealing appearance she was much like Lisa. I could see her in the girl in the short time she was here. Why she even tried on occasion to lure my boy, her own cousin, with her wanton looks. You can be sure that I put a swift stop to such behavior in my inn, sir. But now

I am afraid that you will be wanting your coins for the marriage bargain back?" She looked across at him and put on a sad expression. "I am sorry that the girl has turned out this way, but perhaps it is for the better. A man of your means will be much better off forgetting all about such a one as her."

"No indeed, ma'am. I would not think of asking for the coins that I gave to you. I can see that you acted in good faith. My wife's care is no longer your problem."

Brandy brought a tray with a steaming hot meal upon it, and the conversation at the table quieted for a moment.

Adell Simmons smiled to herself. How stupid this old man was. It had been much easier than she had thought it would be to talk to him about his wife. She had been dreading this meeting since the night Willie had left with the girl, knowing that upon Craig Rollins's return he would find his wife missing and would surely come to her kin. She decided that this man must not care too much for the woman he had wed and that this situation was surely better for her and her son.

Seeing the way that Brandy was preening and smiling at the gentleman across from her, an idea came to Adell's mind. What better way to ensure that he forgot about her chit of a niece than to provide him with another woman. "Our Brandy here"—she smiled as she looked toward the buxom girl—"is quite beautiful, wouldn't you say?"

Craig Rollins, taken aback by this statement,

half choked on the food he had been swallowing. What was this fat woman up to now? he wondered as he looked over his spectacles at her. Instead of voicing a reply, he nodded his head, indicating that he did agree with her speculation.

"Perhaps some sort of arrangement could be made between the two of you?" Adell did not mince words but brought the subject into the open.

Craig Rollins had to hide the grin that threatened to burst from his lips at this woman's simple ploy. She surely must think him quite dim-witted, he thought as he looked first to her and then to the serving girl, Brandy. Did the pair of them think that he could so easily be set from his wife? Would he so quickly cast her golden beauty from his mind?

"I am afraid that an agreement would be quite out of the question." Then seeing the frown that quickly appeared upon the younger girl's face, he quickly tried to mollify his words. "You see there is the matter of my wife, and while I do not know of her whereabouts, surely you can see that I could never take advantage of any woman while married to another."

This seemed to pacify Brandy and a smile once again appeared upon her features. When the older man had refused her attentions for no good reason, an angry fury had possessed her, but she found no fault with the reason he gave for his refusal.

However, Adell Simmons was not so easily put off. She wanted Craig Rollins to become involved with another woman so that she could feel reassured that his interest in Lisa was finished. "The matter of my niece could quite easily be set aside. It would entail little effort to spread the word that the twit ran off with an Indian." As Craig Rollins watched her, his interest piqued, she went on. "No one would fault a husband who found some consolation in another woman's arms if his wife had run off with a stinking Indian."

"But we do not know this to be the case," Craig murmured, drawing his black eyes from this monstrous woman to his plate and taking a bit of the food before him.

Adell decided to tell him some of the story she had been told by her son. She would not tell him everything, but she could twist the facts to suit her purpose. "I am afraid, Mr. Rollins, there is something that I have kept from you. Brandy, go about your duties now and let us talk. We shall send for you if you are needed." She ordered the girl away, not wishing her to hear what she wanted to tell this malinformed man.

Craig set his fork down upon the table, his curiosity aroused.

"You see, Mr. Rollins, I wished to spare you this bit of news about my niece."

"Which is?" the dark eyebrows beneath his white wig rose.

"The truth is that Lisa did, indeed, leave with

an Indian. My own son, Willie, saw her with this Indian at the edge of the forest that leads to your own property."

Craig Rollins watched the woman intently for a moment, his features revealing little of his thoughts. He had thought that Willie had taken Lisa and now he was sure.

"So you see it certainly would be no dishonor if you were to take another in her place."

"Madam, you greatly underestimate your niece's charms if you think that I could so easily be led from my marriage vows."

"But she herself has broken them first. Surely you would not wish her back since she has found herself an Indian lover?" Adell played the part of an enraged aunt to the hilt.

"I am afraid that my relationship with my wife is my own affair." Craig Rollins rose from his chair and looking toward the bar he signaled Adam that he was ready to leave.

"But you have not finished your meal." Adell also rose to her full height. With some concern she tried to read the other's thoughts. Had she said too much? she wondered. Surely she had not. What could he think except that his wife was being unfaithful with an Indian? Perhaps she had been a little too quick in trying to push Brandy upon him, but as she watched him walk toward the door, a smile formed upon her face. What did it matter? Willie was in England, gaining their fortune, and Craig Rollins could not possibly know of his wife's whereabouts. He would have to believe that she had left with an Indian; no one would tell him anything to the contrary.

As Craig Rollins stepped out into the cool night air, he filled his lungs with the clean smells about him.

"Did you find out anything?" Adam asked as he walked alongside the older man.

"Aye, quite a bit. We shall head for England as soon as we can secure passage."

"They have taken her there then?" The little man looked to his master, some concern upon his features. "Do you think that she is all right?"

"There must be some reason they took her there, and if what Brandy said is true, it concerns a great deal of wealth. I am sure that she is alive but I haven't the slightest idea whether or not she is all right. But Willie and anyone else involved in this matter had best pray that they have not hurt a hair upon her head."

Chapter Twelve

To exist without love and kindness is to exist in a vacuum. To occupy one's mind only with thoughts of days gone by and to wish to be left alone is a flight from this world into oneself. But Lisa Rollins was in just such a situation.

The trip back to England seemed endless because she was forced to stay in her cabin, her door being locked throughout the entire voyage. The only person she saw regularly during these long days was Willie, although upon occasion Joby brought her meal on a tray.

Lisa felt her very flesh crawl whenever her cousin's friend entered the cabin. With a sly grin he would place the tray upon the table and then stand and watch her every movement until she finished and he took the tray.

Lisa barely touched the food that was brought to her because her situation had made her lose her appetite, but the presence of this dirty man caused her to eat even less.

One evening, toward the end of the voyage, Willie entered the cabin with her dinner. He did not, on this evening, leave the tray as he usually did, but instead like his friend Joby, he stood and waited for her to finish.

Lisa tried to ignore him. She just sat upon her bed, lost in thought. In her mind only she and Silver Fox existed, and their love was free and giving. But a shout from her cousin pulled her from her daydreams.

"You will come over here and eat what is upon this tray, Lisa." His voice was a command.

For a second longer Lisa looked at him with glazed eyes. What was this strange man talking about? she wondered absently, but as his hands grasped her shoulders and shook her harshly, she came to her senses.

"I said you will come and eat this food." Willie was fast losing patience with this woman, his cousin.

Lisa's answer was slow in coming, but when she spoke Willie's face turned bright red with anger. "I am not hungry and you cannot force me to eat."

Willie realized what she was trying to do. She intended to starve herself to death in order to join her dead Indian lover, but that did not suit his plans for her so he had best change her thinking quickly, he told himself as he stood and looked down at the frail woman before him. He mentally reviewed the threats he could use. He felt that only one might touch her and that was the threat of Joby. He had seen the fear in her eyes whenever the other man was about, so now with a sly grin on his face, he spoke. "I am afraid that you are forcing my hand, dear cousin." As she looked toward him he continued. "If you will not eat the meals I bring to you, I will be forced to have Joby take my place and he shall help you with each mouthful."

Lisa knew full well what her cousin had in mind. With a slight shudder she pictured Willie's dirty, rough-looking friend. She knew that man did not care whether she ate or not. She sensed his evil intent whenever he was about. She knew he wanted to possess her, to show her that he was a man.

"I can see that you grasp my meaning, Lisa. And I assure you that I will not think twice about calling Joby into this cabin. So I would suggest that you pull yourself together and eat the meals brought to you. You are growing far too thin." He stood back from the bed and waited for her to come to the small table on which he had set her tray.

Knowing she could not face what was in store for her if she did not do as he bid, Lisa slowly went to the table, the food upon the tray there arousing a swift unsettled feeling in the pit of her stomach. Exerting her will power, she forced herself to swallow some tiny bites.

"That is much better, sweet cousin. I knew you would see reason." Willie grinned, feeling some pleasure in bending her to his will. "We would not want you to pass from this life before we have settled matters about your estate." He chuckled loudly at his jest.

Lisa did not respond to his humor. It took all her control just to sit there and try to eat the food before her. In the past weeks it seemed that each time she looked at food her stomach rebelled. She had assumed this was caused by her wish to leave this life and to be with Silver Fox, but lately she was beginning to doubt this. She had begun to wonder if she were in the first stages of pregnancy.

"I shall leave you now, but let's not have any more of your games. I can squelch any resistance on your part. Do not think for a second that I would think twice about having Joby take care of you. He doesn't mind taking seconds from an Indian." Laughter again filled the air as Willie unlocked the cabin door and left.

Lisa ate all that she possibly could without making herself ill. Then she went back to her bed and lay down. How alone and frightened she felt here in this cabin, Willie's prisoner.

He had told her upon boarding the ship that the captain and the passengers had all been told she was mentally disturbed and that he, as her cousin, had taken on the responsibility of caring for her. That was the reason given for locking her cabin door. That being the case, Lisa knew that any plea she might make to anyone aboard ship would not be listened to. Her fellow passengers all thought her mad and would not help a mad person to escape. Sighing, she lay back, her blue eyes shutting out the cabin and everything about her as she returned to the realm of her thoughts.

Silver Fox stood tall and strong beside her, his arms encircling her and holding her securely in his grasp. No pain or sorrow could touch her here. She was free to love and to feel. Shining, glistening tears touched her cheeks for even in her dreams she felt her tremendous loss.

Days passed and on a fair morning when the wind was blowing slightly from the north and sending a brisk chill about Lisa Rollins, she and her cousin Willie Simmons stepped onto the London docks.

Willie was in complete control as he steered her to a waiting carriage and, after asking a few questions, climbed in beside her, leaving Joby to ride outside with the driver.

"I think we shall spend the night here in town before going out to Culbreth manor. I shall set up an appointment with the Culbreths' attorney and arrange to have all legal matters settled as soon as possible."

Lisa did not respond as she had in the past. What did it matter to her if Willie got the Culbreth fortune? She did not care about the money. All that she had ever wanted had been taken from her. But as this thought came to her, she thought about her changing body. During the past few days she had become certain that she was carrying Silver Fox's child. Reflecting on this, her hand went to her waistline.

Willie also saw her movement and a sly grin came over his features. He, too, had been thinking along these lines. He had suspected this to be the reason she had eaten so little and he had noticed a slight thickening to his cousin's body, which had previously been quite trim. But the knowledge that she was bearing a child did not deter Willie from his intentions. If anything this new gambit would favor him. Threatening her with Joby might well wear thin, but threatening her Indian lover's child would ensure that he had the upper hand.

Weeks turned to months and Lisa's cheeks now took on a gentle glow because of the added life within her. She tried to ensure that her child would be healthy and well.

Willie had changed all of the servants at Culbreth manor, sending some of the most valued to the town house in London where he spent most of his time and leaving Joby to watch over the country estate.

Lisa had been given her old chambers, and though the door was kept locked, she seemed not to mind that as much as she had in the past. She was given whatever she wished by one of the servants, and was allowed cloth to make baby clothes or books with which to entertain herself.

She rarely saw her cousin except on the occasions when he came to the estate. When he arrived he would make an appearance, pretending to be checking on the welfare of his cousin.

Lisa ignored the nasty remarks about her condition and she swept from her mind the sly grins he cast toward her protruding belly. But occasionally he made some jest about Craig Rollins and about what his reaction would be if he knew that his lovely wife was to bear the babe of an Indian.

At these times Lisa thought of the older man who had braved her kin and married her, only to have her disappear on their wedding night, and her heart constricted with pain.

She could see the hurt expression on his kind face when he learned of her condition, and each time Willie mentioned him tears came to her eyes.

Willie delighted in the rare visits he made to his cousin, finding a certain satisfaction in visiting her in the fancy clothes that her money had purchased and then upsetting her with his references to the babe in her belly.

He quickly became bored with life in the country, however, and after a couple of days he headed back to London to enjoy the many parties to which he was invited. Being in charge of the Culbreth wealth gave him status in London so many sought his favor.

Some of the servants who tended Lisa's needs told her about the rich life her cousin was living, but that did not matter to her.

She felt Silver Fox's child moving inside her body, and to her that was all that mattered. She told herself time and again that after the baby was born she would flee from this house which was now her prison and make a new life for herself and her child.

It was most important to her that nothing happen to the babe she carried. It was all she had of Silver Fox and though the pain of losing him pierced her like a knife, she had learned that she could go on. She had another life to think about—an offshoot of the love she had known. In no way would she risk losing this life too.

As she sat sewing the tiny clothes that would adorn her child, she sometimes pictured Silver Fox smiling down upon her and watching her. Their love had been so strong that she knew she would never love again. All she would ever have was the babe they had created out of their love.

At such moments, tears came quickly to her eyes, but dashing them with the backs of her hands, Lisa admonished herself to endure.

Chapter Thirteen

As the vehicle pulled to a halt in front of a brownstone town house Craig Rollins stepped to the sidewalk with the aid of Adam.

"This is the Culbreth town house. Do you wish me to come with you?" the shorter man asked.

"Nay, Adam. Stay with the carriage. Perhaps it will be better if I venture forth alone." Having said this Craig Rollins started up the stone stoop, his cane tapping each step.

He rapped upon the front door with the head of his gold-handled cane and a servant came running to answer.

"I wish to be taken to Mr. Simmons," Craig Rollins commanded as he entered.

The servant left him standing in the foyer and hurried to tell Willie Simmons that a visitor had come.

Not knowing the name of this visitor, Willie presumed him to be one of the friends he'd made since arriving in London, so nodding his head, he ordered the servant to show the guest into the large front parlor.

With a frozen grin upon his features Willie turned from the fire in the hearth to face the solemn glare of his cousin's husband.

"Do not look so surprised to see me, Willie." Craig Rollins entered the room and, without waiting for an invitation, went to a chair and sat upon it. "I hope you do not mind but I seem to tire easily these days."

It took a full moment for Willie to regain his wits and for his frantic mind to come up with a plan of action.

"I came here to London on some business and you can imagine my total surprise when I was told that you were here."

Willie smiled thinly toward the older man, knowing that Rollins probably was also aware that his wife was at Culbreth manor.

"I was also told that Lisa was at the manor house. There is some talk of her not being quite herself?" Rollins cocked a dark eyebrow.

Willie decided that the best approach to take with this man would be to attack his pride. "What you have heard is correct, but I am afraid that

Lisa does not wish to see you or anyone else. You see, things have happened to her that no one but myself know of, and though I know she would rather die than have you find out about her, I feel that as a man you have a right to know."

"Well, that is mighty nice of you, Willie." Craig Rollins tapped the cane against his boot. "Go on. Tell me this news of my wife."

"I see no other way than to be direct. Your wife, my cousin, took a lover right after you were wed." Willie waited for a shocked reaction to come to the features across from him, but since it did not, he went further. "Her lover was an Indian who is now dead. But I am afraid that her sin cannot remain a secret. She is with child."

Craig Rollins now looked interested. "With child?" He did not know whether to believe the man across from him or not.

"Aye. That is why she wishes not to show herself in public but insists on keeping to the manor."

For a few minutes there was total silence, and then Craig Rollins spoke. "I cannot believe what you are telling me is true. Lisa did not appear to me to be the type who would so freely give of herself."

Willie grinned as he viewed the anger of the man opposite him. "Aye. She can fool anyone she sets her mind to," he agreed readily enough.

"I shall have to confront her myself," Craig Rollins said, and rising to his feet, he added, "You do understand that I must deal with her and let her know that I cannot accept her actions."

The grin never left Willie's features. This was better than he could have imagined. What better than to have Lisa's husband confront her? Then she would know for a fact that her cousin was her only support. "Aye. I can see that you wish to face the little tart." Willie also rose to his feet.

"Would the morning be convenient for you to make the trip?" Craig Rollins asked as he started from the room. At Willie's nod, he went on. "I shall have my carriage stop by at first light. I wish to get this over with as soon as possible."

After the older man left the town house, Willie sat in the parlor for some moments before demanding pen and parchment from a servant. He composed his message; then he ordered the letter to be taken to Culbreth manor and delivered to Joby. They would have to agree on some plan of action in case the old man was taken in by his wife's plight and decided to take her with him. He could not have that. It would mean the end of all that he had gained. He had even decided against his mother sharing in the wealth that now belonged to him. If she ever did come to London, he would have her taken care of.

He intended to keep everything he had and to do that he had to have control of his cousin. He hoped she would be truly ashamed by this confrontation with her husband and that she would learn her true place. For he had decided that no man would want as his wife a woman who was to bear an Indian's brat.

Early the following morning Craig Rollins's carriage approached the town house, drew up, and waited for Willie Simmons to enter before heading out of London.

The ride was quiet. Both men were deep in thought, and Adam was riding atop with the driver.

A few hours later the equipage pulled into the long drive leading to Culbreth manor. Craig Rollins looked with some interest at the large mansion where Lisa had been raised and had known so much unhappiness.

"It is beautiful, is it not?" Willie asked as he noticed the other man's interest. "Myself, though, I prefer the stimulating company one finds in London to the life of a country gentleman."

For a second, Craig Rollins had to stop himself from laughing at Willie, who could never claim to be a gentleman of any degree. But keeping his thoughts to himself for the time being, he trained his dark eyes on the scenery before him.

Soon Adam handed them down from the vehicle.

"Your man there can go to the kitchen with the driver and find something to refresh himself," Willie said, leaving Adam no choice but to do as he bid.

But first Adam looked quickly toward Craig Rollins. At the slight nod of his master's head, he did as he was bid and started toward the back of the house, his mind already deciding how he might get away from the driver once inside so he might be near if his master needed him.

"Come this way, Mr. Rollins. I sent word yesterday that we would be arriving. Perhaps a meal has been prepared for us."

"I care nothing for food. Take me to my wife, if you will be so kind."

Willie grinned again, his anticipation mounting at the thought of how this man might abuse the woman upstairs—his wife.

"If that is your desire, I shall take you right up." They entered without knocking, and as they started up the steps Joby approached the stairway.

"I have brought Mr. Rollins to see his wife. Wait down here for me, Joby."

"Aye," Joby replied as the two men ascended.

At the end of the hallway Willie drew a large key from his vest pocket and unlocked the door.

Craig was not surprised that he kept the door locked, for knowing Lisa he was certain she would not stay in seclusion in this manor. Baby or no, she loved life.

The interior of the room was dark, for the drapes at the windows were pulled tightly together. But near the burning hearth his dark eyes could make out the shape of a woman sitting in a chair, her feet pulled up under her skirts, her golden head leaning back and her blue eyes shut as though she were sleeping.

"You can see for yourself that she stays mostly in this state, dreaming about her Indian lover." Willie sneered as he spoke.

At the sound of his voice, Lisa opened her eyes wondering what new torment her cousin was preparing for her. And when her blue eyes touched upon the features of the man next to Willie, tears started from her eyes. It was like her cousin to bring her husband here so that he also could be hurt by her downfall.

Keeping a grip upon his emotions, Craig Rollins looked upon the beautiful face before him; then turning, anger in his stance, he spoke aloud. "Leave her to me."

Willie took his anger to be directed at Lisa, for it was obvious how large she was with child. He hoped that all of this man's fury would be vented upon the girl. "If you wish, Mr. Rollins. I shall go down and enjoy my breakfast. Perhaps you shall feel more like eating with this business at an end."

"Perhaps," was all that Craig Rollins could say, and as the other man left the room, he went to the woman's side.

Lisa's tears flowed because she realized the full extent of the hurt she had inflicted upon this kind man. "I am so sorry, Craig. I did not mean for things to happen as they did. I fell in love with Silver Fox and I shall always love him." Great

375

wrenching sobs filled the room as she hung her head and wept.

Craig Rollins's heart went out to her and pulling the wig from his head he knelt beside her chair. "Oh, my golden flower, what have they done to you?" Her pain was his own.

But Lisa did not hear his words. All she knew was that Willie had won again. He had brought about her total humiliation. Her husband had seen her when she was with child by another man.

Craig Rollins rose, knowing that he had to penetrate Lisa's grief, and pulling the jacket and shirt from his body he stood before her. "Golden flower, I am not dead but alive." He pulled her from the chair and wrapped his arms tightly about her.

Lisa's head swam as she looked into the black eyes above her.

"Silver Fox." The name burst from her lips.

In reply he lowered his head and took the lips that were so near his own, drinking in the taste of his love, and giving her strength.

Her mind a blur, Lisa tried to get a grasp of the situation. How was Silver Fox standing before her? Where was Craig Rollins? Was she dreaming once again? Had she finally gone insane? She pulled herself free and looked at Silver Fox, trying to clear her senses and recover her reason.

"It is I, my love." Aware of her confusion, Silver Fox spoke gently. "I was going to tell you that day when we were headed for the manor that

I and your husband are one and the same, but things went amiss and it was put off."

Lisa shook her head, not believing her ears. "But how?"

"The wig, my spectacles, and the stance of an elderly man all helped to aid in my disguise. You see I live the life of an Indian, but as Craig Rollins I can help my people. I first met you as Craig Rollins, and that first day aboard the *Sea Maid* I knew that you would be mine."

"Then you are Silver Fox?" She still looked as though she could not believe her eyes. Her blue orbs scanned his body, and then she touched the large scar where Willie's bullet had made contact with his chest. With a soft cry she flew back into his arms, now shedding tears for a love lost and found again.

"Do not fear my sweet." Silver Fox lightly brushed the golden strands from her face. "Nothing can keep us apart. The fates will not allow it. I have been brought back from the very door of death so that I can be beside you and our child." His large hand reached down and touched the small mound of her belly.

Lisa's happiness knew no bounds as the reality of what was happening sank into her brain. Her Silver Fox was here beside her—her love, her very breath. "I thought I would die without you until I realized that I would bear your child." Tears of happiness came to her eyes. "I thought that your child would be a part of you that I could still love.

Oh, Silver Fox, you have come back to me." She wrapped her arms about the strong neck she had never expected to touch again and her lips went to the lips of the love she had so desired.

"We shall both delight in the child of our love. But for now we must see to the finish of the game at hand. Your cousin will be back soon, and I do not wish you harmed. You are to get down near the bed and not make a sound. I shall not let any harm come to you." Seeing a worried look cross her features, he took her lips with his own, in a long kiss full of ardor. He drank of her lips as if their kiss must sustain him for an extended time.

When he released her, Lisa went to the bed, her blue eyes not daring to leave him lest he disappear as suddenly as he had come back to her.

As she watched, he kicked off the boots and trousers that he still wore to stand tall and massive in the center of the room, wearing nothing but the breechcloth of his people.

Going to the end of the bed, he picked up a blanket and draped it about himself and then he went to the chair before the hearth—the one on which Lisa had been sitting when he entered— and there he waited.

His wait was short-lived for Willie was much too eager to see what this man was doing to his wife to remain downstairs long.

Silver Fox heard the key turn in the door, and his blood began to boil. This man was the cause of his pain. He had shot him and left him for dead and then he had taken his wife and had held her captive in this house. He could well imagine what Willie had planned for his child.

When Willie opened the door his eyes darted about the room, and seeing only Craig Rollins sitting in a chair with a blanket wrapped around him he wondered what the man had done with his cousin. Perhaps it had been a mistake to leave him alone with the girl. Had he harmed her and left her in a corner of the room dead? Willie had not foreseen such a possibility. "Where is the wench?" he finally got out as he started toward the older man.

Silver Fox, eager to take care of Willie Simmons, rose to his full height, pulling the blanket from his body and the wig from his head. "The wench you speak of is my wife and she carries my child." The deathlike tone of his voice chilled Willie's soul.

"You?" Willie choked, not believing that this Indian could be before him. "Where is Craig Rollins?" But quicker than Lisa, he realized the deception. "It was you all along. That is why none of the men in Missouri could find you. You are also Craig Rollins."

Silver Fox laughed loudly, not caring that this man knew his game. Willie would not live long enough to carry any tales. Then with murderous intent in his black eyes, he advanced upon Willie.

Turning, he started to flee from the room but large hands grabbed him and slung him to the floor, barely leaving him time to shout for Joby before the Indian was upon him.

Silver Fox was relentless. He was determined to protect Lisa and his unborn child.

Willie was no novice at fighting, and with a power that no one would suspect he possessed, he fought off the powerful Indian. But it was soon apparent that his strength was no match for Silver Fox's. Just as he thought he was finished—his windpipe was being squeezed—he heard the voice of his friend Joby, shouting for the Indian to get up. Then he saw the gun.

Silver Fox saw the gun too, but still determined, he brought Willie to his feet by the front of his shirt, and with a shove he slung him toward the other man. Joby, not expecting this action, squeezed the trigger. The gun went off, the bullet striking his friend who stood before him a moment, disbelief upon his features, before he slumped to the floor.

Silver Fox reacted quickly and before Joby could recover, he had grasped the gun.

Adam entered the chamber seconds later and took in what had just taken place.

Handing him the gun, Silver Fox hurriedly went to Lisa's side and took her up in his arms, leaving Adam to tend to Joby and to Willie's corpse.

Lisa went willingly with him. And entering a chamber down the hall, he took her to the massive bed and gently laid her down.

"Are you all right, golden flower?" he bent over her, hoping that the excitement in the other room had not been too much for her.

With a small cry Lisa pulled him down next to her, her blue eyes rising meanwhile to the portrait of her mother.

This was her father's chamber and the smiling features of the woman above her who resembled her seemed to reassure her. "I am fine now, my love. As long as you are with me."

Silver Fox held her tightly against his chest, drinking in the sweet pleasure of her nearness, something he had sorely missed during the many days she had not been by his side. "Never again will anything separate me from you. I could go on only because I knew you were alive and somehow I would find you. When I lost you my heart cried out for your return. I can endure all things as long as you are with me." Looking deep into her eyes, he became lost in the love he saw in them—a love that time would only deepen. Nothing would ever be able to drive a wedge through it. Their love would last forever.

MORE SEARING ROMANCE
by Elaine Barbieri

Available wherever paperbacks are sold, or order direct from the Publisher. Send cover price plus 50¢ per copy for mailing and handling to Zebra Books, Dept. W27, 475 Park Avenue South, New York, N.Y. 10016. DO NOT SEND CASH.